THE MIDNIGHT SUN

NENE ADAMS

Bella
BOOKS
2013

Bella Books, Inc.
P.O. Box 10543
Tallahassee, FL 32302

Editor: Katherine V. Forrest
Cover Designer: Linda Callaghan

ISBN: 978-1-59493-352-3

About The Author

Nene Adams is a Florida native and part-time historian living and working with her inamorata in the Netherlands. She and her partner share an epic love affair, three cats, and a mutual book collection that is slowly taking over the premises.

Dedication

Dedicated with gratitude to my Aunt Chris, whose real life Yukon River Race provided the inspiration that set this story in motion.

"There are strange things done in the midnight sun…"
—Robert W. Service, "The Cremation of Sam McGee"

"What sets a canoeing expedition apart is that it purifies you more rapidly and inescapably than any other. Travel a thousand miles by train and you are a brute; pedal five hundred on a bicycle and you remain basically a bourgeois; paddle a hundred in a canoe and you are already a child of nature."
—Pierre Elliot Trudeau, 1944

CHAPTER ONE

Whitehorse, Yukon
Canada

Her heart sinking, Tabitha Knowles stared at the woman in the bed.

"I waited in the gym for twenty minutes but you never showed," she said, "so I finished my workout without you. Where've you been? Why didn't you answer your phone? I called you three times. Come on, Vic. Don't do this. The race starts in less than twenty-four hours and you're not...you're just...oh, God," she groaned, words failing her.

Huddled under the comforter, Victoria Wallace sniffled, dabbing at her nose with a tissue. "Sorry, I turned off my phone," she gasped wetly.

"Well, what it is? What's wrong?" Tabitha flopped down on the second bed, noting Victoria's swollen, red-rimmed eyes. Not good, not good, her mind chanted, but at least a fixable problem. "Are you sick? Is it the flu? A cold? I can order chicken soup from room service. There's a drugstore around here somewhere. I'll get some decongestant, Tylenol—"

"Stop," Victoria interrupted. "Just stop, okay? Give me a minute." She took another tissue from the box on the nightstand. "Not a cold. Not the flu. Chicken soup and Tylenol won't cut it." After a pause, she blurted, "I've got cancer."

The news struck Tabitha like a fist. Gasping, she tried to articulate her horror but the words jammed in her throat, a choking mass of protests and denials refusing to be uttered. After a time, enough of the shock receded that she could at least speak. She managed to say in a reasonably calm tone, "Tell me what happened."

"Dr. Kyeong called right when I was about to leave the room this morning."

"Okay."

"You know I had some tests done before we left, right?"

"Right."

"Kyeong called with the results. He told me I've got Stage Four breast cancer. It's spread to my lungs, both lymph nodes, pelvis and two vertebrae." Pushing off the comforter, Victoria sat up in the bed, looking miserable and scared. "He says I've got a chance, the odds are three in a thousand, but I have to start chemo as soon as possible. You understand, Tabby? I can't wait, not even a day. I've got to bail. I'm headed home on the next flight to Florida, and I'm really, really sorry about the race."

Tabitha moved across the room to sit next to Victoria, perching on the edge of the mattress. The clenching in her gut intensified at the guilt she read on her friend's face. "Screw the race," she said. "I mean it. Go home. Do what you need to do. Don't worry about anything or anybody but yourself."

"But we worked so hard, so goddamn hard all these months," Victoria almost wailed, shredding the tissue in her agitation, "and this was supposed to be our year, Tabby, our year, and now I've ruined everything!"

"Hey, hey, cut it out, Vic." Realizing she sounded angry, Tabitha took a deep breath, willing herself to calm, and put an arm around Victoria. "Sure, we worked hard, but we also had a lot of fun, didn't we? And after the treatment, when you're all better, we'll practice and work like crazy, and next time will be our year. We'll be the queens of the Yukon River Quest, I promise. No, don't argue. You get well first. That's your priority."

"God, Tabby, you have no idea how much I wish—"

"I wish, too, Vic. I wish like hell."

Hugging Victoria, Tabitha felt a damp warmth spreading over the front of her T-shirt. She let the fabric absorb the tears, stroking Victoria's back and rocking her a little. Three in a thousand…Jesus Christ! Presently, she heard a murmur that resolved into muffled words.

"My flight leaves in two hours," Victoria said, "and I have to pack."

Tabitha let go. Her arms were empty, her heart filled with grief. "I'll go with you," she offered. "Let me call the airline, see if there's a seat available."

Victoria shook her head. "Absolutely not," she said. "I'm a big girl, I know not to take candy from strangers, thank you. I think I can fly home without a chaperone."

"But—"

"I already called Lil, she'll pick me up and take me straight to the hospital."

"Nice to have a partner who doubles as a free taxi service," Tabitha attempted to tease, her voice breaking.

"Free? Oh, Lil will make sure I pay, one way or the other. She hates the airport in Orlando. Way too many tourists." Victoria tossed the mangled tissue into the wastebasket beside the bed and scrubbed her face with both hands. Straightening her shoulders, she stood and said, "Right. I need to pack and call a cab." She seemed more her usual self, but Tabitha detected brittleness around the edges of her smile.

"I'll take my regular clothes, but I'm leaving the rest of the stuff with you," Victoria went on. "Keep it or give it away, I don't care. I'm not lugging that crap through security."

"I'll handle everything on this end," Tabitha promised, willing herself not to cry.

"The Atherton case is almost wrapped up, and don't forget the meeting with ATF about Dolohov next Monday," Victoria said, opening the dresser drawer to retrieve her FBI credentials.

"I'll call Strickland on the way to the airport and tell him I'm taking emergency medical leave. He's a decent boss, he won't give me any hassle. God, so much to organize…getting sick is damned inconvenient."

"Is there anything else I can do?" Please, please give me a task, give me something to do or I'll go crazy.

"No. And before you ask, no, you may not go with me to the airport. I'll see you when I see you. Stay and watch the race. Call me when you come home." Victoria put her arms around Tabitha and whispered in her ear, "Love you, Tabby. I'll be fine, I swear."

"Love you, too." Tabitha clung to Victoria, cherishing the strong, solid feel of her best friend since their Academy days. The thought of losing that strength, that precious partnership, brought stinging to her eyes. She wanted to weep, beg for more reassurance, rage against life or fate or God, but she dared not add to Victoria's burden. "I guess you'd better start packing," she said. "Don't want to be late for your flight. Can I help?"

"You can get out of here," Victoria said gruffly, turning away to fumble an empty suitcase onto the bed. "Don't hang around on my account. Go on, shoo! You know how much I hate to say goodbye."

"Then I won't say it. See you later, alligator." Tabitha grabbed her purse from the dresser where she'd dropped it and picked up a navy blue sweater. When she opened the door, she heard Victoria make the traditional reply, "After a while, crocodile."

Her control breaking, Tabitha blindly stumbled down the corridor.

CHAPTER TWO

The hotel bar resembled a holdover from the Gold Rush days, Tabitha thought. Brown wood paneling, leather chairs, and old-fashioned fixtures including a brass rail—even a bartender flourishing a handlebar moustache waxed into points—but Leonard Cohen and Michael Bublé played from hidden speakers, the walls were covered in modern sports memorabilia, and the cranberry spiked beer came from a local microbrewery.

Perched on a stool, Tabitha tried not to fret, but failed miserably. Her mind wandered to dark, resentful places, more bitter than the beer she nursed. How could this have happened? Victoria was a healthy, active woman, never sick in her life. Didn't smoke, didn't drink except the occasional cocktail. Shot twice, minor wounds, no complications. Why her?

A selfish, unworthy voice intruded in her head: why now?

Sipping her beer, she thought about both of them stealing precious time from work to prepare for the race. Nine months paddling practice, three days a week. Ten- to fourteen-hour trial runs on the Wekiva River every month of endurance training. Blisters, pulled muscles and sprains, exhaustion, mild heatstroke. And always Victoria sharing the pains and triumphs, closer than a sister, more constant than a lover, unchanging and as dependable as the sunrise. Such a waste…She broke off her musings, her chest tight, her cheeks hot with shame.

Victoria still lived, but chemotherapy and the cancer itself would ravage her body and steal the familiar, leaving a shell of the woman she knew. The odds were stacked high against survival. Three in a thousand, the doctor said. Part of her already mourned her friend's loss, which felt like the worst kind of betrayal.

A pile of colorful brochures on the end of the bar caught her eye. She picked one up. Yukon River Quest, screamed the headline over a photograph of a sunrise. Race to the Midnight Sun - 740 kilometers/480 miles - Whitehorse to Dawson City. World's longest canoe and kayak marathon. She replaced the brochure on the stack with a sigh, considered ordering something fattening from the snacks menu, and started when someone bumped her shoulder.

"Hi, gorgeous," chirped the leggy brunette.

Recognizing the woman, Tabitha groped for the facts. Cynthia, that was it. Cynthia Piggott. Member of the Klondykes team from Alabama, women's Voyageur class. Friendly but kind of pushy, never without immaculate makeup and hair, a real flirt.

"Hi," she replied without enthusiasm, returning to the menu and its promise of poutine. She hoped Cynthia would take the hint.

"Excuse me for saying so, but you look like you're two bites into a big ol' shit sandwich. Somebody bust your dolly, hon?" Cynthia asked, hopping onto the stool next to her and signaling to the bartender.

In their previous encounters in the hotel, Tabitha had found Cynthia's cheerfulness refreshing, but at the moment, the perky attitude grated on her nerves. "My friend's going home. I'm out of the race," she said coldly.

The rebuff didn't faze Cynthia. "Oh, I'm so sorry, hon," she said, grimacing. "You're women's tandem canoe, yeah?"

"Uh-huh."

"You poor thing, having to drop out so soon. That sucks."

"You don't know the half of it," Tabitha muttered into her beer.

"Breakups are the worst," Cynthia went on. The bartender slid a cocktail in front of her—fruity from the color, adorned with maraschino cherries, and very alcoholic from the smell that hit Tabitha's nose. Cynthia took a gulp from the glass, crunching ice between her teeth. "Two years ago, a girlfriend broke up with me right before the Neches Wilderness Race in Texas. Didn't have the guts to tell me to my face. She sent a text message. Can you believe that? I killed half a bottle of Jose Cuervo and blew the race next day, sick as a dog for a week. Glad she dropped me, though. That bitch was nuttier than a squirrel turd."

"Me and Vic are friends, okay? Best friends. Not lovers," Tabitha gritted, dropping any pretense of politeness. "I don't really give a crap about your love life, so fuck off."

"Whoa! Sorry, sorry, my bad," Cynthia replied, raising her hands as well as her plucked eyebrows. "Jeez, you don't pull any punches, do you? But you're upset, so no hard feelings, yeah? My gal Tracy tells me all the time that verbal diarrhea of mine's going to get me in a peck of trouble one day. Let me make it up to you. Buy you another beer?"

Tabitha flushed and mumbled an apology. "I'm not fit company."

Cynthia shrugged. "I've got a temper when I'm riled too. No harm, no foul. It's cool. You want to talk about it, hon? I've got a great shoulder you can cry on." She winked.

"Thanks for the offer, but no. I'll be fine." Tabitha ordered a shot of Maker's Mark from the bartender. The bourbon traced a trail of smooth heat down her throat, pooling in her stomach like a banked fire. The temperature in the bar suddenly felt like a sauna, the air stale. "Listen, I'm going for a walk or something. See you later," she said, slipping off the stool.

"Hey, before you go, maybe I've got a solution to your problem," Cynthia said. "I heard about a gal looking to get into a team or something. Tracy talked to her the other night. I forget her name. Doreen? Diana? Dee Dee. No, still not right." Her lips pursed in thought. "I think she's staying at the Tremblay B&B. Know where that is?"

"I think so," Tabitha said. "Why's she trying to get a team at the last minute? Don't you think that's odd?" she asked, frowning.

"Oh, Lord, I don't remember her sad, pathetic story right this second. As for odd, hon, considering y'all are in the same boat, so to speak…Ha! You hear that? 'In the same boat.' That's pretty funny. I got to remember to tell that to Tracy. She'll pee herself laughing." Cynthia called the bartender over, already repeating the joke as he moved toward her.

Tabitha made her escape, yanking her sweater over her head as she fled.

The weather in Whitehorse was dry, the temperature holding steady at around sixty-eight degrees, but walking through the downtown area, Tabitha shivered in spite of her sweater and wished she'd ordered coffee at the bar instead of bourbon. She could always find a restaurant, she decided. The town might be in the Yukon wilderness, but it boasted modern amenities like golf courses, shopping malls, even a hot springs just outside town.

A long, low, hooting blast resonated through the air, startling her: the steam whistle of the SS *Klondike*, a paddlewheeler turned tourist attraction docked on the waterfront. The sound signaled noon. She checked her watch to be sure. Recalling how charmed Victoria had been by the historic buildings when they first arrived in Whitehorse from the airport, she smiled. One thought led to another. Victoria would have zero patience with her wallowing in pity. She had to pull herself together before she went home. Victoria needed her to stay strong so she could help, not collapse into a blubbering wreck every five minutes.

Walking on, she avoided a group of men and women clotting the sidewalk, probably racers or team supporters from the snatch of conversation she heard. She turned onto a different street and spotted a sign that read Tremblay Arms B&B hanging on the front of a brick building. She stood in front of the building, torn between satisfying her curiosity, or going back to the hotel and drowning her sorrows in more bourbon.

Curiosity won. Reaching for the doorknob, she let herself inside.

A bell fastened over the door jangled.. After passing through a vestibule cluttered with winter coats, boots and miscellaneous junk, she came to a dim room where a balding man read a magazine behind a wooden desk. The reek of booze and stale cigarettes hung like a haze in the air. Facing the desk, she cleared her throat.

The man turned a page, pointedly ignoring her.

"This is going to seem like a weird question," Tabitha said, damning the curiosity that had brought her here. The need to know might make her a good investigator, but it sometimes caused trouble in other ways. "I'm sorry to bother you, but do you have a guest staying here, a woman named Doreen, or Diana, or something like that?"

He glanced up from the magazine. "What are you, a cop? I know all the cops in town," he said, his hostility clear. "You're not one of them."

"No, I just—"

"Unless you want a room, you've got no business here."

"Fair enough, but—"

"Get out."

His chill, flat tone made her hackles rise. "I'm looking for information, not picking a fight," Tabitha said, putting some sharpness in her tone. "There's no need to be an asshole."

"I don't like people like you. Know why? You Americans think you're better than us," he said, rising from his chair. The magazine fell unheeded to the floor. He was a big man, tall, broad shouldered, a solid belly swelling the front of his shirt. "Think you're entitled. Special. Come here with your money, your attitude, your bad manners. You want this. You want that. Like what I want doesn't count." His hand balled into a fist at his side.

The situation with Victoria had already eroded her self-control. Now the man's implied threat brought her temper roaring to life. She stood her ground, knowing defusing the situation would be better, but feeling rash enough not to let it go. "You know what? I work for a living, just like you," she spat. "As for bad manners, have you listened to yourself?"

"Do I need to throw you out?"

"Oh, please, don't even think about starting something with me."

He sneered. "Why? You'll call your lawyer and sue?"

"No, I'll put your ass on the ground." Fine tremors ran through her muscles. Not fear—if she chose to run, she could be out the door and gone before he made it around the desk— but adrenaline. "You don't want to help me? Fine. You want me gone? Fine. But don't try to intimidate me. I won't be bullied by a drunk."

His voice dropped to a growl. "I'll show you how we treat rich bitches around here."

"Hey, Artie, what's up?" interrupted a barefoot woman as she came through a doorway at the back of the room. "Your mama's looking for you. She's in the kitchen." When he didn't respond, she poked him in the shoulder with a finger. "Hey, I think your mama's out of smokes. You know how she gets when she ain't got those cancer sticks of hers."

He fumed, his gaze traveling from Tabitha to the newcomer, and back again.

"Artie." The woman drew the name out, her voice rising on the first syllable, dropping lower at the end. It sounded like she was calling a dog, Tabitha thought.

With a final glare, Artie snorted, turned, and stomped through the doorway, leaving a vaporous trail of alcohol fumes in his wake.

Tabitha blew out a sigh. "What's that guy's problem?" she asked, willing her heart to stop thumping against her ribs.

"He's like a pit bull-poodle mix I had once. Quick to go on the offense, showed teeth at every little thing, but no follow through. Don't get me wrong, sugar. Artie's no saint, and he's got some major bugs up his butt, but his mama would strip the hide off him if he started a fight in her house and he knows it." The woman eyed her, an unreadable expression on her face. "Who'd you say you were looking for?"

"Someone named Doreen or Diana? Damn it, this is such a mess." Tabitha rubbed her neck, so grateful for the rescue that she felt she owed the woman an explanation. After all, she'd come close to causing an international incident by kicking a Canadian citizen's ass. "I was supposed to be in the race tomorrow, women's tandem canoe. My paddling partner had to go home on an emergency. Do you know Tracy? With the Klondykes? Her friend Cynthia told me somebody named Diana or Doreen wanted to get into a team. That's why I came."

"Oh." After a moment's hesitation, the woman stuck out her hand. "I met Tracy the other night at the Gold Rush. My name's Diana Crenshaw. You can call me Di if you want."

Tabitha shook Diana's hand, giving her name and taking a moment to study the woman. A fellow American, a Southerner from the drawled accent, she noted. Tanned skin visible on her bare arms, a brown ponytail sprinkled with gray, pleasing freckled features, blue eyes darker than her own. More importantly, Diana appeared fit and strong despite some extra weight carried on a stocky frame, enough to broaden her hips and thicken her waist.

"Where're you from, Di?" Tabitha asked, pleased with her initial impression.

"Itty-bitty place called Lightning Ridge in Georgia." Diana seemed slightly tense, but her smile didn't waver. "And before you ask, I was supposed to compete with a mixed Voyageur team. We sent in the forms, paid the fees and deposits, reserved a campsite, the whole nine yards, then the captain's appendix blew, and Bob's wife had to have a C-section, and Marley Jo decided she couldn't leave her sick cat, so the trip was canceled. I figured what the hell, I'd visit the Great White North anyhow. Thought I'd ask around town, talk to the other racers, see if I could find me a place on a support team. You never know."

"Well, I need a bowman if you can handle the position," Tabitha said.

"I can do as I'm told. Bow suits me fine."

"You done much adventure racing? Marathon canoe racing?"
Diana obliged with an impressive list of races.

Tabitha whistled. "Busy girl."

"Sister, you ain't seen nothin' yet." Diana flashed a grin. "Though I've always done the mixed team thing before, you know. Going to be mighty quiet in that canoe with just the two of us." She colored faintly. "That is, if you decide you want me."

Amused, Tabitha raised an eyebrow.

"Oh, sweet baby Jesus in velvet pants!" Diana cried, blushing more furiously. "You are a bad woman with her mind in the gutter. I don't mean anything by it except if you want me as a paddling partner, and you know it."

Her excitement welling, Tabitha considered the possibility she might not have to quit the race. For a moment, doubt intruded. She and Victoria had planned so long, trained so hard, it seemed horribly unfair, not to mention disrespectful, to continue as if her best friend could be replaced by a stranger. What would Vicky think? How would she feel?

In her heart, Tabitha knew going on was the right thing to do. She and Diana had very little chance of winning, but she would finish the race for Victoria's sake as well as her own. Besides, she had taken an instant liking to Diana, who appeared friendly and experienced—an excellent combination for an event that would take them to the edge physically and mentally.

"Tell you what," Tabitha said, trusting her instincts and making a snap decision. "Let's go on a trial run, put you through your paces, see if we mesh. That sound all right?"

Diana brightened further. "Bring it on."

Tabitha imagined she felt Victoria's approval warming her heart.

CHAPTER THREE

Three days later, waiting with the other racers near a gazebo on a grassy field in Rotary Peace Park, Tabitha squinted at the sun. This time of the year in Whitehorse, daylight came early, around two o'clock in the morning. Despite the hotel's blackout curtains, she had been awake since four thirty, too keyed up to sleep.

After drinking more coffee than practical or advisable, she'd spent the time before breakfast checking and rechecking her gear, getting GPS coordinates off her laptop, and going over the maps just one more time until the lines blurred together.

Now with her belly full of oatmeal, her head full of cautions and strategies, and her heart full of excitement made bittersweet by Victoria's absence, Tabitha forced herself not to look at her watch for the umpteenth time. Officials had just completed the last mandatory equipment checks. The race would start right after the team announcements.

Next to her, Diana was in the middle of thigh stretches, a calm presence unable to soothe her prerace jitters. She focused on the weather to distract herself.

The sky looked clear, though contrary to the reports she'd heard, heavy, black-bellied thunderclouds had begun piling up over the mountains, threatening a storm later in the day. Tabitha hoped the rain and wind would either hold off or blow away. She'd heard from veteran racers that Lake Laberge, a challenging stretch of the river about thirty miles away, was a bitch to traverse in anything except the mildest weather.

She shot another look at her teammate. Diana had stuffed her long brown hair under a white baseball cap. A sheen of balm coated her lips, and she smelled faintly of coconut from the sunscreen on her face and neck. The artificial scent usually made Tabitha a little sick to her stomach, but she had found herself almost liking the stuff on Diana.

Wrenching her mind back to the race, Tabitha began performing triceps stretches, sparing a glance at the shore where canoes and kayaks were lined up. Her canoe—their canoe, she corrected—stood out like a beacon.

Double Jeopardy, as sleek and elegant as an eighteen-foot long razor blade honed to a killing edge. The spruce and cedar gunwales pulled in sharply at the seats, giving the racing vessel a rakish appearance. She knew the canoe like a favorite child, intimate with all its quirks, and utterly in love with the sweet, smooth way it glided through the water.

Had *Double Jeopardy* been a woman, she'd have married her.

During her trial runs with Diana over the last few days, she thought the woman had demonstrated the strength and experience needed by a paddler. As a bonus, Diana's open admiration of *Double Jeopardy* tickled her pink, as Victoria would have said.

Glad to have a competent paddler on her team, she'd given Diana some of Victoria's abandoned gear, mostly fleece jackets and thermal leggings, as well as a pair of Lycra and synthetic leather fingerless gloves, but not without a pang. A call to Victoria earlier that morning had gone unanswered.

"Hey, you okay?" Diana asked, glancing at her with concern.

"I'm fine," Tabitha answered, startled out of her worried thoughts. "Just a little nervous, I guess."

"I wondered why you were shaking like a poodle crapping peach pits." Diana let out a cackle when Tabitha snorted so hard she inhaled a flying bug and sneezed violently.

"Sorry," Tabitha wheezed, signaling Diana to stop whacking her on the back. "I never heard that expression before."

"Really? Where're you from? I forgot to ask."

"I live in Clermont, Florida. It's close to Orlando."

Diana nodded. "Sounds like a nice place. Plenty of sunshine."

"And plenty of rain. Don't get me started on hurricane season." Tabitha took off her floppy boonie hat and reached up to tighten the knot that held a red kerchief tied over her short blond hair. She eyed the race marshal, but he seemed busy arguing with another man. Anticipation tightened the muscles in her neck and shoulders. She hadn't felt this edgy since testifying in an Albanian gang leader's trial last year.

"Relax, would you?" Diana said out of the corner of her mouth. Her gaze remained fixed on the vessels three hundred meters away. "You're making me nervous, sugar. Just think, compared to the Everglades Challenge, this puppy's a piece of cake."

"Piece of cake...yeah, right." Tabitha sought the petite form of Betty Hollis or the heavily bearded Dusty Singer, local volunteers and members of her support team. Both of them ought to have been near the canoe, waiting for the start signal. After a panicked moment, she saw Betty headed toward *Double Jeopardy* with an empty orange garbage bag fluttering in her hand. "Talk to me again after we get through Five Finger Rapids."

"I'm serious. The Everglades is tougher. Forget the wildlife. They got mosquitoes down there so big, they could stand flat-footed and screw a punch buggy," Diana said, "but I guess you know that already, living as you do in Mickey Mouse land."

"Like I said, don't get me started. Hey, check around, will you?" Tabitha asked, growing increasingly anxious about Dusty. Both helpers were needed to push off the canoe at the start. She switched her focus from the shore to the park. The milling crowd included members of the seventy-six teams participating in the event plus support personnel, volunteers, race officials, locals, tourists, journalists, photographers and gawkers.

"I'm trying to locate a male Caucasian," she continued, "six feet tall, hundred and eighty pounds, redhead, big bushy beard and moustache."

Diana frowned, giving her a curious look, but did as she was bid. Suddenly, her face paled under the tan. The freckles peppering her nose and cheeks stood out like ink spots on vellum. "Shit," she breathed.

"What's wrong?" Tabitha reacted automatically by scanning her surroundings to identify any anomaly, any threat, but found nothing out of the ordinary. "Di, talk to me," she prodded after Diana remained silent too long.

Diana licked her lips, her gaze darting back and forth. "Uh, nothing. It's nothing."

"I'm not buying that story. What's got you so worked up?" Tabitha asked, only afterward remembering this wasn't an interrogation and Diana wasn't a suspect.

"I don't want to talk right now." A blank expression slammed over Diana's face and her gaze went flat, giving nothing away. When she continued speaking, her tone was mild but cool. "Let's concentrate on not falling over our own feet when we have to make a run for the canoe. Look over there, somebody from the pizza parlor is giving away free slices. Let's grab a few for later."

Wondering what had caused Diana's upset, Tabitha tucked the incident away in a corner of her mind and decided to bring it up again later.

CHAPTER FOUR

"Five…four…three…two…one!"

The crowd's enthusiastic chanting and cheering was drowned out by a hoot from the SS *Klondike*'s steam whistle, followed by frenzied drumming from a man wearing a First Nations costume. At the signal, Tabitha and Diana took off at a run, scrambling with a stampede of other racers to get to the riverbank as quickly as possible.

Tabitha winced when her ankle turned slightly on a stone, but she righted herself and reached *Double Jeopardy*, happy to find the mandatory spray deck already fastened down. Betty and Dusty stood nearby, nodding at the unspoken question she glanced at them. Everything was ready, no need to delay.

After the barest pause to fasten the personal flotation device over her fleece jacket, Tabitha hopped into the rear of the canoe and sat on the padded bench, arranging her legs to fit in the space, her feet on either side of a five gallon plastic jug of water. A flexible plastic tube threaded through the lid served as a straw.

Helped by a long, smooth shove from Diana, Betty and Dusty, *Double Jeopardy* slid into the shallows, bobbing a little when Diana splashed up and stepped into her place ahead of Tabitha's seat without overbalancing the canoe.

Itching with impatience, Tabitha waited a bare second for Diana to settle before dipping her paddle in the water to make the first strokes, sending the canoe darting into the Yukon River where she felt the keel bite into the current.

Sunlight had turned the river's surface to gold from a distance—sweating in the heat while standing in the park, she had scoffed at warnings from veteran racers—but in reality, the water was the color of lead, laden with silt, and swollen with cold glacial runoff. A significant wetting would require stopping to change into dry clothes to avoid hypothermia.

Hundreds of cheering, shouting people lined the riverbank. Tabitha noticed a man standing thigh-deep in the water beside the prow of a Voyageur canoe, sprinkling tobacco in a traditional offering to the river spirits. She hoped he prayed for a good wind and no rain.

Moving the canoe past the old shipyards and leaving the town behind, Tabitha worked at a practiced and easy pace of forty-five strokes per minute, her shoulders and back muscles loosening when her body fell into rhythm. The initial chaos at the start soon resolved as other canoes and kayaks spread out, some pulling ahead, the rest scattering.

When a motorboat with several photographers on board buzzed ahead of her canoe, she quickly used her paddle as a rudder to steer *Double Jeopardy* away from the choppy wake. Another boat pulled over, the police officer inside shouting something at the motorboat's pilot. Tabitha couldn't make out a single word, but from the officer's irate tone, it sounded uncomplimentary. She grinned. Idiots deserve a chewing out.

Diana never paused in her powerful strokes, the paddle lifting and coming down sharply to slice into the water. As agreed earlier, she switched from one side of the canoe to the other to avoid overtiring her arms. Tabitha did the same.

When they approached the sandy beach at Policeman's Point—the first checkpoint twenty-five miles from the start—Tabitha called her team's number to the clipboard-carrying race marshal. A glance at her watch told her *Double Jeopardy* was making good time, well within her planned schedule. She and Diana celebrated by taking a simultaneous five-minute break, eating a banana and a slice of pizza each from the provision box provided by Betty and Dusty, and chasing down the hasty meal with cans of lukewarm energy drink.

Ten minutes later, Diana stopped paddling, turned her head, and said over her shoulder, "Hey, over there to starboard, looks like somebody's in trouble. No, sugar, your other starboard. Do we render assistance?"

Tabitha glanced to the right, where a yellow fiberglass tandem canoe had overturned about a kilometer from shore. Kind of early in the race for an accident, she thought, shaking her head at the two crewmembers splashing in the water, trying and failing to prevent their canoe from drifting away on the current.

"They'd do better to get their butts out of the water and dry off," she replied. "Speaking of assistance…" Spotting a rescue boat crisscrossing the river, she waved a paddle to get their attention and directed them to the distressed crew.

Continuing paddling toward Lake Laberge, Tabitha settled into a pattern. She worked for a half hour, and then gulped water from the five-gallon jug to ease the rawness in her throat before wolfing down a granola bar, a handful of cold pasta, or slices of ham sandwiched between pancakes pilfered from the hotel buffet. In the bow, Diana did the same, staggering her rest periods with Tabitha's so they wouldn't lose too much progress.

Eating gave Tabitha a chance to admire the landscape, so different than tropical Florida. On either side of the river, the land was peppered green with trees. Behind the trees rose irregular lumps of hills overshadowed by mountains streaked with blue and white. No matter where she looked, she saw beauty.

Every fiber in her body singing, she refocused on the race, digging her paddle's blade into the water, stroking or steering as needed, her body reacting without conscious thought.

This is what I want, she thought, shifting on her seat to ease a slight sore spot on the back of her thigh. What I've been craving all these months. Nature that isn't manicured to death. A vista without a palm tree in sight. A physical challenge for a change instead of criminals, court appearances, meetings, paperwork.

A sound from behind caught her attention. Twisting around, she found a bright red solo kayak drafting off *Double Jeopardy's* wake.

The kayaker was a woman singing in a glassy soprano in time with her strokes, "My paddle's clean and bright/Flashing like silver/Follow the wild goose flight…"

When Tabitha scowled, the woman gave her a cheeky grin and a wave, but kept her position. Rather than make a fuss—drafting wasn't against the rules, and in fact, the technique was encouraged by professional racers—Tabitha threw back her head and sang an off-key rendition of "The Good Ship Venus," the dirtiest version she knew. After a startled look over her shoulder that turned into a wink and a smirk, Diana joined in.

The kayaker gave up. Shooting ahead of them, she quickly disappeared from sight.

"'Twas on the good ship Venus/By Christ you should have seen us—" Diana broke off her warbling and threw Tabitha a wide smile. "I see we lost our hitchhiker, along with everybody else. We're all by our lonesome out here."

"Well, Miss Red Kayak doesn't need to draft off us to make her life easier. Let her do her own work." An eagle's piercing shriek caused Tabitha to glance at the sky. Ahead of them, clouds boiled as if stirred in a cauldron. "I think we're in for a real drenching," she said. "Do you need to pee before we hit the lake?"

Diana shook her head. "Think I sweated it all out." Strands of hair had escaped her ponytail and stuck wetly to her freckled face.

"You're not drinking enough."

"If I drink any more, I'll founder."

Tabitha was about to point out the follies of dehydration when a very familiar, very unwelcome, and very unexpected sound split the air: the flat crack of a rifle shot.

The next second, Diana cried out in what sounded like pain.

Cursing the lack of cover—sitting in a canoe in the middle of an empty river was the very definition of a sitting duck—Tabitha scanned the nearby shoreline for the source of the shot. She ducked instinctively when another bullet struck the water near the hull.

"Diana, where are you hit?" she asked. The bullets weren't stray shots from a hunter, she realized, but must have come from a sniper shooting at them deliberately.

"I'm okay," Diana gasped. "Just scared shitless."

Tabitha bitterly regretted leaving her firearm at home. "We need to get the hell off this river. I think the shots are coming from that rise on the right. Let's go left, get up on that spur of gravel, and take cover under those trees, okay? Can you paddle?"

"Sugar, I'll walk on water if I have to," Diana replied, gripping her paddle.

A third shot came, also missing the canoe by a hair. Paddling as fast as she could, her heart hammering in her chest, Tabitha bit the inside of her cheek to keep from screaming blasphemies. She felt as if a bull's-eye hung on her back. The skin between her shoulder blades itched with each second that crawled past.

The river had apparently widened to an impossible distance. No matter how hard she stroked, it seemed the canoe drew no closer to shore.

No help from from the authorities, no backup, no miraculous escape, she thought. She and Diana were dead unless they saved themselves.

CHAPTER FIVE

At last, after what seemed like hours of desperate paddling, *Double Jeopardy's* keel crunched on gravel.

Without hesitation, Tabitha leaped out and into the shallows and shoved the canoe higher on the pebbled shore. She expected another bullet any moment. Adrenaline burned in her veins like fire. Grabbing Diana's wrist, she hustled away from the water, finding shelter in a stand of stunted spruces that had looked much denser from the river.

Another shot struck a tree trunk, scattering splinters. Tabitha went a little further inland, towing Diana with her. Panting, she finally squatted down, her back against a fir tree. "Damn it," she muttered, unfastening and shrugging off the bright orange PFD that restricted her movements and made her even more of a target.

Putting a hand on Diana's shoulder, she wasn't surprised when the woman flinched violently, jerking away from the touch. "Sorry," Diana whispered through stiffened lips, her face gone paper pale. Tears trembled on her lashes.

Shock, Tabitha thought. "You're okay, understand? Nothing to be sorry for. But I've got to go back to the canoe. No, listen to me…whoever's up there with a rifle, he's either a terrorist, a thrill killer or he has another agenda. Every racer, every volunteer on the river is in danger. I have to get the satellite phone and alert the RCMP in Whitehorse."

"No!" Diana looked wild around the eyes. "You'll be hurt. Maybe killed."

"Don't worry. I'll be fine. He shot at us four times, but he missed, remember?" Tabitha tried to sound more confident than she felt. True, the shooter had missed, but perhaps those had been ranging shots. If he hit his stride, the moment he had a clear shot, she'd be dead. However, she had a duty to report the situation to the authorities.

"Don't go. Please, don't leave me here."

"You'll be okay, Di, I promise. Just stay put. I'll come back as fast as I can."

Despite Diana's tearful protests, Tabitha started walking back to the canoe. As she came nearer, she bent low, trying to present a smaller target. Some of her tension eased when no bullets answered her appearance out of the tree line, but she took nothing for granted. Feeling horribly exposed, her skin crawling, she moved to Double Jeopardy.

The shot she half expected did not come.

She shifted cautiously to keep the side of the canoe between her body and the river. Using fingers made clumsy by haste and nerves, she worked to unfasten the center spray deck covering the cargo space, an area amidships between the front and rear seats.

A noise from the river made her glance up, her heart freezing mid-beat when she saw a Zodiac boat bearing toward the gravel bar. None of the men inside looked very friendly. All of them carried rifles. They were definitely not race marshals or safety personnel.

"Shit!" she exclaimed. The shooter had brought his friends to the party.

The spray deck strap loosened. Reaching inside the canoe, she grabbed the first pack that came to hand, then a second, but not the third. No time, no time, no time…beat through her head. A pack in each hand, she bolted for the trees and heard the men shouting behind her. A shot slapped into the ground next to her feet as she ran, her pulse pounding.

The moment she reached Diana, she threw her a pack. "Come on, we need to go right now!" she said, adding when Diana snatched at her abandoned PFD, "Leave it!"

Diana scrambled to her feet, pulling the pack straps over her shoulders, and took off at a run with Tabitha right behind her.

Tree branches seemed to deliberately reach out to snag her pack, the kerchief covering her hair, her clothes, the exposed skin of her face and neck. Tabitha tore free, heedless of the damage or the signs they must be leaving. The men might be skilled trackers, but the most important thing right now was to put distance between herself and Diana, and the threat.

When Diana stumbled, she took hold of her arm, dragged her upright with an effort that made the world spin, and pushed her forward. "Keep moving," she gasped, trying to ignore the pain burning like hot coals lodged under her ribs.

At last, after crashing through a thick growth of bushes, Tabitha paused to take stock of the situation. She whispered to Diana, "I think we've got a few minutes' grace to catch our breath. How are you doing?"

Diana shook her head, scattering sweat droplets. "What the hell's all that about?"

"Looks like our sniper has buddies and they're definitely unfriendly. Four Caucasian males armed with rifles just landed a Zodiac by our canoe, and one of them took a shot at me, which puts a different spin on things." Tabitha rubbed her forehead, feeling an unpleasant stickiness on her skin. Glancing down at the livid, bleeding scratch on her wrist, she frowned.

"Oh, my God." Diana clutched at Tabitha's arm.

"Keep it together, Di," Tabitha said, touching Diana's knee. "Look at me. Come on, let me see those baby blues."

When Diana turned wide, terrified eyes on her, she went on in her best authoritative voice, "We'll get through this. We just have to circle around, get back to the canoe, paddle like hell to the Lake Laberge checkpoint, and we'll be home free. Stick with me, do as I say, and we'll both walk out of here, I swear."

"He's going to kill me," Diana muttered, her gaze sliding away from Tabitha to focus on some private nightmare. "Jesus Christ, Blair's going to kill me."

Realization struck Tabitha like a blow, stealing her wind and her wits so she gaped like an idiot for several seconds. Stunned surprise gave way to the rage bubbling in her gut. "You know the shooter? Who is Blair?" she demanded.

Diana didn't answer.

Tabitha grabbed Diana's chin, wrenching the woman's head around with just enough force to make her fury known. "Who is Blair?" she repeated. "Why does he want to kill you? Those shots that missed us...we were herded here. This is a killing ground, goddamn it, so answer me, Di, and no lies, or I swear to God, I will leave your ass right here to die."

Diana stared at nothing for several long seconds, her fluttering pulse visible in the tanned column of her neck. She released Tabitha's arm. Her tongue crept out to wet her lips, and finally she spoke. "Blair's the man who killed my brother, and now he's after me."

Tabitha fought to contain her dismay and anger, not only at Diana, but also at herself. Everybody lies: one of the first and more difficult lessons to learn in law enforcement. The innocent lied because they were afraid, the guilty lied to hide their sins. She knew better than to believe anyone without verification.

Listening intently, she heard nothing out of place in the wilderness—no sounds of approach, no men's voices, not a single snap of a branch to betray a footfall. It seemed they had lost their pursuers. She saw no reason to delay getting an explanation.

"Is your name really Diana Crenshaw?" she asked. "Bear in mind that as soon as I get access to a computer, I'll check on your story."

"Yes, that's my real name," Diana replied. Her shoulders slumped. She took off her baseball cap to reveal brown hair unraveled from the ponytail and matted by sweat. "And I was born and raised in Lightning Ridge, Georgia. That's all true."

"Now tell me the rest of it." Tabitha sat down on the ground next to her.

Diana grimaced, but complied. "My twin brother, Jack…I loved him, you know? He was always getting into trouble, even when we were kids. I protected him, I tried to help him." She paused, scrubbing roughly at her eyes with the heel of her hand. "Jack was an alcoholic and a compulsive gambler. We used to joke that I didn't have many bad habits because he inherited enough for both of us." She gave Tabitha a wan smile.

Tabitha was unmoved. "Go on," she said, not only hearing Diana's words, but keeping a close eye on the woman's demeanor and the nuances of her body language. She ought to have used her training as a skilled interrogator when they first met in the Tremblay Arms, she thought…but apparently my bullshit meter was on the fritz that day.

"It wasn't too bad at first, but he got worse after his wife divorced him," Diana continued. "Anyway, the drinking and gambling were a lot worse after they split. The dumbass lost his job, his house, his car, everything except a big mountain of debts he couldn't pay even if he won the state lottery. But nothing was his fault. You've met the type, right? Jack was like that. Blamed everybody but himself for his troubles. Maybe Mama spoiled him too much. God knows, she sure as hell didn't spoil me—"

"Let's keep on track," Tabitha interrupted. "What happened to Jack? Why did Blair murder him?"

Diana flinched, the picture of misery. Her fingers knotted together in her lap. "Jack got himself tangled up with a nasty piece of work named Blair Montoya. Way I heard it, Blair bought up Jack's IOUs, then threatened to make his ex-wife the star of a torture snuff film if he didn't do what he was told. Jack still loved her, so he agreed." She looked at Tabitha. "You heard about that payroll robbery in Flathead?"

Tabitha recalled an alert that crossed her desk about a month ago. She dredged her mind for details. The payroll truck servicing several logging companies in Flathead, Georgia, had been robbed by a team of five well-armed, well-organized experts with automatic weapons. The robbers had used a spike strip on a stretch of road in a cell tower blind spot, ambushed the truck when the tires blew, and escaped in a blue van. Had Blair Montoya's name come up on the suspect list? Since it wasn't her case, she couldn't be sure.

"Anyway," Diana went on, recapturing Tabitha's attention, "Blair had to have a man on the inside of the armored car company 'cause the head office kept changing the routes as a security precaution. Every day the routes were chosen at random according to some computer algorithm to keep the trucks' movements unpredictable. Nobody knew which truck would go out when or what roads it would take to its destination. You see?"

"I'm beginning to."

"One of the company managers, Charlie Whitehead, was Jack's best friend since grade school, but when Jack started drinking so heavy, they kind of lost touch. So Jack goes to Charlie with some story about being on the wagon. Charlie felt sorry for him and gave him a desk job. Once Jack was in the office, he sent Blair information on the daily truck routes."

Tabitha nodded. A professional operation, flawlessly executed, planned for minimum violence and maximum payoff. She wondered why Montoya had killed Jack Crenshaw. A quarrel between thieves? The discovery of a murder victim shortly after a robbery raised all kinds of red flags, which she'd have thought a pro like Montoya would want to avoid.

"What went wrong?" she asked.

"Jack thought he was done, I guess. He asked Blair for a cut. Can you believe that greedy fool?" Diana asked bitterly. "When Blair told him no, Jack stole the money. All of it. He stole it and ran with it, and sent me this in the mail, along with a letter telling me what he'd done." From beneath the neckline of her shirt, she drew out a key on a silver chain. "A week later, Jack was found shot in the back of his head in an alley in Atlanta. I know Blair killed my brother. I know it! And now the bastard's after me."

Tabitha peered at the key dangling from the chain. It looked ordinary, like it fitted an automobile rather than a safe deposit box. "Montoya's after the money, you mean." When Diana blinked in confusion, she added, "Your brother's dead. There's no need for Montoya to come after you unless he thinks you know the location of the money. How much?"

Diana tucked the key back under her shirt, her hands shaking. "Two million dollars. And I don't know where the money is," she muttered. "Jack never said."

Tabitha smelled a lie. The sum seemed suspiciously low, for one thing. She let it pass, thinking she could get clarification later. "I take it you left town."

"You'd better believe it. My mama didn't raise no dummy. A couple of guys tried to grab me in the supermarket parking lot one night, then my apartment got broken into when I was at work. I lit out of there in a hurry, let me tell you."

"Why go to Canada? Why not report Blair to the police?"

"Are you kidding me? Go to the cops?" Diana let out a scoffing sound. "Hell, sugar, ain't nobody can help me except myself. I learned that lesson a long time ago. As for Canada, I was already living here. Last three years, I've been working for a natural gas company as a chromatography tech. They're based in Toronto, and these days, so am I."

"Toronto's a long way from Whitehorse," Tabitha pointed out, wondering why Diana had such mistrust of the authorities. Did she have a criminal record?

Diana nodded. "Blair's right on my tail. I didn't dare stay in Toronto. I knew about the Yukon River Quest. Thought I'd blend in with the out-of-towners in the ass end of nowhere, and I've got a friend in Dawson who'll help me out, which is why I was looking for a team or a support crew spot. I didn't think Blair would try to kill me with witnesses around."

"This morning in Rotary Peace Park, you spotted someone," Tabitha said, recalling Diana's pallid face right before the race began.

"One of Blair's goons. They've been stalking me since I arrived in Whitehorse. I figure they've got the roads out of town covered, but so far I've managed to stay ahead of them by the skin of my teeth—"

Tabitha cut her off with a gesture. A scuffling on the forest floor had caught her ear, along with a murmur of human voices. Four men, she thought. Same number as the riflemen in the Zodiac. She decided not to stick around for visual confirmation. She rose to her feet, flashing four fingers of her free hand and drawing a thumb across her throat.

Diana's eyes widened in understanding.

Trying to move as quietly as possible, Tabitha led Diana deeper into the woods.

CHAPTER SIX

Three hours later, Tabitha had to admit she was lost.

She and Diana had been within a half-hour's paddle of the Lake Laberge checkpoint, but in avoiding their pursuers, they'd wandered along the trails and side-trails. Worse, she found while searching both packs during a rest break that the GPS navigation device had taken a stray bullet and neither pack contained a compass. That wilderness essential, as well as the satellite phone, must have been in the third pack she hadn't had time to grab.

"We're screwed," Diana said wearily. She sat on the ground with her back against a white spruce tree, her knees drawn up, her arms wrapped around her legs.

"I don't know about you, but I'm tired and cold. We need to warm up and we need to eat," Tabitha said. She found a single extra fleece jacket in the second pack and pulled it on. It had been warm on the river, but under the trees, the temperature was decidedly cooler. "There's a camping stove here, and we've got survival blankets and food. I'll go find something to burn. You stay here," she went on, passing Diana a light, silvery emergency blanket. "I'd rather we weren't separated, but if you hear or see Blair's men, I want you to head east toward the river, which I think is that way. I'll meet up with you, okay?"

Diana nodded and wrapped the blanket around herself.

Taking a long bladed knife out of the pack—a military surplus Ghurka kukri, she noted, home modified with a paracord wrapped handle—Tabitha left Diana behind while she went in search of wood.

While gathering dry sticks from the forest floor, she thought of *Double Jeopardy* with a pang of regret. Survival-wise, abandoning the canoe had been the smartest move. They couldn't have continued paddling with a sniper taking shots at them. Perhaps Blair's men had left the canoe alone, but she doubted it. Holing the hull would have taken seconds.

Victoria, who had treated the canoe with the tenderness another woman might show a child, would be furious, Tabitha thought. Wondering if Victoria was already sick from the initial cancer treatment made her heart hurt, but she pushed her emotions aside. Right now, she had more pressing concerns.

Retracing her steps, she returned to the clearing to find that Diana had already set up the camping stove and pulled a couple of MREs from one of the packs. The stove was collapsible, low emission and virtually smokeless, weighed less than two pounds, and burned almost any flammable fuel. Not mandatory gear for the race, but she was grateful that Betty and Dusty had included it in their supplies.

Once she used the kukri to whittle down some sticks into rough chips, she loaded a big handful of the chips into the camp stove, adding more finely shaved wood for kindling. From a survival kit in an army surplus magazine pouch, she took a lighter.

"No matches?" Diana asked, leaning forward to poke at the survival kit.

Tabitha shook her head. "Magnesium and flint are more useful. And this, too." She pointed out a credit card-sized magnifying lens. "A pyromaniac's dream come true. Just add kindling." Using the lighter, she soon had a fire going in the camping stove. "You know much about camping?" she asked, pushing some longer sticks into the ground on one side of the stove and draping the second emergency blanket over them to reflect the heat while she and Diana sat side by side on a folded plastic tarpaulin.

Diana scooted closer. "Not a damned thing, sugar," she admitted. "Closest I ever got was a sleepover in a tent in the backyard."

"I used to be a Girl Scout, but I'm hoping we can reach the checkpoint or maybe flag down a safety boat before the sun goes down. I don't really want to spend the night out here." Tabitha studied the two MRE packages. "We don't have much water, so I'd rather not waste any heating these up. What's your poison—chicken fajita or beef ravioli?"

"Which one has a brownie? Hey, don't look at me like that. Everybody knows chocolate is survival food," Diana said, chuckling.

The rich, warm sound slightly lightened Tabitha's mood. She tossed Diana the chicken fajita MRE with a wry, "Bon appétit."

As it turned out, the beef ravioli wasn't bad, even eaten cold. An awakened appetite insisted she devour every bite including the atomic orange cheese spread, jalapeño crackers, chocolate chip toaster pastry, oatmeal cookie and candy. She tucked the package of caffeinated mints into a pocket in case she needed a quick energy jolt later.

Her belly full, her body warmer, she said to Diana, "If you need to pee, I'll stand guard. You can do the same for me, okay?"

"And here I thought you had a cast-iron bladder," Diana replied, hopping to her feet with the blanket clutched around her shoulders. "My back teeth are swimming." She paused, eyeing the open packs. "Do we leave this stuff here or what?"

"We're not going far. I think I saw a collapsible shovel in that pack. Do you want it?" Tabitha hinted, flushing with embarrassment.

"Do you?" Diana asked, grinning. "Hey, don't be delicate on my account. When I did the Texas Water Safari, I came down with a serious case of the runs about halfway through the course. I spent more time with my butt hanging over the edge of the canoe than paddling. Sure felt sorry for the folks downstream."

Choking back a laugh, Tabitha rose. "Come on, let's go find a friendly bush."

A few minutes later, squatting with her pants and underwear around her ankles, the waistbands pulled forward to get the garments out of the line of "fire," Tabitha released her bladder with a happy sigh. When she pulled up her pants, she heard a noise coming from the direction of the clearing.

"Do you hear that?" she asked Diana, who had been standing nearby with her back politely turned. Not waiting for an answer, she hurried to their makeshift campsite to find a fat black bear pawing through the packs, no doubt searching for food.

The bear had already chewed on their discarded MRE packages. While she watched, frozen in a combination of indignation, horror and fury, the animal knocked over the camping stove, scattering coals and embers over the ground.

A touch on her shoulder had Tabitha whirling around, her heart in her mouth, but it was only Diana.

"What do we do?" Diana asked, her voice barely audible.

Tabitha tried to recall the advice given by the race organizers. Unlike grizzlies, black bears were timid by nature. Any bear was dangerous at any time, of course, but more so if starving or with cubs in tow. She didn't see a cub and this bear seemed well fed to her inexperienced eye. If they'd had a bear banger, the noisemaker might have served to drive the animal away. Under other circumstances, it might be less risky to leave their supplies, but what was in those packs might mean the difference between survival and death.

Before she could make up her mind, Diana stepped out into the clearing, looking scared but resolute. She put up both arms to make herself appear bigger and began clapping her hands, calling loudly, "Go on! Go on or I'll knock you on the head and eat you myself!"

Though startled, the black bear stood its ground, its muzzle shiny with the blobs of petroleum jelly it had been licking out of a broken jar.

"Go on!" Diana yelled. "I said go on, damn your eyes! Scat!" Sticking two fingers in her mouth, she blasted out a shrill shriek of a whistle.

To Tabitha's amusement, the bear bolted, crashing into the undergrowth.

Diana dusted her hands together. "And stay out!" Turning to Tabitha, she said with an air of satisfaction, "That's how we do it in Georgia, Ms. Knowles."

Tabitha applauded. "Good job, Ms. Crenshaw. Now we just need to figure out what we can salvage from this mess—shit!"

Interrupted by a rifle shot that sounded appallingly close, she snatched at the survival kit, the kukri and the second emergency blanket. Glancing toward Diana, she saw the woman already in motion, bending to snag the shoulder straps of a half-empty pack and disappearing into the woods as quickly as the bear.

She regretfully turned her back on their precious supplies and followed Diana.

CHAPTER SEVEN

The trail led upward into the hills, but Tabitha's primary concern was escape, not finding the river. They had one advantage: the men on their tail wanted to take Diana alive.

According to her watch, the time was edging into early evening. The temperature had fallen further, and now she felt a definite nip in the air, especially where the sweat cooled on her exposed face and neck. She also heard the reedy whining of mosquitoes.

Diana swore fervently under her breath, slapping at her neck. "Sucker bit. This keeps up, I'll need a blood transfusion."

"Any mosquito repellent in that pack?" Tabitha asked, halting to lean on a tree.

Grumbling, Diana shrugged off the pack and began rummaging through the contents. "Here we go," she said, pulling out a spray bottle.

"Does it have DEET in it?"

"Right at this moment, I'd marinate in DEET if it kept the skeeters off."

After Diana sprayed her neck, face and hands with the repellent, Tabitha accepted the bottle and did the same, wrinkling her nose at the fake lemony odor that reminded her of rest stop toilets. "Any water in there?" she asked, nodding at the pack.

Diana shook her head. "Sorry, not a drop."

Learning they had no water made Tabitha thirstier. "I've got water purification straws in the survival kit," she said. "As we move, keep an ear out for a stream."

"Well, ain't you little Miss Wilderness?" Diana heaved a sigh. "I have got to sit still for two minutes. If I keel over, you'll have to haul me along by the hair like a caveman."

"That's cavewoman, thank you very much, and there will be no hair dragging without a club and a leopard skin bikini."

"Into role-playing, huh?"

Tabitha flushed. Was Diana flirting with her?

"That's okay, my last girlfriend liked to pretend she was Annie Oakley," Diana said with a wicked chuckle. "You do not want to know what that woman did with a cap gun. No, seriously. You don't want to know. Get that image out of your head."

Resisting the urge to laugh, Tabitha prowled around the immediate area, finding nothing more threatening than a profusion of animal tracks. "Okay, we can take a break," she said, turning around to find Diana sitting cross-legged on the ground and using a log as a backrest, with the silver emergency blanket draped over her shoulders.

"Could use a cup of coffee," Diana said, opening a flap of her blanket in invitation when Tabitha joined her.

After hesitating a moment, Tabitha scooted closer, so that her side was pressed against Diana's. Even through the double layers of her fleece jackets, she felt a bloom of extra warmth. "And a fire," she murmured. "And a sandwich."

"Applewood smoked bacon, lettuce and tomato on whole wheat, country-style bread with just a smidgeon of homemade mayonnaise," Diana replied promptly.

Tabitha's stomach rumbled. "You're an evil, evil woman," she mock complained.

Diana suddenly turned to face her, looking sober. "Tabs, I am so, so very sorry I put you into this mess. It wasn't my intention to involve anybody else in my problem. Had I known Blair Montoya was crazy, I'd have found another way to get to Dawson."

This close, Tabitha was surrounded by Diana's scent: a bit smoky, a bit salty from sweat, a general muskiness overlaid with a chemical citrus smell from the mosquito repellent. It should have been repellent to her, too, but the smell made her inner muscles clench. Instant desire fluttered in the pit of her stomach like a trapped bird.

The lines at the corners of Diana's mouth deepened. She wanted to kiss the frown away. Instead, she cleared her throat. "Uh, sure, Di, it's okay. You aren't to blame."

"It's my fault if we die out here."

"We're not going to die."

"But—"

"But me no buts, Diana Crenshaw, and trust me when I tell you that I have no intention of dying in the woods, today or any other day," Tabitha said more sharply than she intended. "So suck it up, put your big girl panties on, and help me figure out what to do," she went on, glad to see the fear in Diana's eyes retreating.

"Yeah, yeah, okay, I'm done wallowing," Diana said, "but for the record, although I'm not a dainty girl, my panties can in no way, shape or form be called 'big.'"

Tabitha smiled. "So noted."

Diana handed her a granola bar. "I found two at the bottom of the pack," she explained, "and I thought you'd prefer the chocolate chip to the apple cinnamon. Better eat up. Food's better in your body than carried around in your hand." She paused. "Peace?"

"Peace." Tabitha took the bar, tore open the wrapper, and made herself take small, deliberate bites instead of gobbling it whole. She even licked her fingers and the inside of the wrapper, chasing every trace of sweet stickiness. Her stomach still ached a little, but she wasn't starving. Not yet, she corrected herself silently. But their immediate priority was finding water. Apart from preventing dehydration, if they located a stream, they could follow it downhill to the river.

After sitting quietly for five minutes and listening to the rustling leaves, the skittering of a small animal in the underbrush, and the sound of Diana's breathing, Tabitha leaned her head against the tree trunk and closed her eyes. She was tired, hungry and thirsty, and would have sold her soul for a firm mattress, a fast-food hamburger and a glass of iced tea. Not to mention a round dozen FBI agents armed to the teeth.

"Why didn't you go to the police?" she asked.

Diana jerked in apparent surprise. "I thought you were taking a nap."

"Nope," Tabitha said, opening her eyes. Focusing on Diana, she continued, "When you knew what your brother did, why didn't you go to the police? Why run?"

"Because the police are lying assholes," Diana replied, sounding irritated. "When me and Jack were ten years old, my father saw a guy get shot in the street by another man. Daddy stepped forward as a witness. Said he had to do his duty. The shooter turned out to be a drug lord on the police's Most Wanted list, and Daddy's testimony was the DA's case."

"He was offered protection?"

"Oh, sure, witness protection program, new identities for his family, the whole nine yards. Would've been peachy keen except for one thing: on the day of the trial, the cop supposed to escort my father left him alone in the courthouse men's room."

Tabitha's throat tightened. She already knew the end of the story.

"Somebody stabbed Daddy to death while that cop walked away," Diana went on harshly. "There was an investigation, but nothing happened. Not enough evidence, they said. That cop—his name was Beckett, by the way, I'll never forget him—got two weeks' suspension. That's it. But it gets better, you know. The DA wasn't interested in protecting us anymore. Without Daddy's testimony, without a case, we were worthless to him. Then the day after the funeral, Mama found our dog, the sweetest Lab in all creation, on the front porch. He'd been butchered. She got the message. She packed us up and took us the hell out of there. We made a new life, but poor Mama spent years looking over her shoulder.

"So you see, I don't trust the police. Far as I can tell, ain't nobody in law enforcement worth a good goddamn. Once they have what they want from you, they'll leave you high and dry. Screw 'em, every last one of them sumbitches. Can't rely on help from nobody but yourself. I learned that lesson young, and it stuck for life," she concluded.

"Okay," Tabitha said after a pause, deciding she would keep her FBI identity to herself. No need to unnecessarily antagonize Diana when she needed the woman's cooperation for them to survive. "So why don't you just give Montoya the key?"

"Because Blair killed my brother," Diana said, her expression pinched with dislike, "and I sure as hell won't give him millions for his trouble. I'll burn that money first."

"Then you know where it is?" Tabitha asked, the question popping out of her mouth in such an eager tone, she winced. Way to go, Knowles, she said to herself. If this was a real interview with a suspect, you'd have blown it.

Diana stiffened, drew away from her, and glared suspiciously. "You never did tell me what you did for a living," she said, sliding further away so that the folds of the blanket fell between them.

Already mourning the loss of warmth, Tabitha began, "Ah, about that—"

She broke off when Diana leaped to her feet, brandishing a long, heavy stick she snatched from the ground. The splintered, pointed end was aimed directly at her throat.

"Are you working for Blair?" Diana demanded, practically vibrating with tension.

"No! No, of course not," Tabitha replied, striving to keep her voice calm. "Think about it. If I worked for Montoya, would I have saved your life on the river?"

Diana said through clenched teeth, "Yes, because the last thing Blair wants is my corpse. He needs me alive because he hasn't got the first clue where Jack hid the money." She held the makeshift spear poised to strike.

"Do you?"

"What's it to you? Just answer my question."

Tabitha didn't reach up and simply remove the stick from Diana's grasp, although she could have disarmed the woman if necessary. She'd save force as a last resort. Panic made otherwise reasonable people do stupid things, made them unpredictable. No need to exacerbate the situation with a confrontation. Instead, she leaned back against the log, relaxing in a deliberate effort to ease Diana's anxiety. The pose was deceptive. She had positioned her body so that if an assault occurred, she could defend herself.

"I am not working for Blair Montoya," she said, meeting Diana's glittering gaze.

"Then who do you work for?" Diana asked, trembling a little.

"The government of the United States of America," Tabitha answered, keeping her hands in her lap to avoid making any gestures that might be misinterpreted. The stick didn't look that sharp, but if Diana hit hard, putting her weight into the blow, she'd be pinned through the neck like a butterfly specimen.

Diana frowned. "What do you do for the government?"

"I work for the FBI," Tabitha said while evaluating Diana's body language. The woman seemed more perplexed and hurt than angry. "I came to Whitehorse with my partner. My FBI partner," she clarified when Diana arched a brow. "She and I trained a long time for the race, but she had bad news at the last minute and had to back out. That's why I went to the Tremblay Arms looking for you. I didn't know anything about you or your brother, or Blair Montoya for that matter, until I heard your story."

"You should have told me."

"It didn't seem important at the time. I know better now and I apologize."

Still frowning, Diana lifted the stick away and let it drop. "I thought…no, it doesn't really matter. Shit," she sighed. "Sorry."

Tabitha stood and moved over to Diana, incidentally stepping on the stick to prevent it being picked up again. The emergency blanket had fallen to the ground, forgotten. She stooped, picked up the blanket, and put it around Diana's shoulders, holding the edges closed.

"Di, what happened to your father and your family…well, for lack of a better word, it sucked," she said. "My sole concern at this point is keeping us alive and getting us back to civilization. Anything else can wait."

"Have I broken the law?" Diana asked in a small voice. "You going to arrest me?"

"Not me, but I can't predict what the District Attorney in Flathead, Georgia will do. He could possibly file charges against you for obstruction, maybe even try for conspiracy. I don't know. But right here, right now, we have bigger problems."

"Like getting away from Blair."

"Yes, exactly. You need to trust me, Di," Tabitha said, giving Diana an impatient little shake. "I am not the enemy. I'm on your side. Give me a chance, will you?"

Diana stared. At last, her wariness crumbled. "I don't know what to do," she whispered, looking lost. "I'm so scared, Tabs. So tired, and so damned scared all the time…"

Obeying an impulse to comfort, Tabitha wrapped her arms around the shuddering woman, inhaling sharply when Diana pressed a wet face against her neck. The first soft sob, the first desperate clutch of hands in her fleece jacket left her undone, unable to do much more than rock Diana back and forth, rub her back, and murmur platitudes until the storm passed, the sobs turning into hiccups.

"Now listen to me," Tabitha said, drawing back to inspect Diana's face. Her eyelashes, surprisingly thick and dark, were wet and starred into points, and her freckled cheeks and nose had turned pink with weeping. "We'll work together," she went on. "I'm not going to let Montoya hurt you. But you need to be honest, Di. Don't keep anything from me. And when this is over, maybe I can help you in a more official way. Talk to the DA on your behalf or something." Why she made the last offer, she couldn't say, but it seemed right.

Diana seemed guarded, the stiffness warring with the fragile hope in her eyes. "You'd do that? Really?"

"I promise. Cross my heart."

"Just don't hope to die, okay? I don't think my nerves can stand it."

Reluctantly, Tabitha released Diana and knelt on the ground next to the pack. "Better take an inventory, see what we've got to work with besides the survival kit," she said, not taking out any items, but committing the pack's contents to memory. She needed a distraction. Diana was too damned attractive. The woman smelled too good, felt too good, and pressed all her buttons—a complication she didn't need. Want, certainly, but need…

"Those were the only granola bars," Diana said, coming to stand beside her.

Tabitha resisted leaning against Diana's muscled legs. "Flashlight, tissues, collapsible mess kit, some freeze-dried emergency meals, water purification tablets, a tarp, laser pointer, and a handful of tampons. Betty must've stuck those in. Two empty water bottles. That's it. Next time we stop to eat, let's avoid leaving any food where the bears can find it. Now we just need water." She stuck the survival kit inside the pack.

"Wouldn't want to choke down freeze-dried chicken without water," Diana said, smiling down at her. "You don't happen to have a gun in there, do you?"

"Nope, sorry. The paperwork required to bring a weapon into Canada is a nightmare. And I left my FBI credentials in the hotel room, not that Montoya is likely to be impressed." Tabitha rose, dusting off the knees of her khaki pants. "I didn't think I'd need to fend off bloodthirsty felons while paddling a canoe on the river. Speaking of which, I'll have to make a report to the RCMP as soon as I hunt down a constable."

"I understand." Diana picked up the pack. She tried arranging the emergency blanket around her body, but the pack on her back made it difficult.

"I've got an idea," Tabitha said, removing the kukri from its sheath. She used the blade to cut a slit in the center of the blanket, which allowed Diana to pull it over her head like a poncho. A length of paracord unwound from the kukri handle worked as a belt.

"Very fetching. You ready to go?" she asked, tucking the re-sheathed kukri into her waistband so it lay flat against the small of her back, within easy reach.

"Yeah." Diana bit her lip, appearing faintly embarrassed. "Thanks for...um, you know. When I had a meltdown. You didn't...you were nice to me. Thank you."

An unexpected feeling of affection rose in Tabitha's chest, expanding like a bubble and lodging under her heart. "You're welcome," she replied.

CHAPTER EIGHT

She found a stream by accident.

While walking downhill, following a narrow trail peppered with animal tracks, the toe of Tabitha's shoe struck a root or a rock, she couldn't be sure, but the impact caused her to stumble. Instead of solid ground, her foot hit soft earth under the leaf litter and sank down several inches, throwing off her balance. Arms windmilling, she fell on her side.

"Oh, my God! Are you okay?" Diana cried, scrambling after her.

After doing a quick mental check—all her limbs seemed intact—Tabitha rolled over, mortified by her clumsiness. "I'm fine, I'm fine, just...wet? What the hell?" The fleece jacket repelled water, but her trousers were soaked along the hem, as were her shoes.

Diana knelt to push dead leaves and fallen branches aside. "You found it," she said, holding up fingers stained with muddy earth. "You found a stream."

"I did? I did!" Tabitha pushed herself upright. The stream was tiny, barely more than a trickle running through a channel clogged with forest debris. Gripped by an overwhelming need to quench her thirst, she scrabbled to enlarge the stream, digging with her hands until she had widened and unblocked enough of the channel that the stream gushed more forcefully. She gestured at Diana's pack, ignoring the clots of mud that caked her hands to the wrists.

"Give me a straw out of the survival kit," she said.

Diana found the kit, opened it, and passed her a water purification straw, somewhat thicker than a normal straw and about ten inches in length. Tabitha bent over and stuck the end of the straw into the water, sucking hard until she feared the veins in her head might explode. Finally, after what seemed like an agony of suction, water surged into her mouth. The liquid tasted a little flat, but she kept drinking greedily until she felt almost bloated.

"Hey, take it easy," Diana said, resting a hand on her shoulder. "Drink too fast, sugar, you'll puke it out again."

Aware of Diana watching the straw and the stream with naked longing, Tabitha washed her hands and surrendered her place.

She stood and groaned, wondering if her stomach sloshed. The filtering straw helped them avoid waterborne diseases like typhoid, cholera, dysentery and E. coli infections. Far from any hospital or emergency clinic, unable to rely on medical evacuation by helicopter, the last thing she and Diana needed was a serious illness. Even a minor case of the runs would be more serious than inconvenient at this point.

Four years ago, a long weekend in Mexico had taught her the absolute necessity of clean water. Montezuma's revenge, indeed. She wondered what they called traveler's diarrhea in Canada. Probably Fox's trot, she thought with a grin, blessing Betty and Dusty for including three of the purification straws in the survival kit.

While Diana drank, she surveyed the area. The stream was close to a patch of ground surrounded on three sides by a ring of birch, lodgepole pine and white spruce trees. On the fourth side, the forest opened to reveal an expanse of mottled green and brown mossy tundra rising as if to meet the mountains in the distance, all snowy stone peaks and jagged edges thrusting against an endless blue sky. The sheer, aching beauty made her breath catch.

"Here," Tabitha said when Diana joined her. "We should stop here."

"Stay overnight? You sure?"

"I don't think we'll find the river today and navigating the woods at night doesn't appeal to me. They may call it the midnight sun around here, but it still gets pretty damned dark. Besides, I'll bet Montoya's men are holed up till morning."

A corner of Diana's mouth twitched. "No bet. I'm sure you're right. Hey, do you think it's safe to light a fire? We need boiling water for those freeze-dried meal pouches, and I'd really, really like to feel warm sometime this century." She grinned, a bright flash in her dirt-smudged face. "I'd also kill for a cup of coffee."

Tabitha considered. "If we're careful and keep the fire small, it should be okay. Let's scout around, see if we can scare up fuel and something to use as kindling. Try not to go too far into the open, Di. It's safer to stay in the trees. We don't want to be spotted."

Muttering something under her breath that sounded suspiciously like "grandmother" and "eggs," Diana walked away.

Smiling, Tabitha began collecting dry sticks off the ground. When she moved closer to a huge, wild tangle of bushes, she noticed the branches had grown up and over to form a distinct peaked shape. Could it be a roof? Her stomach knotted. She walked around the bushes, peering under and around the masses of leaves until she found the outline of a dark rectangular shape. Dropping the sticks she had collected, she took out the kukri. Cutting away the growth eventually revealed a door, which opened at her touch.

The interior of the roughly crafted wood cabin appeared spartan at best: a partially collapsed cot, a few hooks screwed into the wall near the door, two large metal storage chests and a woodstove in the corner that looked somewhat rusted but still sturdy, including the chimney pipe piercing the roof to vent smoke. Tabitha sniffed at the pungent odors of animal urine, mouse droppings, decay, mold and the dry, dusty scent of neglect. Whoever owned this cabin hadn't visited in quite some time.

Opening another door set into one side of the cabin, she discovered a lean-to with a composting toilet, thankfully clean and ready for use. A bag filled with a mixture of dried moss and woodchips showed signs of being nibbled by mice. No sink, but a metal bucket hanging from a nail would probably suffice for washing hands if filled with water. Primitive, she thought, but at least the cobwebs in the corners of the low ceiling didn't appear occupied.

She turned her attention to the two metal storage boxes. Neither was padlocked, but both were secured with a bolt to keep out scavengers. Opening the first, she found several folded blankets, a couple of thick flannel shirts, woolen gloves, a pair of snowshoes, a Bible, three boxes of copper jacketed, .223 caliber ammunition for a rifle, a scrap of soap, matches, lighter fluid and a mess kit. No rifle, which came as something of a disappointment. The other box contained food items, mostly canned fruit, dried beans, containers of salt and sugar, a jar of instant coffee and a bottle of off-brand whiskey.

Tabitha patted the bottle fondly. Rising to her feet, she went outside.

Diana returned bearing an armful of sticks. On seeing Tabitha standing by the bushes, her brow furrowed. "What's up?"

"I found a cabin. Looks abandoned, but I think you'll like it," Tabitha answered, trying to contain her glee. She swept an arm at the half-hidden cabin in invitation. "We'll have a roof over our heads tonight, a soft bed to sleep on, and a wood stove for warmth and cooking. I'll even make you an Irish coffee after dinner. How's that for service?"

Diana went into the cabin, her expression filled with wonder. "Damn it, Tabs, I love you so much right now," she said, tossing her armload of sticks on the floor near the stove. "In fact," she went on, "I'm going to give you something I've wanted to give you since we met in that crappy B&B in Whitehorse." In a shaft

48   Nene Adams

of sunlight slanting through a hole in the roof, her eyes seemed to catch fire, bright and as luminous blue as the heart of a candle flame.

"Oh, yeah? What's that?" Tabitha asked, laughing to cover the sudden nervousness constricting her chest. She waited, frozen to the spot, while Diana stalked closer. Her gaze settled on Diana's mouth. She found herself fascinated by a gleam of moisture on the full bottom lip. Her heart pounded, sending an insistent rush of blood to her head.

"A kiss," Diana murmured, stopping when she stood directly in front of Tabitha, their bodies almost, but not quite, touching. Under her jacket, the rise and fall of her breasts quickened. "You know, sugar, I've got a crush on you somethin' fierce."

Tabitha wavered. If she let Diana kiss her, that would lead to complications. For all she knew, the story about Blair Montoya might be a fabrication. Diana could be involved in the payroll truck robbery. Hell, she might've planned it herself.

No quicker way to tank her career at the FBI, she thought, than to be romantically tangled with a suspect or worse, a known criminal. Even a one-night stand compromised her integrity. A man might survive the indiscretion. A woman, never. The double standard was worse for an "out" lesbian since antidiscrimination laws only went so far. She knew at least two people above her at the regional office who would throw a gleeful "don't let the doorknob hit you on the ass" farewell party if she crossed the line.

Hook up with Diana and she stood to lose everything she had worked hard to achieve. She could say goodbye to the respect of her colleagues and especially to Victoria's friendship. Close as they were, she couldn't imagine Victoria giving her a free pass for behaving like a horny teenager with a case of raging hormones.

It was stupid. It was folly. A mad, impulsive attraction to a woman she knew virtually nothing about. Common sense dictated a retreat, a gentle rejection, an excuse, but the words sounded like falsehoods when she tested them in her mind.

Diana's hands slid into her hair, strong fingers curling around the back of her neck. "You want this," she said, her voice searing through Tabitha and sending hot shivers to the pit of her stomach. "You want this as much as I do."

A current of desire coursed deep within her, as strong as the tide and just as irresistible. Fuck it. Tabitha gripped Diana's hips, closed the distance between them, and took that tempting mouth in a kiss.

She deepened the kiss and parted Diana's lips with her tongue, a touch of warm, soft heat that burned like white fire to the very core of her.

Diana made a sound deep in her throat, her fingertips digging into Tabitha's scalp.

Breaking the kiss, Tabitha nuzzled Diana's throat, pulling aside the jacket collar to nip at the tendon standing taut under skin tinged faintly pink with sunburn. She licked the livid mark her teeth had made, tasting salt and a lingering trace of coconut sunscreen.

"Christ, I want to eat you up," she murmured, feeling Diana's pulse beat faster against her lips. Irresistible impulse. She had never believed a temptation existed that couldn't be resisted by the strong-willed, but now she understood the truth of the phrase.

Too late, her mind sang, the sentiment echoed by another, more primitive part of her anatomy. Too late. Desire demanded satisfaction. She wanted to sweat, to rut, to wallow in pleasure until she was lost to herself.

"God, I hope so," Diana moaned. She took a step back, her palms flattened on Tabitha's chest to prevent the automatic surge forward. "Unless you plan for us to do the dirty deed on the floor in the mouse shit and who knows what all else," she said, "I suggest we take five minutes to do something about it. Something comfortable if possible."

Tabitha shook her head. "This isn't a suite at the Ritz," she protested, but went to the metal storage box to grab a stack of blankets. No broom, but a couple of leafy branches from outside swept the worst of the litter out the door. Laying down the plastic tarp from the pack, she heaped blankets on top to make a cozy nest in front of the woodstove.

While she worked, the first blaze of lust settled to a warm simmer, a hum of anticipation sharpening her senses.

"Very nice," Diana purred, "and I'm not just talking about the accommodations."

Bent over to start a fire in the stove, Tabitha wiggled her ass and chuckled at Diana's wolf whistle of appreciation. She glanced over her shoulder to find that Diana had already stripped down to bra and panties, revealing a body that wasn't perfect, though hard work and exercise had toned her arms and shoulders nicely. Her waist was thicker, her breasts and hips rounder, her curves riper than a young girl's.

Womanly. Luscious. Powerful. Perfect, Tabitha thought, licking her lips.

Diana's smooth, lightly tanned skin was sprinkled with darker brown freckles like a scattering of crushed peppercorns. The freckles were clustered thickest on the tops of her shoulders, thinning out on her chest and dusting the tops of her breasts.

"It's not particularly cold right this minute and I'm horny as hell," Diana said, startling Tabitha out of her momentary reverie. "Quit messing with that stove, get your precious little butt over here, and fuck me already."

After tossing a few more pieces of wood into the stove, Tabitha straightened. "My, my, Ms. Crenshaw, such language," she mock-chided, wiping off her hands on her trousers. "Tell me, do those freckles go all the way down?"

Diana crooked a finger. "Come and find out."

The teasing flirtation felt unexpectedly comfortable to Tabitha, as if she and Diana were old friends, old lovers who had done this a hundred times before. Walking over to the pallet, she shed her jackets and shirt, dropping each piece on the floor. She toed off her shoes without bothering to untie them, and then her trousers, kicking them across the room.

She wrinkled her nose at her body's odor. Paddling plus running around in the woods for hours evading hunters had taken its toll. However, she was certain Diana didn't smell as fresh as a daisy either, so she refused to be self-conscious about it.

When she approached the pallet, Diana's smile turned predatory. "Mmm, you look yummy, like the world's best dessert," she said, giving Tabitha a flattering, frankly appraising glance. "Or maybe a soufflé, all sweetness and light. I'll bet you taste delicious. So tell me, sugar, are you a natural blonde?"

Tabitha stood hipshot, her fingers working on the hook and eye closures in the front of her cotton sports bra. "Come and find out," she said, pulling the bra's cups apart to free her breasts. Cooler air and excitement tightened her nipples.

Diana removed her bra, slung it away, and stepped out of her panties. "Get over here," she growled, a glint in her eyes. "Or else."

"Or else what?" an imp of mischief made Tabitha ask.

"Or else I won't do filthy, nasty things to you," Diana replied, "that are probably illegal in most states except California. And maybe West Virginia."

Swallowing laughter, Tabitha lay on the pallet on her back. She reached up to grasp Diana's wrist and pull her down. Rolling on her side, she kissed Diana, an almost chaste meeting of their lips, all breath and sighs.

After savoring long, languid kisses that stretched on and on until she was passion drunk and light-headed, Tabitha felt Diana roll down the waistband of her panties till the garment bunched like a band around her upper thighs. She gasped, the banked simmer of desire leaping up to a blaze.

"Oh, hello there," Diana said with evident delight. She pinched Tabitha's nipple. "Yours are darker than mine. Look."

Tabitha glanced at the place where Diana held their breasts pressed together. Diana's areola was large and rosy pink, her breast heavy and full, the skin creamy, blue-veined and sporadically spotted with freckles. Tabitha's breast was smaller, firmer, the areola dusky, drawn up in crinkles and dotted with bumps. The biggest bump in the center, her nipple, was almost brown. The sight gave her a hollow feeling, as if almost everything behind her belly button had been scooped out, leaving hunger behind.

Diana began to rub her nipple back and forth against Tabitha's, the rubbery sensation sending jolt after jolt straight to her clitoris, making it throb and twitch.

"Tell me," Diana whispered. "Tell me where you want to be touched."

"Do it, Di," Tabitha said, hardly able to speak through the ache in her throat. "Do it. Make me come."

A hand squeezed between Tabitha's legs, cupping her pubic mound before two fingers pushed through her folds and slid into her dripping entrance. She stiffened when Diana started thrusting her fingers in and out with subtle, twisting movements. The panties still bound her thighs, making it impossible to obey her instincts and spread her legs further apart.

The somewhat rough callus on Diana's palm rasped against her vulva, driving her higher. Each stroke drew a grunt from her. The grunts turned to a shuddering gasp when a thumb began circling her clitoris, gliding from one side to the other, sweeping over the sensitive tip and back to the top.

"You like that, sugar?" Diana asked, quickening her movements.

Tabitha nodded, too far gone for speech. She looked at Diana. The little details stood out: the sheen of sweat on the woman's face, the tendrils of dark, silver-laced hair trailing across her neck, the lust-filled eyes watching her, eating her alive.

She was swollen with need, trembling on the edge. When Diana pressed a careful thumbnail into the tip of her clitoris, the world vanished as she came with a shout, nothing existing anymore except wave after wave of blinding pleasure.

Panting, Tabitha opened her eyes to find Diana smiling at her.

"Good?" Diana asked, her fingers still seated but not moving.

"Great," Tabitha replied. She was tired, but ready to satisfy another desire. She let her gaze drift past Diana's full breasts, past the gentle little swell of belly, to the dark brown, crisp curls on her mound, shaved to a thin strip that seemed to point the way to Paradise.

"I want to suck you," she said, low and intense. "I want to eat you out like it's my last meal. I want to taste you. I want you to come on my face."

Diana removed her fingers and licked them clean. "Lovely and earthy, just the way I like it," she said with an exaggerated roll of her tongue across her lips, turning it into a show. She rolled over on her back, spreading her legs far apart.

"You want to eat my juicy pussy, sugar?" she asked, patting her plump mound. "Go to it. Bon appétit. Make me scream."

Tabitha did.

CHAPTER NINE

Unconcerned by her nudity, Diana used the kukri to slit open both freeze-dried meal pouches from the pack, carefully poured an amount of boiling water into each, and sealed the tops. The smell of chicken teriyaki filled the cabin.

Also naked, Tabitha added more wood to the fire. The mess kit had provided two pots, one of which sat on the stove, full of simmering water intended for coffee and general use. She planned to top up their water supply before she went to sleep.

"Don't burn yourself," Diana said, laying back on the pallet and propping herself up on an elbow. "You know, this isn't exactly what I had in mind when I ran to Whitehorse." She fingered the key on the chain around her neck.

"I wasn't planning on running away from payroll truck robbers, either, but here we are. It's not so bad," Tabitha replied, sweeping a hand around to indicate the cabin. "We've got food, water, blankets, and a functional toilet. What more do you want?"

"Room service would be nice."

"Best I can do is breakfast in bed."

"Ooh," Diana breathed, her eyes wide and sparkling with mischief. "That's about the best offer I've had all day."

"Woman, it's the only offer you've had all day, but I appreciate your appreciation." Tabitha went to the open pack, conscious of Diana's gaze as she walked, which felt warmer on her skin than the stove's heat. After a brief rummage, she held up two freeze-dried meal pouches. "I can give you a Denver omelet or spaghetti and meatballs in the morning."

"Shouldn't we conserve our food?"

"What for? We should reach the river tomorrow. Besides, calories are more useful inside your body than carried around in a backpack."

Diana looked thoughtful. "True. Hey, what's in those storage boxes? Anything to eat that's not spoiled?"

"There's some supplies, dried stuff and canned fruit, but I don't know how old they are," Tabitha said, moving to the pallet and sitting down. "Why?"

"Maybe I can rustle something up better than powdered eggs for breakfast." Diana hopped up and moved to the storage boxes. Glancing at Tabitha to confirm her choice, she opened the one on the left. "There's flour in this tin, packed in a vacuum sealed bag," she said after sorting through the contents. "Looks like the mice left it alone. Might still be okay." Cutting the bag open with the kukri, she rubbed a bit between her fingertips. "Feels like a mix. There's fat in it for sure. Smells fine."

Tabitha shrugged. "What can you do with it?"

"Ever had bannock? Camp bread, very nice."

"I thought you said you had no experience with camping."

After taking a can out of the storage box, Diana returned to the pallet and tucked the can in her lap, which hid the label from view. She sat cross-legged facing Tabitha, long strands of her hair falling over her breasts.

"When I was a girl, my daddy used to take me and Jack to this fishing camp on Lake Qwinetta," she said. "We thought it was the coolest place on Earth. Big hunting lodge kind of place that belonged to a friend of his. We'd go up there, just the three of us, and spend a couple of weeks fishing and goofing off. Mama never went 'cause she couldn't be away from her soap operas. That's where I learned how to make bannock."

"I never had time to learn how to cook," Tabitha said. "There's a retired lady who lives in the condo next to mine. She owned a restaurant and her food is fabulous. I pay her to make me freezer meals every month." She paused. A memory of Victoria, who'd enjoyed eating at her house when Lil was out of town, came to mind. "My FBI partner used to tell me Mrs. Famosa's kitchen put out better eats than most restaurants in Orlando."

"Your partner used to tell you? Oh, sugar, I'm so sorry. What happened?" Diana asked, her voice filled with sympathy.

Realizing she'd referred to Victoria in the past tense, as if her partner had already died, left Tabitha stricken. Her throat closed. She pressed a hand to her mouth.

"What's wrong?" Diana persisted, scooting over to put an arm around her. When Tabitha didn't answer immediately, she flushed and mumbled, "Sorry, sorry, I'm too nosy for my own good. I didn't mean—"

"No, it's okay," Tabitha managed to interrupt, gripping Diana's hand where it rested on her thigh. "I just…my partner has cancer," she blurted.

Diana hugged her. "I'm sorry," she repeated.

Tabitha stared down at her lap. "Breast cancer. Stage Four."

"Are you and her, uh…" Diana trailed off delicately, raising an eyebrow. "I mean, if it's none of my business, tell me and I'll shut up."

Taking a deep breath, Tabitha said, "Her name's Victoria Wallace. We met at the FBI Academy in Quantico. I swear, it was like I'd known her my whole life. She's my best friend. Not lovers," she added to forestall the question lurking in Diana's expression. "Vicky's been in a serious, long-term relationship with her girlfriend for years."

"Victoria sounds amazing," Diana said. "Maybe one day you'll introduce us."

"One of these days, sure." Tabitha didn't know what Victoria might make of Diana, but if the opportunity presented itself, she'd like to get her friend's opinion. Too many goddamned ifs. If Vicky lives through the treatment, if the cancer doesn't come back or spread, if I even survive this place to get back in time to see her…Wiping her eyes and deciding to change the subject, she asked, "That food done yet? I'm starving."

"Think so. They've been cooking long enough." Diana opened one of the pouches and gave the contents a stir with a plastic spoon. "Dinner is served," she said, handing the pouch to Tabitha along with a plastic fork. She took the other pouch for herself.

Tabitha ate, her stomach demanding food despite her upset over Victoria. As a freeze-dried, reconstituted meal, it wasn't bad. The chicken was spongy, the slivers of mushroom and bamboo shoots rubbery, the rice sticky and the sauce sweet and very salty, but hunger made it delicious. The pouch was supposed to serve two people, but she ate the whole thing.

Afterward, Diana showed her the can from the storage box: cling peaches.

"Wow," Tabitha said, running a thumb over the faded label. She hadn't eaten canned peaches in syrup since…startled, she realized she could not remember the last time.

Whenever possible during their training year, she and Victoria had driven to the local market every Saturday to stock up on fresh fruits and vegetables. Also during the right season, farmers from Georgia often loaded their trucks with bushel baskets of fresh peaches, drove across the state line into Florida, and hawked their wares from the side of the road. Nothing better than a fresh, ripe peach dribbling juice down your arm.

She frowned. "Is there a can opener in there?" she asked. "Otherwise, we're going to have a problem. I wouldn't want to try prying this can open with the kukri, not if I can help it. Good way to lose a finger."

"Would I offer you my peaches if I didn't have a way for you to get at 'em?" Diana asked, giving Tabitha an exaggerated, eyebrow-waggling leer that made her choke. Producing an old-fashioned, pressed metal church key, she handed it over with a flourish.

Tabitha had never used a church key, but the device wasn't hard to figure out. As soon as she had the lid open, careful not to cut her fingers on the jagged rim, she sniffed at the syrup, which smelled fine, if cloying. No sign of mold. The peach halves inside looked acceptable, she decided after poking them with the plastic fork.

Lifting out a peach, she let the syrup drip a moment before slurping it into her mouth. She ignored Diana's indignant, "Hey!"

The sugary taste exploded on her tongue, so sweet it hurt her throat. She ate another anyway, mischievously holding the can out of Diana's reach.

"Give me that!" Diana squawked, snatching at the can and missing, and almost ending up sprawled across Tabitha's lap. "I want my share, damn it. Don't be such a hog. Gimme!" Another lunge jostled the can, spilling syrup over her hand and down her front.

Glancing down at the sticky, shiny stream of syrup drizzled on her breasts and belly, Tabitha asked with a pretend scowl, "For heaven's sake, who's going to clean up this mess?" She gestured at herself with the fork.

Diana's wide, white grin was dazzling in its sheer greed. "Heaven ain't got a thing to do with it," she said, tossing the spoon over her shoulder. Leaning in, she licked at a trail of syrup on Tabitha's breast, making her whimper. "Better put that can down, or we'll have peach juice in places we didn't know we had," she warned before lowering her head again.

Suddenly breathless, everything else forgotten, Tabitha obeyed.

CHAPTER TEN

Tabitha awoke somewhat disoriented, feeling ragged around the edges in a way that meant really good sex in the recent past. She lay on her side in the dark, her head pillowed on her arm, a warm body curled behind her. Victoria? No. Hell, no. Recalling Diana and the cabin, she relaxed, only to stiffen when unexpected sounds broke the silence: crunching footsteps and a violently expelled, "Shh!" that could only have issued from a human throat.

Montoya's men had found them.

Cursing herself silently, she rolled over and clapped a hand over Diana's mouth to stifle a startled scream. "It's okay, it's me," she breathed. The whites of Diana's eyes gleamed in the darkness, reflecting an orange glow from the banked fire in the wood stove. "Not a word," she went on in the barest whisper possible. "Somebody's outside. You good?"

Diana nodded, her body still rigid under Tabitha's.

"Can you get to your clothes? Okay, get dressed. Shoes, too. Pick up everything, put it in the pack as quickly as you can. And be quiet. Got it?" Satisfied by Diana's second nod, she rolled off, reaching for her shirt and trousers.

Donning her clothes took longer than she liked. The lack of light and the need for stealth as well as speed hampered her. She first put her trousers on backward, and had to kick them off and try again. Any moment, she expected the door to burst open and shadowy men to rush inside, shattering the night with shouts and shots. Why were they waiting?

Stupid, stupid, stupid! I should have anticipated this, I shouldn't have been so damned complacent. She yanked her shirt over her head without bothering to don her bra.

Finally tying her shoes, she stood up, thinking frenziedly about their exit while she zipped up the second of her fleece jackets, stuffed the bra in her pocket, and tucked the kukri into her waistband. The cabin had no windows. There was only one way in or out, currently blocked by their pursuers. Was there an alternative?

Moving across the room, she found Diana. "Ready? Got our stuff?" she asked softly. "Head to the other door."

"Toilet?" Diana whispered back, sounding unsure.

"Yes." Tabitha led the way, certain with every footstep that they were about to be attacked. She opened the door of the lean-to and pushed Diana inside. Once there, she risked flicking on the lighter from the survival kit she'd kept in her pocket.

Light blossomed, pushing back the darkness. Tabitha ignored the scurrying sound made by a fleeing mouse. Examining the walls of the lean-to, she found several boards loosened by the weather and by the bushes growing right outside. The invading branches had pushed through cracks and loosened nails.

"We can get out this way," she said. "There should be room to squeeze through once I take off a few boards."

Diana shrugged on the pack and pulled her makeshift poncho over her head. "Won't that make too much noise?" she asked in the same hushed tone while scraping her lank hair into a ponytail secured with an elastic band.

Tabitha went to examine the rotting boards more closely. Several appeared loose enough that a tug should pull them away from the structure's rough frame. She snapped the lighter closed and whispered, "It'll be okay. Let me move this first."

Grabbing the sack that held peat moss and wood shavings, she shifted it away from the wall, exposing a long, narrow metal box. Like the storage boxes, it wasn't padlocked. Signaling for Diana to examine the contents, she turned her attention back to the wall.

The cabin door opened with a bang that seemed so shockingly loud, for a moment Tabitha thought the men had fired a rifle inside.

"She isn't here," said a male voice which sounded deep and resonant with a trace of a drawl. "You told me you could track that bitch, Robertson, and I'm paying you for results. Don't tell me I came all the way out here for nothing."

"It's him," Diana mouthed after getting Tabitha's attention with a waved hand. "Blair." Looking terrified, she clutched a thin fleece bag, more than two feet long, closely to her chest. Tabitha thought she must have gotten the bag out of the box, but had neither the time nor the inclination to satisfy her curiosity.

From the crack at the bottom of the flimsy door, Tabitha saw a flashlight beam sweeping back and forth. Ice water trickled through her veins. She began pulling boards, one by one. Every tiny squeak or crack made her flinch. The cabin had only one room, quickly searched. She and Diana had mere seconds, if that, before they were found.

To her relief, Robertson seemed inclined to mollify his employer. His voice covered the small sounds of Tabitha's hurried work. "Mr. Montoya, the Yukon's a very big place, like I told you. I wish you'd wait at the lodge. We can move a lot quicker if—"

"Shut up. You aren't going to leave me sitting around with my thumb up my ass while you and your boys take a weekend vacation on my dime."

"I'm a professional, sir, and I resent the implication."

"A professional what? You're a fuckin' taxidermist, Mr. Robert Robertson. You stuff bears and fish for a living. You like to go moose hunting with your redneck friends. Christ, I should've hired a real guide. You know what? Screw you. The point is, when I'm paying you a hundred grand, you'll take my orders or I'll find somebody who will. Understand?"

"Yes, sir." Robertson sounded weary.

"The woman has something I need, or she knows where I can find it," Montoya went on. "Frankly, I don't trust you not to screw this up, so you'll just have to get used to me lagging behind and plan accordingly. Now you've been leading me around the goddamned wilderness all day and I've got nothing to show for it but blisters and a rash. Find her."

"Look, Mr. Montoya, the dust's been disturbed, and the stove's still warm, so your woman can't have gotten far."

"Maybe she's in here, boss," piped up a new voice.

Fuck! Abandoning caution, Tabitha tore the boards off faster. "Hurry," she said, pushing Diana out sideways through the hole she had made.

Her heart froze in her chest when she realized Diana was stuck, the pack on her back caught on the splintered wood on either side of the hole. Gathering her strength, she shoved hard, hearing cloth rip. Diana tore free, stumbling forward as the door opened and two men spilled inside the lean-to with two more crowding into the small space behind them.

Tabitha slid through the hole and ran into the night. Although not truly dark, the low angle light caused by the "midnight sun" effect grayed the shadows to twilight under the trees where she and Diana fled. A bullet zinged past her ear. She heard Montoya bellowing curses and admonitions. From the sound of the shouted orders, he wanted Diana taken alive.

Behind them came the crashing noises of pursuit.

CHAPTER ELEVEN

Walking through the woods at night was not a good idea. Running through the woods at night went beyond foolhardy, edging into insanity.

Tabitha ran with a ball of ice in the pit of her stomach, a sick, cold feeling that left her graceless while she tried to avoid getting tangled in branches or tripping over logs. Knowing the men pursuing them weren't professional killers did not ease her mind. In fact, that made the situation worse. To a certain extent, a professional's behavior could be anticipated, but civilians were prone to panic, their reactions unpredictable. She couldn't count the number of times a would-be criminal turned murderer told her, "I didn't mean to do it."

They weren't lying.

Diana kept up, sometimes a silhouette beside her, other times a pale and grainy figure racing through the gray-drenched twilight.

Tabitha stayed on a downhill course, hoping to find the river. She prayed they weren't going around in circles. When she and

Diana stumbled out of the tree line and onto an open patch of tundra, she stopped, her muscles quivering. Too exposed. She and Diana melted back into the trees to find a large, rotten tree trunk to crouch behind.

"Two minutes," Diana panted, offering her the long fleece bag she had carried from the cabin. "Let me catch my breath."

"Take five," Tabitha replied, trying to control her own breathing. After taking the bag, which weighed about nine pounds, she opened it and found a rubber case inside. A familiar odor hit her nostrils the moment she unfastened the case. Gun oil. She breathed in the smell, a low burn of excitement in her gut. Her hands trembled slightly. She lifted out a Remington 700 centerfire rifle, the steel barrel and wooden stock gleaming like salvation in the dim light.

"Oh, my God." Diana sounded awed. "Tell me I'm not seeing things."

Tabitha tested the bolt action and examined the barrel as well as she could, finding no rust. The rifle's owner had cared for the weapon far better than his cabin. "Well, unless we have ammunition, this amounts to an expensive and very awkward club," she said. The disappointment was far more bitter than she expected.

Diana fell silent, squirming around under her makeshift poncho. At last, she pulled out the pack, opened it, and began rooting around inside. "You remember back in the cabin, when you told me to grab everything I could?"

"Uh-huh."

"I wasn't sure, but you said everything, so do you think these will fit?" On her palm, Diana balanced a box of .223 ammunition.

Tabitha recalled the bullets had been in one of the storage boxes. "I could kiss you on all four cheeks," she said, her mood lifting. Being armed evened the odds somewhat. Of course, if she actually shot someone, Canadian law enforcement would likely have a polite shit fit. She'd be answering questions and filling out paperwork for the next decade.

"I may take you up on that offer later, when we're not running for our lives," Diana replied, fluttering her eyelashes like a Southern belle. "I guess that means I done good."

"You done great." Tabitha loaded bullets into the magazine. She tipped half the ammunition out of the box to filled her outer jacket's pockets and returned the rest to Diana. "Keep 'em close to hand," she said.

Diana shoved the box in the pack. "Now what?" she asked, wiping her sweaty forehead with her wrist and leaving a streak of dirt on her skin.

"We still need to get to the river. And listen," Tabitha said, "I'm not planning on firing at Montoya's men unless they leave me no choice, understand? This isn't an action movie and I sure as hell ain't Bruce Willis. I'd prefer not to get into a gun battle."

Diana scowled. "Do you really think Blair's going to let me live once he has the key?"

"The bad guys don't have to play by the rules, but I do. So the plan is, we keep heading for the river. Once we find it, we flag down help. At no time, under no circumstances will you touch this rifle, you hear me?"

"What if one of Blair's taxidermy weekend warriors shoots you? What am I supposed to do to defend us? Throw rocks?"

Tabitha leaned forward, catching Diana's wide blue gaze and holding it. "If I go down, you run like hell. Do not stop," she said gravely. "Do not turn back. Just run for help."

"I am not leaving you—" Diana began, but Tabitha interrupted.

"You don't have a choice. You run." She softened her tone. "Look, Di, getting the RCMP involved is the best chance for both of us. Montoya won't kill me. Just put your fear aside and pay attention. Montoya doesn't want to kill me, I promise. He's too smart. He knows if he murders a federal officer, he'll be hounded for the rest of his life and I'll proclaim my law enforcement status loudly enough for them to hear me across the border."

"Like he cares."

"Oh, a man like him cares. The payroll truck robbery was meticulously planned. No one got hurt. Montoya's a professional bank robber, not a killer. The best thing you can do is escape. If you shoot at them, they'll shoot back. Don't give them a reason to kill you."

"Blair is dangerous," Diana said mutinously. "I won't be safe until that shitheel's dead or jailed for life."

"Or until the money from the robbery is in federal custody," Tabitha pointed out.

Diana shrugged. "You see that money here? Fat lot of good turning it over to the cops does me unless you've got a posse and an arrest warrant in those pants, not to mention a first-class airplane ticket to Fort Gill, Georgia 'cause I prefer to travel in style."

"The money's in Fort Gill?"

"Ask me no questions, I'll tell you no lies."

Tabitha said nothing.

After a moment, Diana relented with a harsh bark of laughter that grated on Tabitha's ears. "Okay, since I'm not sure I'm getting out of this cluster fuck alive, I'd rather you have the loot than Blair Montoya," she said. "If ever a pile of cash was cursed…but that's neither here nor there. They say confession's good for the soul. Well, here's mine: you want them millions, Agent Knowles, you go to Buddy Rinker's junkyard. Junior, not Senior."

"And?"

"You just go there with the key I showed you. See what happens."

Tabitha committed the names to memory. "I'm serious about the rifle, Di," she said. "Hands off, no matter what happens. If the shooting starts, you rabbit out of here."

"You just make sure not to get hurt, otherwise I may shoot you myself." Diana settled on the ground, arranging the poncho over her lap and legs like a small tent.

Closing her eyes, Tabitha rested her head against the mossy trunk, the rifle held securely in her grip. She would have sold her soul for a cold beer and a GPS. "Don't worry," she said after a while. "I don't plan on taking a bullet anytime soon."

Diana muttered, "It's always the ones you don't expect that get you in the end."

Tabitha knocked gently on the tree trunk to ward off bad luck.

CHAPTER TWELVE

What she could see of the morning sky through the treetops was tinged salmon pink, the color filtering down below the canopy to a paler hue, like water with a drop of blood in it. Tabitha covered a yawn with her hand, amazed she had actually fallen asleep for—she checked her watch—a little more than three and a half hours.

Beside her on the ground, Diana still snored lightly, huddled under her poncho and using the lumpy pack as a pillow.

"Hey," Tabitha said, trailing her fingertips over Diana's face. "Wake up, sleepyhead."

"Coffee?" Diana mumbled drowsily.

Tabitha laughed. "You wish." Getting to her feet, she spent a few minutes stretching the stiffness out of her muscles. "Christ, I could use a toothbrush," she said to herself, running her tongue over her teeth. "Tastes like a camel took a dump in my mouth."

"No good morning smooch for you," Diana said, sitting up. She knuckled the sleep out of her eyes and yawned. "I'd trade my left tit for a cup of joe."

"Considering we're a long way from the nearest coffee shop, I'm pretty sure your breast is safe," Tabitha replied, hoping her hair didn't look as disgusting as it felt. She had lost the handkerchief she used as a head cover last night. Just as well, she thought, since the red stood out like a sore thumb in the middle of the forest. "By the way, how do you take your coffee?" she asked out of curiosity.

"Strong and black. No mocha-choco-latte foo-foo stuff for me. You?" Diana asked.

"Cream with a pinch of cinnamon." Victoria had taught her to appreciate subtlety. "Sometimes café cubano in the morning, or café con leche with strawberry French toast."

Diana's stomach growled. She stood. "Will you quit that?" she moaned. Putting both hands on the small of her back, she bent this way and that, cracking her spine. "Sweet baby Jesus in velvet pants, I'm so hungry, I could eat my shoes." She held up a foot, showing a high-cut, neoprene paddling bootie caked with filth. Dead leaves stuck to the rubber sole. "Does that look remotely appetizing to you? I didn't think so."

"Anything left in the pack?" Tabitha asked hopefully.

"A couple of freeze-dried meals, but without hot water… on the other hand, I did manage to take some stuff out of the storage boxes last night," Diana said. "It was too dark to see what I was grabbing. Maybe I got lucky."

"Some stuff" turned out to be a can of apple slices in water, a paper wrapped twist of salt, a bag of dubious pinhead oatmeal, the bannock mix and a container of homemade jerky that looked shiny and hard, uncomfortably reminding Tabitha of a cockroach's carapace. Nevertheless, she decided to try it.

"Good," she said after she'd sucked on a strip of dried meat to soften it before risking her teeth. Although she had anticipated the worst, the flavor was fairly palatable. She couldn't identify the source. Moose, maybe? Venison? She asked Diana, who grunted and shrugged.

After managing two pieces of jerky—she quit because her jaw was sore, and vowed next time to find a rock and beat the stuff into submission—Tabitha was thirsty. Her bottom lip had cracked and split while she slept, and now stung like fury from the overly salted meat, while her throat felt like it had been scoured with wire wool.

"I don't suppose you have anything to drink?" she asked, already knowing the answer. Her heart sank. Running blind through the forest had left her unable to find the stream. Unless they reached the river or came across another stream by accident, she would have to go without water. The prospect wasn't pleasing.

As an athlete and a Florida native, she was painfully familiar with mild dehydration. In her mind, she ran through a checklist of symptoms: dry mouth, headache, weariness, light-headedness. In its more severe form, which she had never suffered, she knew the condition caused lack of sweating, dry skin that didn't bounce back when pinched, rapid heartbeat, rapid respiration, low blood pressure, eventual fever, delirium and death.

What had a coroner once told her about human survival? Three minutes without air, three days without water, three weeks without food. Gross generalizations, of course. Humans could and did survive for longer periods than stated, but the basic principle was sound. Going too long without water would have serious health consequences.

She was confident they would find help well before either of them fell truly ill, but as a precaution she said to Diana, "Be sure to check the color of your urine."

"What's with the kinky interest in my pee? Didn't know you were into golden showers," Diana quipped. She sobered quickly under Tabitha's steady regard.

"The darker your urine, the more dehydrated you are," Tabitha explained.

"Good to know." To her surprise, Diana suddenly grinned. "And to answer your previous question, yes, I have something to drink," she said, holding up two plastic bottles from the pack. "After you sacked out last night, I filled 'em up with the water you left in the pot on the stove. Should be safe enough. Only half a liter, so don't waste it."

Tabitha accepted a bottle, grateful for Diana's foresight. Unscrewing the cap, she took a careful swallow, mindful of her lip. The cool liquid slid down her throat, tasting and feeling heavenly. Almost as good as sex, she thought, reluctantly returning the bottle to Diana for safekeeping. She picked up the rifle and slung the strap over her shoulder.

Once they were ready to go, Tabitha scanned the surrounding area. She saw no trails, no animal tracks, just a line of trees thinning out where the tundra began. Crossing the flat, open space seemed inviting, but she rejected the idea at once. Her skin crawled at the thought of being so exposed and vulnerable.

Judging from the conversation she had overhead when hiding in the lean-to, Montoya's guide was a recreational hunter. What was his name? Robert Robertson. How good was Robertson? How much control did he have over his men? How far was he willing to go to earn Montoya's money? Lacking data, she could only guess at the answers, and decided evasion remained their best option. She wanted to continue east toward the river, but had to confess herself baffled since the terrain had no clear downhill direction.

Eying a tall white spruce gave her an idea. She said, "I can't see the sun's position while we're under this heavy canopy, so I'm going to climb a tree to get above it. Once I figure out which way is east, we should hit the river today."

"Why not just go out there and look?" Diana asked, pointing toward the tundra.

"What if Montoya's hunting party is close by?" Tabitha asked. "There's zero cover on that flat plain, and they'll spot us in a heartbeat. Easy to draw a bead and put a bullet through my head. Montoya doesn't want to take me alive, after all."

"I thought you said Blair wouldn't kill you," Diana accused.

"No, I said he wouldn't want to murder a federal officer," Tabitha said, pinching the bridge of her nose to ward off the headache she felt blooming behind her eyes. "Only the race organizers know who I am. Montoya doesn't, and I won't have time to convince him if he shoots me out of hand. And he might just kill both us out of sheer frustration." The mulish set of Diana's jaw made her continue, "Look, we don't have a choice, Di. Montoya isn't likely to add murder to the list of charges, but he's got two million reasons to eliminate anyone preventing him from getting what he wants, which is you and that key around your neck."

Diana grimaced. "Shit."

"Don't worry, okay? I'll climb the tree, figure out where we are, and come back down lickety-split. You'll never know I'm gone."

"I don't like this, Tabs. Not one bit."

"You don't have to like it." With misgivings of her own, Tabitha handed the rifle to Diana. "Hold this for me. Do not use it, remember? Not under any circumstances."

Diana took the rifle, holding it awkwardly at arm's length.

Tabitha grabbed the lowest branch and hoisted herself up into the tree.

She hadn't climbed a tree since she was twelve years old, when she had not yet "sprouted" breasts. Back then, she'd worn braces, played stickball with the boys, and suffered a major crush on a girl in her homeroom who'd refused to sign her slam book. A lot of time had passed. Still, her body remembered, her muscles stretching in familiar patterns while she made her slow, careful way from branch to branch.

Fortunately, the white spruce's branches stuck out fairly straight and regularly from the trunk, so it was mostly a question of maintaining her balance while she climbed from one to the other. Rough bark scraped her palms raw, but provided decent footing. The needles prickling against her face and neck smelled resinous and musky, reminding her of cat pee.

The higher she climbed, the more she became aware of the diminishing ground beneath her. She wasn't exactly afraid of heights, but her heart fluttered fast and light in her chest like hummingbird wings. Despite the need for haste, she took every precaution, making sure of her grip before transferring her weight.

When she was halfway up, just as she reached for a new handhold, her paddling bootie's sole slipped, pitching her forward. Fear caused an instant flush of panic, leaving her mindlessly scrabbling for a branch with one hand and clawing at the tree trunk with the other. Her world narrowed to spiky evergreen needles, clusters of cones dangling from too-thin tree limbs, and glimpses of the ground that seemed a hundred miles away.

Her balance teetered. Gravity exerted its long pull. In the split-second before the fall became inevitable, Tabitha's hand closed over a branch that cracked, but held. Panting, she righted herself, clinging to the trunk while she closed her eyes and willed her pulse to slow before she stroked out.

When the dizziness churning her stomach finally ebbed, she opened her eyes and glanced down, seeing Diana looking up, her face a blot of paper whiteness in contrast to the brown and yellow leaves littering the forest floor.

After a moment, she forced herself to go on.

At last, Tabitha reached an area at the top of the spruce where she could look out over the treetops and see the sky, a swath of pale blue perfection unrolling from horizon to horizon. Grinning in triumph, she drew the crisp air deep into her lungs, letting it out in a little chuff of laughter. Her palms throbbed and burned with pain, she stank like she'd been marked by a tomcat, but she had made it.

Almost directly ahead, a hot yellow sun rose above distant mountains. Better still, she glimpsed a glittering ribbon of water that must be the Yukon River about a half day's travel away. If she and Diana managed to travel in a more-or-less straight line without getting turned around, if they avoided Montoya and his hunters, if they flagged a safety boat or another racer before dark… A lot of ifs, she thought, and damned few certainties.

But first, she had to get back to earth without breaking her neck.

Pushing aside a twinge of guilt for leaving Diana waiting below, she delayed her return, enjoying the freedom as well as the view and, if she were honest with herself, taking the time to work up the courage to climb down.

She had reached the halfway point when she heard a shout. Straining her neck, she turned her head to look over her shoulder. Horrified, she watched three men in hunter's gear move toward Diana. No, four men. Someone who must be Blair Montoya stumbled along in the rear, swatting at a bush.

"Gotcha, bitch!" Montoya crowed.

In answer, Diana pointed the rifle at him.

No! Tabitha wanted to scream, but she dared not make a sound, dared not give away her position. Unarmed, she could do nothing against the hunters. If Diana survived and was captured, she would have to stage a rescue. Witnessing a crime and doing nothing about it went against the grain, but she gritted her teeth and hung on.

"Aw, Ms. Crenshaw, you make me feel like I'm not welcome," Montoya said, spreading his arms apart as if prepared to hug her. "I think you have something of mine."

"Screw you," Diana replied defiantly, her voice easily reaching Tabitha's ears although she didn't seem to speak very loudly.

Montoya's expression was impossible to make out from her position, but Tabitha had the impression the man smiled. "C'mon, what's all this about, anyway? Money that doesn't belong to you. Why not give it up and save yourself a lot of grief?" he asked.

"You killed my brother."

"Jack Crenshaw, that goddamned punk. That thief stole our payoff."

"Don't you talk about Jack that way!"

"Darling, if I could raise Jack from the dead, I'd cut off his dick and fuck him with it before I killed him again. I might go dig him up anyway, just so I can violate his stinking corpse." Montoya's tone hardened. "Where's my money?"

Diana held the rifle steady. "Screw you," she repeated.

Robertson and the other two hunters kept their weapons trained on Diana, clearly waiting for a signal from Montoya. Tabitha couldn't predict what any of them might do if ordered to fire. She shouldn't have left Diana alone, she thought, guilt eating at her.

"You can tell me now, or you can tell me later when I'm done with you, but you will tell me," Montoya said matter-of-factly. "A car battery, a pair of pliers, a screwdriver…real torture isn't anything like TV. I'll hurt you in ways you'll never forget until death takes away the memory. You won't hold out. You can't. But we don't need to go through all that unpleasantness, Diana, do we? I'm a reasonable guy. Give me what I want, tell me what I need to know, and I'll let you have a small cut, okay? Say, two percent. You can walk away with a little money in your pocket, buy your brother a memorial if that's what butters your muffin. We can both profit here, and nobody needs to lose."

"I burned it," Diana choked, visibly shaking but still aiming the rifle at Montoya. "I burned every bill, you sick bastard."

He made a flat, unpleasant buzzer sound. "Nope, sorry, that's a lie."

Tabitha tried to will Diana to shut her mouth, to surrender her weapon, to stay safe by giving up, but the woman kept tempting fate. "I gave the money to the police," she said.

Another buzzer sound from Montoya. "Wrong again, that's lie number two." His amusement made Tabitha's hackles rise.

She had speculated that Montoya was ex-military, but his current demeanor didn't seem very disciplined to her. His moods were too mercurial. She detected something "off" about him, something dangerous lurking under the affable surface.

Striding forward, Montoya stopped when the muzzle of Diana's rifle pressed against the center of his chest. "I'm getting bored, darling. Playing your little game isn't very exciting, but I think I know how to spice it up." He grabbed the rifle's barrel and yanked the weapon out of Diana's grasp. Diana tried to hit him, but he evaded the blow, laughing. "I tried to be nice about it," he said, "and you just keep lying to me."

Suddenly, his open hand cracked across her face, making her stagger, trip over a root, and fall flat on the ground. "Every lie you tell me is only going to make the pain last longer, you know," he said. "That's okay. I'm patient. I can wait for the truth." He nudged her with the toe of his shoe. "How long can you wait, hmm?" The next nudge turned into a vicious kick that caught Diana in the side, rolling her over. He tossed the rifle into the bushes. "Fun's over, darling. You brought it on yourself." He paused. "By the way, where's your friend?"

Diana didn't respond.

Tabitha closed her eyes a moment. She opened them because whatever happened, she had to bear witness. Diana's chances of survival plummeted with each moment that passed, and the longer Montoya kept up his brutal interrogation, so did hers.

CHAPTER THIRTEEN

Montoya stooped over Diana, a black-clad figure as threatening as a predatory bird. He took hold of Diana's left hand and bent her wrist until she whimpered in pain. "Last night in that rundown cabin, you had somebody with you. Man, woman, I don't care. Where are they?" he asked, bending her wrist further backward.

Diana's scream was muffled by Montoya stepping on her face, grinding the sole of his shoe over her mouth.

"No need to terrify the local wildlife, darling," Montoya said, his voice chillingly normal. "I'll ask you one more time, and if you don't tell the truth, I'll give you to my boys."

Digging her fingernails into the spruce's trunk to keep herself from doing something suicidal and useless, like leaping down in a rage and getting shot for her trouble, Tabitha glanced at the waiting hunters and tried to assess them. Would they kill Diana? Humans had a powerful need to fit into the herd, to follow the leader, and she knew that given the temptation of sex without the need to consider consequences, an average man with low impulse control might succumb to the worst parts of his nature.

She prayed matters wouldn't go so far. She couldn't remain in hiding if Diana was sexually assaulted, or if the torture continued right in front of her.

"She…she…she got lost," Diana stammered when Blair removed his shoe from her mouth. "Last night. We ran. She got lost."

"What's her name, this friend of yours?"

"Not my friend, just somebody who lost her paddling partner. I agreed to help out."

"Her name? I won't ask nice again."

"Tabitha Knowles," Diana answered hastily. "Her name's Tabitha Knowles."

Montoya turned to the hunters. Fearing he might give the order to rape Diana, Tabitha gripped the tree trunk harder, biting her tongue to keep from crying out when one of her fingernails broke down to the quick. She stuck the finger in her mouth, tasting blood.

"Robertson, you guys seen any sign of another person?" Montoya asked.

The man he addressed shook his head. "No, sir."

"Okay, let's go. That cabin's not too far away. Me and the lady have some business to conduct." Shifting his grip to Diana's upper arm, he hauled her to her feet. "You can walk or I'll get my guys to carry you, but you'll have to pay for the ride. Understand?"

Whimpering, Diana nodded.

"Good girl. Cooperate and you can still get out of this alive." Taking his attention off Diana, Montoya focused on Robertson. "I have what I want. Any of you see the other bitch, this Tabitha Knowles, you shoot first, got it? I'm not interested in taking any more prisoners."

"Uh, Mr. Montoya, I'm not sure about—"

"Did I ask you to think?" Montoya snarled. He turned on Robertson, who quailed. The taxidermist topped Montoya by a good head and was heavier by about forty pounds, but he treated Montoya with the same caution one might use toward a rabid dog.

Smart, Tabitha thought. People like Montoya were as unpredictable as the weather. You may know there's going to be a thunderstorm, but exactly where the lightning's going to strike always comes as a surprise.

Montoya jabbed Robertson in the chest with his forefinger. "So smart guy, am I going to have a problem with you? Can't do what you're told?"

Robertson took two steps back. "Sorry, sir, you never said we had to kill somebody. A woman. I'm not comfortable…" His voice trailed off.

Tabitha almost groaned. The only man in the group with a conscience, but he lacked the willpower to back it up.

Montoya grinned. "That's okay, Bobby. Seriously, I'm not mad. If you can't do it, you can't do it. No balls. I get it. *Y qué*, huh?"

"Sorry," Robertson repeated, not rising to the insult.

"It's cool." Montoya walked over to one of the other men while Diana remained rooted to the spot behind him. "What's your name?" he asked.

The man answered quickly. "Barry, sir. Barry Tsosie."

"Shoot him, will ya?" Montoya waved a hand at Robertson.

"Hey, what the hell?" Robertson continued backing up.

"How much you gonna pay me?" Tsosie asked Montoya.

"Want me to sweeten the deal?" Montoya shrugged. "This once, seeing as he's a friend…how does an extra twenty grand sound to you?"

Without more than a second's hesitation, Tsosie raised the rifle to his shoulder.

"C'mon, Barry, buddy, don't do this," Robertson pleaded. "We went to school together. We married sisters. I'm your little boy's godfather, for Christ's sake!"

"I got bills to pay, Bobby. It's twenty grand. I need the money. My son's sick, you know that. We got no insurance. I have no choice." Tsosie fired point-blank at Robertson. The man fell over, quivered a moment, and went still.

The third man watched, but did and said nothing.

Tsosie led the way when the group filed off, moving deeper into the forest and leaving Robertson's body where it lay. As soon as they disappeared from sight, Tabitha stayed in the tree counting the seconds until a full minute had passed before scrambling to reach the ground, heedless of scrapes and scratches as she half climbed, half slid to earth.

She wasted another minute locating the Remington 700 rifle Montoya had tossed into the bushes. Her hands shaking slightly from the adrenaline surge, she reloaded the weapon from the stash of bullets in her jacket pocket.

Her handgun proficiency was better than average in Hogan's Alley, the FBI's tactical training facility. On the firing range, her scores were more than good enough qualify, but the rifle was an unknown weapon. She would have felt much more confident with her service pistol. While working the bolt to arm the rifle, she thought, Needs must when the Devil drives.

She spared a single glance at Robertson. The dead man lay on his back, his blind eyes staring up at the sky. A bloody, scorched hole marred the center of his forehead. Leaf litter around the body was splattered with blood, skull fragments, and bits of brain matter. In a matter of days, between normal decomposition, and insect and animal activity, there would be little left of Robert Robertson. She turned away from the body. As much as she regretted the man's death, she had to concentrate on the living.

After putting the rifle sling on her shoulder and picking up the abandoned pack with its meager supplies, Tabitha began following Montoya's group. She wasn't a hunter and would have been lost if required to track them, but Tsosie seemed uninterested in hiding the obvious signs of his group's passage. She easily picked up their trail.

Once she spied the cabin, she lurked in the bushes beside the lean-to, considering and discarding plans. She heard the murmur of conversation, occasionally recognizing Montoya's voice, but nothing intelligible. No screams at least, but her relief faded when her mind conjured up several reasons why Diana might not be able to make a sound. She had investigated too many crime scenes to hold any illusions.

Think! Think, you stupid cow! she ordered herself, wracking her brain for a workable idea. While she squatted here giving the mosquitoes a free meal, anything might be happening to Diana. Worse, once he had the information he wanted, Montoya had no reason to keep his captive alive. As for Tsosie and the other man, she had no doubt they'd do as they were told.

Near frantic with worry, she closed her eyes and concentrated. Her teeth ground together in frustration until her jaw ached, and suddenly, she knew what to do.

Making for the river and alerting the proper authorities was a far, far smarter way of dealing with the matter, but that would take too much time. As much as a full day for all she knew, not to mention convincing the RCMP she wasn't a crank. Furthermore, could she even find the damned cabin once she left the area? Without GPS coordinates, the best she could do was a rough estimate, worse than useless in the wilderness.

No, this time she was not playing by the book.

Resolved not to let Diana die at Montoya's hands thinking she had been abandoned, Tabitha took the survival kit out of the pack. Snapping open the lid as silently as possible, she searched through the contents: several folded sheets of waterproof paper and a pencil, roll of paracord, whistle, fishing line and hooks, small suture kit in an old peppermints tin, water purification straws and a handful of tablets, aspirins, package of scalpel blades, anti-diarrhea pills, snare wire, lens, magnesium/flint fire bar, and finally, an unbreakable mirror.

She found a reasonably long, sturdy stick on the ground and stripped off the leaves and smaller branches with the kukri. From the suture kit she took a thin roll of surgical tape, using it to secure the mirror to one end of the branch.

Before she could rescue Diana, she needed intelligence on the situation inside the cabin. Identifying the locations of any persons or weapons in the room was critical to a tactical operation. Going over her plan, nothing more than bare bones and ideas at this point, she heartily wished she had a hostage rescue team handy.

Put your big girl panties on, she told herself, it's time to kick this pig till it's squealing from the feeling.

Tabitha left the pack next to the hole she had made last night in the lean-to, and adjusted the rifle sling so the weapon hung straight down her back, out of the way. Controlling her breathing, her heart drumming against her ribs, she paused to peer around the corner of the cabin. No guard posted in front, which made her uneasy. Such seeming carelessness might conceal a trap. She stiffened. Scanning the area, she found no immediate threats, but didn't relax her vigilance.

Sidling to the front of the cabin, she found the door had been partially closed, leaving a gap about two fingers broad. Dropping to her belly in the dirt, she used the stick to carefully hold the mirror in position near the bottom of the door, glad there were no windows that might betray her position with a flash of reflected light.

Sweat prickled her skin, gathering in rivulets to pool between her breasts, under her armpits, and in the small of her back. Stinging droplets ran into her eyes. She felt like she was burning up, trapped in a sauna made by the two fleece jackets she wore and her own body heat. Blinking, she managed to wipe her face on her sleeve while she tilted the mirror at various angles, trying to see into every corner of the room.

Montoya sat on the cot, peeling an apple with a knife. Tsosie and the other man—Tabitha decided to call him Smith—sat on the floor, passing a can of stew back and forth. Smith held an iPod in his lap, earbuds in place, his head bobbing while Tsosie leafed through a hunting magazine between bites. Their rifles were close at hand. And Diana…

Tabitha whispered a curse, barely more than a stirring of air, but as heartfelt as a shout.

Diana sat propped against the wall opposite the door, her expression fearful. Her hands were lashed together in front of her. More cord bound her ankles. Someone had taken off her makeshift poncho and cut thin silver strips out of it, knotting one around her throat, with a second longer strip acting like a leash. Montoya held the other end loosely while he continued to peel his apple, but Tabitha had no doubt he would tighten the slack if Diana tried to escape.

She scooted back several feet before getting to her feet and moving around the corner to the lean-to. This situation is a pooch screwing waiting to happen, she thought. The odds of rescuing Diana weren't in her favor by any means, but she wasn't going to give up.

Negotiating with Montoya and his men to surrender had no chance of success without backup, no rationale for persuading him to give up without resisting, and she held no legal standing in Canada beyond professional courtesy. If confronted, he might decide to cut his losses, kill Diana, and escape into the forest. He could be back in the States in less than a day, or anywhere else for that matter. Even without the two million dollars from the payroll truck robbery, he might still own the resources to live in style in a nonextradition country.

On the other hand, a firefight was the last thing she wanted. She'd known fellow officers and hostages killed in cross fire during operations.

Her best bet lay in taking out Tsosie and Smith. They were the only well-armed people in the room. From her recollection of the scene, Montoya had no weapon other than a knife. If she disabled Tsosie and Smith, Montoya might threaten Diana. However, an FBI officer with a well-aimed rifle might persuade him to let Diana go to save his own skin.

Probably. Maybe. Possibly.

Sighing, she reminded herself that she wasn't a criminal psychology expert. On the other hand, she had enough experience working with Supervisory Special Agents at the National Center for the Analysis of Violent Crime in Quantico and with her own cases to make a few observations about Montoya that might negatively affect the outcome of her plan.

He'd exhibited signs of borderline personality, which made him prone to risk taking and disregarding personal safety. Those little facts, as well as the sadistic streak of malignant narcissism she had seen displayed earlier, made Montoya dangerously unpredictable. If threatened, he might take Diana's life as a final act of defiance.

For a short while, Tabitha weighed the pros and cons of various plans. Grabbing Diana and running like hell was appealing, but it would take at least a minute or two to free her from her bonds. During that delay, Tsosie and Smith were free to act unless she disabled them and somehow avoided injury herself. That still left Montoya, a wild card who wasn't going to let her waltz in and out without a fight.

She needed a distraction.

It took fifteen minutes to gather together an armload of dry brush and sticks—about fourteen minutes too long, by her reckoning. Tabitha eased through the hole in the wall and into the lean-to, careful not to catch her rifle on the splintered edges. She piled the brush and sticks into the composting toilet and added dried peat from the bag. The peat served as excellent kindling when she took the lighter from her pocket and set a fire that smoldered rather than burned, quickly sending out gouts of black smoke that trickled under the door.

Pulling the collar of her fleece jacket up over her mouth and nose, she positioned herself with the rifle in her hands, waiting for someone in the cabin to notice the smoke.

Soon panicked shouts told her the men were reacting to the assumption of fire. Tabitha kicked the door open and rushed into the room. Peat-scented smoke began belching from the lean-to, rapidly filling the cabin. Her eyes watering, she headed toward Diana, only pausing to slam the butt of her rifle into Smith's gut when he blundered into her.

Tsosie's yell warned her the man was close. Jumping over Smith, who lay groaning on the floor, she continued moving in Diana's direction. She bumped into the cot with her knees and drew the kukri from the waistband of her trousers. Her anxious heart rose to fill her mouth, but Montoya wasn't there. Feeling her way to the end of the cot, she found Diana.

"Hush," she murmured when Diana twisted away from her touch. "I got you."

"Tabs?"

"Hang on a sec." Tabitha knelt down and tried to cut the paracord binding Diana's ankles without slicing into skin, a task made more difficult by the smoke. The pressure to hurry added to her clumsiness. Her lungs cramped. She couldn't stop coughing, making her hand more unsteady. By the time she sawed through the cords, she knew she had nicked Diana several times, but she hoped the wounds were superficial.

Freed, Diana stumbled her first step forward. Tabitha took hold of her and tried to orient herself. A shape loomed in the smoke: Tsosie or Montoya. Dragging Diana behind her, she hurried to the lean-to, thinking neither man could predict she'd run to a fire instead of away from it. They would more likely be waiting by the cabin door.

When she ran face first into the firm but yielding wall of a man's chest, she realized she'd been wrong.

"Got her," Tsosie croaked.

Without hesitation Tabitha lashed out, throwing a punch that caught him in the throat. The man fell back, gagging. She pulled Diana past him into the lean-to, halting when the woman didn't budge. She tugged harder and heard Diana let out a strangled protest, but couldn't understand a thing she said.

Half blind from the smoke and feeling as if her lungs had turned to concrete slabs in her chest, Tabitha turned around to find Blair Montoya holding onto Diana, his knife at her throat, his red-rimmed, bloodshot gaze filled with menace. The blade was small, but she knew that an instrument as thin as a metal nail file could penetrate the carotid artery or jugular vein if driven through the skin with enough force.

She wasted no time on negotiations. Deprived of fuel, the choking smoke had begun to thin. Any moment, Tsosie or Smith would recover. She and Diana had to get away right now.

She raised her rifle to smash the butt down on Montoya's hand where he gripped Diana's shoulder. Montoya's agonized yell almost drowned out Diana's cry. The blow from the rifle butt had caught her, too—unavoidable but necessary.

Montoya instinctively released Diana to cradle his injured hand against his chest. Tabitha grabbed the front of Diana's shirt, yanking her forward and away from him, and steering her into the lean-to and pushing her out the hole.

Out of the frying pan, out of the fire—she risked a glance behind to see Tsosie barreling through the door—not out of the woods yet.

CHAPTER FOURTEEN

As she exited the lean-to, something hard struck the back of her head.

Her vision graying out, Tabitha scraped through the hole in the wall after Diana and fell to her knees in the dirt, the strength pouring out of her as pain clanged through her skull.

"Get up!" Diana screamed, bending to grip her upper arms. "Get up, goddamn it!"

Tabitha tried to stand. Her knees wobbled, but she slung an arm over Diana's shoulders, accepting help to get to her feet. "Grab the pack. M' okay, go on, just get it," she mumbled. Glancing at the ground, she saw an unopened can of stew with blood on the label.

Tsosie's face, mottled with fury and wreathed in smoke like a demon straight from hell, appeared in the relatively narrow gap between the boards in the lean-to's wall. Roaring curses, he tried to force his big body through, but he stuck and was just able to get an arm free. He held a can of corned beef in his hand, poised to throw.

Behind him, Montoya shouted, "I've got the gun! Get out of my fucking way!"

"The other door! The front door! They're getting away!" Tsosie called. He launched the corned beef can at Tabitha.

She avoided it, but the movement made the world spin.

Seeing that Diana had snatched up the pack, Tabitha forced her legs to carry her into the woods. The further she ran, the more her head hurt, until her vision blurred further, going red around the edges. Every low-hanging branch she dodged, every log she jogged around or over, made it harder to control her vertigo. When she and Diana reached a small clearing, she paused to catch her breath and stood next to a tree, putting a supporting hand on a trunk. Miraculously, she found she was still in possession of the rifle.

"You okay?" Diana asked, coming back to check on her.

Opening her mouth to reply, Tabitha suddenly vomited, surprising herself.

Diana cursed and leaned over to peer into her face. "I'm sorry, sugar, but we need to go, they're right behind us," she said, looking concerned. "Can you walk?"

"Yeah, I'm good." Spitting to clear the taste of bile, Tabitha willed her body to obey. "Concussions suck and I seriously need a toothbrush. And mouthwash. And a dental hygienist or three. I swear my teeth are wearing fuzzy sweaters."

"Do I need to be worried?"

"Told you, I'm good."

"Uh-huh." Straightening, Diana scanned the area. "Which way?"

"Which way what?" Tabitha asked, wondering if she dared take the time to pull an aspirin out of the survival kit in the pack.

"Which way is the river?" Diana asked, making a clear effort to keep her impatience in check. "Or did you do that squirrel imitation just for the hell of it?"

The river…Tabitha tried to recall which way she and Diana had run from the cabin, and where the cabin stood in relation to the spruce tree she had climbed, but found she had difficulty thinking through the fog in her mind. The details wouldn't come.

"Find somewhere safe to rest, let me take a painkiller, and I'll figure it out," she said, "but I can't do anything here and now."

Diana nodded. "Stay here, I think I saw something that way." She trotted away before Tabitha had a chance to object.

Left alone, Tabitha hobbled to another tree to avoid the smell of vomit. She leaned on the trunk, grounding the butt of the rifle in the dirt to use as a prop so she wouldn't tip over. Her eyes closed while she mentally cataloged concussion symptoms. Dizziness? Check. Nausea? Check. Headache? Hell, yes. Seeing stars? A whole constellation's worth, she thought sourly, damning Tsosie and his pitching arm. The last time she'd had a headache this bad, it followed a night of tequila shooters with Victoria at a titty bar in Springfield, celebrating their graduation from the Academy. The smell of lime gelatin still made her ill.

She massaged her forehead, listening for any sounds of pursuit. Above her head, she heard rustling in the leaves—a bird, she thought, or a squirrel. From the left came a louder crunching noise, something large moving through the brush. Opening her eyes and snapping the rifle to her shoulder, she found herself confronting a moose.

She smiled and lowered the rifle. The moose looked comical with its broad, pendulous nose and short, thick neck. It quizzically blinked at her.

Like a big brown cow, she thought. When the animal came closer, her smile faded. The moose was huge, at least six feet long, taller than a horse, and a good fifteen hundred pounds of muscle. The lifted head was topped by spreading palmate antlers. It no longer seemed friendly or goofy. She gulped.

Nostrils flared, the moose pawed at the earth.

Cold with fear, Tabitha took a step to the side to get clear of the tree. Watching her, the moose snorted, its ears twitching back and forth. She froze, desperately trying to remember what she'd been told at the mandatory safety meeting before the race.

Moose attack more people each year than bears. They can see and hear very well, but their eyesight is poor, she recalled.

Do not provoke them. Avoidance is the first step to survival. Oh…oh, shit.

Another moose stepped out of the bushes to join the first.

Recalling a relevant piece of advice, Tabitha quickly put the tree between herself and the two moose, standing so she could peer around the trunk to keep an eye on the animals. If necessary, she could sprint away faster than a gangly moose could dodge around the tree.

She didn't want to shoot them. The sound of the rifle might attract Montoya and his men, and she had to assume they were in pursuit as none of them had been disabled in the fight. She also knew she could not kill both moose cleanly in the split-second she'd have to fire before one or the other charged her. Dealing with a wounded, angry, fifteen hundred pound-plus moose was definitely not on her bucket list.

A moose bawled, picking at the earth with a front hoof and throwing up clods of dirt. The other moose made a moaning sound. Unable to interpret the behavior, Tabitha backed away, using the tree trunk for cover. She was anchored to the site by the need to wait for Diana, who might return any moment, so she dared not go too far.

Convinced it had been at least an hour since Diana left, Tabitha checked her watch and found only five minutes had passed. She cursed under her breath, wishing she had the pack. Then at least she could have dry swallowed an aspirin. She knew from experience a concussion headache usually lasted a while, in some cases as much as a month or two.

The second moose drifted away and disappeared in the undergrowth.

"Hey, where'd you go?" Diana asked, stepping into sight on the other side of the small clearing. She spoke in a near whisper, but the sound carried. Spotting the moose, Diana froze in mid-step. "Uh…nice moose, aren't you a sweetie? It's okay, don't be scared, I ain't going to hurt you," she went on in the high-pitched baby talk reserved for infants and pets. "You're a good moose, aren't you?"

Tabitha moved to the side, within Diana's line of sight. "Come this way," she said. "No, not across the clearing, walk around. Put some distance between you and that moose."

"Is it a boy moose or a girl moose?" Diana asked nervously, sidling several steps closer to a large bush.

"Just get your ass over here," Tabitha said, allowing her exasperation and worry to show. Every movement of her head made the pain worse, but she swung the rifle into position in case the moose decided to charge.

When Diana moved further away, the moose belted out a long, low bugling sound. The hackles rose on the shaggy hump between its shoulders.

Tabitha decided this couldn't be a good development.

"Nice moose," Diana crooned, continuing to pussyfoot around the clearing. "Good moose. You don't want to squish Auntie Di, do you?"

"Quit farting around, damn it," Tabitha ordered through gritted teeth.

Diana halted to glare in her direction. "Don't you get all pissy with me, Tabs."

"Just come on, we need to move."

Making a series of guttural grunts, the moose tossed its head, rubbing its antlers against the trunk of a tree and chipping off bits of bark that flew through the air like confetti. The behavior seemed aggressive, preparatory to an attack. Diana yelped when some of the splintered bark hit her in the face, but she kept going.

Her stomach knotted with apprehension. Tabitha snugged the butt of her rifle into her shoulder and closed an eye to draw a bead on the moose without bothering to use the scope. She kept her forefinger on the trigger guard, ready to shoot if necessary, but silently willing the moose to back down, move away, and leave them the hell alone.

"Any day now, Di," she called. Her voice had gone raspy with irritation, but she didn't give a crap. The stabbing pain behind her eyes made it difficult to focus. "I'm growing roots while you're taking a Sunday stroll."

"Do I really need to tell you how annoying that is?" Diana growled.

Tabitha waited until Diana joined her behind the tree before lowering the rifle. She didn't completely relax, but kept a vigilant eye on the moose, who started lipping leaves off a nearby bush. Her skin felt tight to the point of agony, and she thought her brain might be trying to batter its away out of her skull.

"Okay, what was so important you felt we had to split up just now?" she asked, a potent mix of frustration and anger drawing her muscles tight.

"Huh?" Diana's brow creased in bewilderment.

"I mean when you took off a minute ago," Tabitha said to prevent herself from doing something foolish and destructive, like screaming at the top of her lungs. Fifteen years in law enforcement and she had never wanted to smack someone so badly that her hands trembled.

Diana gave her a careless shrug. "Mountain and molehill."

"Don't do that again," Tabitha ground out, her temper going off like a flash-bang grenade. Every word felt like shards of glass in her throat. "If you want to throw your life away after I went to the trouble of saving it, you might have said so and spared me the effort."

Huffing out a breath, Diana put her hands on her hips. "What's the big deal?" she asked, her chin lifting, her eyes narrowed to glimmering blue slits. "You left me before."

"That's different," Tabitha said, slinging the rifle on her back. Buoyed by righteous indignation, her exhaustion melted away. "I was doing my job, figuring out how to save our asses, not playing hide-and-seek with killers." She turned to choose a direction, intending to lead the way deeper into the woods to put more distance between them and the moose. She also wanted to leave the area before Montoya and his hunting party caught up to them.

After a moment, she noticed Diana wasn't following her. She refused to go back to the clearing, but kept going forward until she heard footsteps approaching rapidly from behind.

"What is your problem?" Diana demanded, putting a hand on Tabitha's shoulder and wrenching her around.

Tabitha dropped her shoulder and rotated on her heel, breaking Diana's grip without hurting the woman. No matter her exasperation, she never wanted to hurt Diana. Not really. Not that way. "My problem, as you put it," she said, "is that I'm trying my damnedest to keep both of us alive. I'd appreciate it if you cooperated a little."

"What do you think I'm doing here?" Diana asked hotly. "At least I'm not just wandering around because I'm too proud to admit I'm lost."

"Now wait a minute—"

"No, you left me, remember? While you were nice and safe in that tree enjoying the view, I was a sitting duck."

"That's unfair. We needed to know which way to go," Tabitha protested.

"You did what you wanted, never mind me," Diana said, a subtle shiver in her muscles that Tabitha read as the inevitable exhaustion that followed coming down from an adrenaline high. "Do you know what it's like to be tied up like that?" she asked, her voice cracking. "To be at an evil man's mercy like that? Not knowing what he'll do to you because he can do anything at all, and there's not a thing you can do about it?"

"No, but—" Tabitha broke off when Diana walked away. "Wait," she said, darting after the furious woman.

Diana did not acknowledge her. Instead, she kept her head down and continued to plod along. Lodgepole pines as tall and straight as spears ran in an irregular line on either side of the trail, eventually thinning and replaced by spruces.

Tabitha followed, feeling like an asshole. In the heat of a panicked moment, she had forgotten that Diana was a victim. Who knew what Montoya had done? Not all hurts were visible, she reminded herself. Her anger faded, changing to rising alarm when she realized she had no idea if Diana suffered any physical injuries. The possibility seemed more than likely.

She studied Diana's gait, looking for tell-tale signs of abuse: a limp, any hesitation in movement, the cherishing of a bruise, a hand flattened over the ribs or other parts of the body. Finding nothing obvious, her mind helpfully supplied a list of hidden injuries, each accompanied by a mental snapshot of a victim or witness from a previous case.

Christ, I really don't need any more nightmare fodder today. She wanted to apologize, but Diana's attitude clearly indicated a desire to be left alone. Best give her some space for now. Later, she'd insist on a visual inspection. The thought of finding evidence of Montoya's violent streak on Diana's body reignited a slow burn of rage in her gut.

Montoya. She found compartmentalizing her feelings toward him difficult. Had she been involved in an official FBI investigation of his crimes, she'd have been forced to recuse herself because of the tangled mess of resentment, hate, anger, and guilt preying on her mind due to his mistreatment of Diana. She wanted Montoya dead. She'd like to kill him herself, and that was not acceptable. Grounds for a psychological evaluation if her boss found out.

She had to cope. If she flaked, if she quit, or if she crossed the line, giving in to the temptation to kill him, no matter how much he deserved to die...well, stepping on that slippery slope only led to damnation. Shooting someone in self defense, yes. In defense of another, yes. But she never, never let it become personal, no matter the provocation.

Trudging behind Diana, she waved a flying insect away from her face. The temperature had gone up, leaving the woods hot, muggy, and airless. Sweat itched in her hairline. A bead of perspiration winked bright in a shaft of sunlight before it shivered off the end of her nose. She desperately wanted a drink of water. Her headache was worse, each step setting new waves of pain pounding in her skull like a storm tide hammering a shore.

She swatted a mosquito, which left a red smear on her palm. "Any chance of stopping a second?" she asked, wiping her hand on the front of her jacket.

"Almost there," Diana said over her shoulder.

Tabitha forced herself to continue without complaint as the downward slope of the ground became more acute.

"You know," Diana said after a few minutes, "I was really pissed at you." She sounded calm. "Still kind of mad as hell, but I'm not likely to stove your head in anymore."

"I'm sorry," Tabitha replied, stepping over a pile of something nasty crawling with flies. Insect wings tickled her cheek when the flies buzzed into the air, disturbed by her passage. "I was careless," she added, surrendering to the sudden, stricken impulse that jammed words in her mouth. "I should've done something, not let Montoya—"

"No, you did what you had to do. If you'd swung down out of that tree like Tarzan, you've have been shot dead. Letting me get caught was logical, I understand that. You had to survive to rescue me. I was just…well, I wasn't feeling very reasonable. I'm better now."

"Are you sure?"

Diana shrugged. "As good as I'm going to get."

"Did he…" Tabitha hesitated and chose a different way to phrase her question. "Are you okay? Are you hurt anywhere?"

"Yes."

"Where?"

"I'll tell you later." At Tabitha's frown, Diana went on, "I'm not likely to bleed out, it's not that serious, don't worry about it."

Tabitha swallowed her concern. She didn't want to rile Diana any further. "You want something for the pain?" she asked, digging the survival kit out of the pack.

Diana stared at the kit in Tabitha's hands. "Aspirin?" she asked.

"No water."

"Don't care. I'll swallow 'em dry."

Tearing open a packet of aspirin, Tabitha gave Diana two pills.

"Lord, that's bitter," Diana said. She shuddered, but managed to keep the pills down. For the first time, her gaze focused on Tabitha. "Shit, girl, are you bleeding?" she asked. "You've got blood smeared all over your jacket collar."

"I'm fine," Tabitha said, trying to evade Diana's scrutiny. "It's a mosquito."

"No, you are not fine. Will you hold still? You're squirming like a three-year-old doing the pee-pee dance. Show me the back of your head." When Tabitha complied, Diana sucked in a breath, letting it out on a whispered, "Oh, my God."

Alarmed, Tabitha spun around, almost falling as a wave of vertigo struck. "What…what's the matter?" she asked, but Diana just stared at her in shocked silence.

She felt her hair at the back of her head, finding the strands sticky and matted together. Steeling herself, she probed her skull, gritting her teeth when even careful pressing on the bone caused a flash of pain that streaked across her vision like a red lightning bolt.

"Don't touch it," Diana said, her voice quavering.

"It's a laceration from where that bastard clocked me with a can," Tabitha said, her fingertips brushing the edges of a small cut. "Scalp wounds always bleed like bastards. If I were near an ER, I'd get stitches, but I'm not. So unless you see brains dripping out…"

Diana let out a nervous little laugh. "No chance of that."

"Good. You ready to go?"

"Yeah, let's get out of here. We're pretty close." Diana walked on, glancing anxiously over her shoulder several times.

Tabitha almost asked, "Pretty close to what?" but resigned herself to following Diana without an explanation.

At last, after pushing past a stand of immature willow trees, Diana came to an abrupt halt. "Here we go," she said, waving a hand.

Realizing the chuckling sound she heard was running water, Tabitha hastened to stand next to Diana. To her astonishment, a river flowed in front of her, a broad, silvery-gray ribbon flashing under the sun. Pebbles and gravel covered the riverbank. She saw a pile of twigs and logs smeared with dried mud—the wreckage of a beaver's lodge, she assumed, having seen several in photographs taken by prior racers. Nothing had ever looked so good to her.

Her view of the river fuzzed as though viewed through static when her vision blurred with involuntary tears.

"I figure that's got to be the Yukon," Diana said with a brilliant, triumphant, and somewhat smug grin. "Sugar, you're not the only one can climb trees around here."

Weak with relief, Tabitha grinned back. "Thank God," she breathed.

"To be fair, it wasn't God who skinned up a tree to look for the river and got pine sap all over His hands and pants," Diana said, wrinkling her nose. She gestured at a blob of sap on the leg of her khaki trousers, hardly distinguishable from other stains. "That stuff's sticky like glue and pure hell to get out in the wash."

"When we reach civilization, I'll buy you a new pair of pants," Tabitha said.

She started to say something else, but renewed dizziness swept over her, leaving clammy sweat in its wake. A very unpleasant sensation followed, as if the entire world had taken one step to the right and she'd stayed behind. Her stomach heaved.

"Hey, Tabs, you okay?" Diana asked, frowning. "You're white as a sheet."

Her balance gone, the forest spinning around her, Tabitha fell into darkness.

CHAPTER FIFTEEN

Tabitha woke to wetness on her face. Her eyes still closed, she licked her lips. Water. Seized by a sudden, terrible thirst, she tried to struggle up on her elbows, whimpering when a spike of pain flared inside her skull.

"Shh, it's okay, stay down," said a familiar female voice.

Tabitha cracked open her eyes. "Di?" she croaked.

"The one and only, sugar." Diana smiled, but worry puckered her brow. She wiped her dripping hands on the front of her pants.

Slowly, Tabitha registered the uncomfortable sensation of rocks under her back. "I guess I passed out," she said, pronouncing each word with care. "That sucks."

"Well, you took a heck of a whack on the noggin, then you got dehydrated, so yeah. It sucks. You feeling dizzy now? Nauseous? Seeing double?"

"No."

"Think you can manage to keep down water?"

Mute with craving, Tabitha decided that nothing seemed painful other than her head. She recalled her earlier headache had seemed much worse. In the debate between satisfying her thirst or coddling a concussion, she chose the former. She sat up a few deliberate inches at a time, relieved when she neither puked nor passed out. In fact, the longer she sat quietly, the less she hurt except for some stiffness in her muscles.

"I'm okay," she said in response to Diana's anxious expression.

"Good girl," Diana said, rising from her crouch. "Now stay there, and for God's sake, stay vertical. You scare me like that again, I swear I'll raise a knot on your head a calf could suck on." She paused, visibly calming. "The bad news is, we lost the cups, so there are two ways we can get you a drink: I can bring a drop of water to you in my hands like I did before, or you can go to the river. What'll it be?"

Tabitha's heart leaped at the idea of drinking directly from the river as opposed to waiting while Diana ferried a mouthful at a time to her. "I'll go," she said, reaching for Diana's outstretched hand. With a little help, she lurched to her feet.

A moment later, kneeling on the riverbank, she bent with a purification straw to her lips. The first sip burst on her tongue like the best champagne, cool and delicious, saturating her water-starved tissues. Greedily, she drank more, swearing she felt herself plumping out as her flesh expanded like a sponge sucking up moisture. The sandpaper ache in her throat eased. Too soon, she felt a touch on her shoulder.

"Not too much, or you'll be sick," Diana cautioned.

Tabitha released the straw. "I needed that," she said. Wiping her mouth, she rose without help this time. Her headache had lessened now that she'd satisfied her thirst.

Diana took the straw from her, knelt, and drank several gulps of water. "You just collapsed. You were breathing, but you wouldn't wake up." She shook her head and stood up. "Goddamn it, Tabitha Knowles," she continued fiercely after a moment, her eyes glinting, "how dare you do that to me? I thought you were dead—"

"I'm sorry, I'm so sorry," Tabitha interrupted.

She threw her arms around Diana and gathered her close. As she hugged the shuddering woman, she felt tears burning her eyes. A flood of emotions poured out of her heart: affection, guilt, gratitude, relief and others she could not name. Putting aside her feelings to examine later, she held on until Diana tried to pull away. Reluctantly, she let go.

"I didn't mean to blubber and snot all over you," Diana said, wiping her face on her shirtsleeve when she stepped away. "And I didn't mean to be such a bitch. No, that's kind of a lie," she went on, preventing Tabitha from getting a word in. "What I mean to say is that I acted badly when I blamed you for what happened. You saved my worthless ass, and not for the first time. You could've left me there and walked away, but you didn't. You risked your life to help me. You faced off against three armed guys in that cabin, and you without so much as a rock to defend yourself. And what did I do? Screech and holler."

"It's understandable," Tabitha said, searching for the right way to comfort Diana. All those years of victim sensitivity training, and she found herself at a loss for words when she needed them most. "You were in shock. You were afraid. You were angry. Montoya's a dangerous man. He threatened you. He hurt you. You needed to blame someone."

"But I shouldn't have blamed you. I thought…I guess I felt abandoned. Betrayed. Stupid, huh? Blair's such a mean bastard, and I was so scared, but you came for me. You didn't abandon me. I know that right down to my bones. So I'm sorry for spewing all that crap. Believe me, I didn't mean it. Not a bit." Squaring her shoulders, Diana let out a mirthless chuckle. "Hell, I ought to be down on my knees thanking you, but gravel doesn't agree with my joints. I swear I'll pay you back someday."

Tabitha blew out a breath. "Di, you don't owe me anything."

"How can you say that? I owe you everything, Tabs. Everything."

"How long was I unconscious?"

Diana seemed surprised and puzzled by the question. "About ten minutes, I guess," she finally said, giving her a concerned look.

"Would you have left me lying there, unconscious and helpless, and walked away?"

"Of course not!"

"Why not?" Tabitha asked, moving a step closer. "Let's face it, you didn't know if I'd ever regain consciousness. In this setting, a comatose woman is a severe liability. Trying to care for me would compromise your survival. You'd have been better off concentrating on yourself." Lowering her voice, she stared into Diana's eyes, bluer than the sky, bluer than the mountains in the distance. "You could have justified your actions, kept your conscience clear by telling yourself that you'd send back help, that leaving me was the right thing to do. So why'd you stick around?"

"Because I'm not an amoral asshole," Diana snapped.

Tabitha closed the last bit of distance between them until she and Diana stood chest to chest, face to face. "And neither am I," she said gently.

Diana's mouth dropped open. She started to say something, stopped, and swallowed. After about thirty seconds, she murmured, "Are you going to kiss me?"

"Yes," Tabitha whispered. She pressed her mouth against Diana's lips, which were dry and chapped, but the touch stirred something complicated in her chest. She didn't deepen the kiss, just held Diana to her for a timeless moment. Nothing existed except the two of them, suspended like butterflies in amber while the world faded to white noise.

Fear had no place here. Neither did lust. Desire remained muted, the merest flicker at the base of her spine reminding her of past pleasures. The hollow spaces inside her filled with warmth. All she wanted was contact, she lied to herself, the fulfillment of a yearning for closeness with another human being. Anyone would do.

No, her heart insisted. Not anyone. Diana.

Her feelings made no sense. She hadn't known Diana long, but she'd never felt so protective, so tender, so willing to cherish and be cherished. Her hands clenched on Diana's arms when her sudden realization shattered the moment. Panting in mingled exhilaration and terror, she tore her mouth away, unwilling to let her emotions dictate her actions.

Diana made a noise that might have been a protest. Her breath came fast and shallow. Raising her hand, she touched her fingertips to her lips. "Wow," she said, a faint pink flush warming her cheeks. "If that's the way you kiss after a knock on the head, I'll have to remember to keep a blunt object handy in the future."

Not sure how she ought to take Diana's statement, Tabitha mumbled an incoherent response while struggling to regain her composure.

"Hey, you okay?" Clearly concerned, Diana tried to peer into her averted face. "If you're getting sick again—"

"No," Tabitha said hastily, "I'm fine. Just tired, that's all."

"You sure?"

"Yes. Are you cold? I'm cold. I think I'll build a fire." Tabitha started for the wrecked beaver dam, eager to avoid any further conversation about kisses.

"What about Blair?" Diana protested, following her as she walked along the bank. "Can't he or his goons use the smoke to find us?"

Tabitha paused and pressed the heel of her hand to her forehead. Her headache had turned to a dull throb between her eyes, but that wasn't her main problem. She took a deep breath, willing the fluttering in her stomach to go away. Forget her feelings. She and Diana couldn't afford distractions.

"I don't want to attract the wrong kind of attention," she said, "but we need a way to signal a boat. A fire is the most practical solution. Besides, there are likely other racers taking rest stops up and down the river, and they'll need fires, too."

"If you're cold, we could cuddle to stay warm," Diana suggested, giving her a sly glance. "I hear sharing body heat is very good at warding off hypothermia."

Her mind scrabbled to find something to say that wouldn't hurt Diana. Tabitha opened her mouth to reply, but the excuse went unspoken when she spotted a canoe on the river, headed in their direction. Inflating her lungs, she shouted, "Hey! Over here!"

The canoeist waved a paddle in acknowledgment and the canoe darted for shore. At last, the canoe came close enough and slid forward, crunching on gravel as the keel grounded on the riverbank. Almost faint with relief, Tabitha grabbed the prow. Diana took the other side. Both of them worked to drag the vessel higher, clear of the river.

As soon as he could manage without getting his feet wet, the canoeist sprang out. "You ladies all right?" he asked, looking from Diana to Tabitha.

"We had an accident," Tabitha told him, taking a mental picture of the man: Caucasian male, early- to mid-forties, tall and rangy, brown hair cut shorter than fashionable, brown eyes. No tattoos, moles or scars, though since he wore a long-sleeved shirt, not much of his tanned skin was visible except his hands and face. He had an upright bearing, not slouching much, but relaxed in what she considered a parade rest stance. "Are you in the race?" she asked.

"Yeah, sure," he replied. "Yancy Warner," he said, not offering his hand.

Tabitha ignored the lack of a handshake. Perhaps he had blisters from paddling, she decided. He wasn't wearing gloves. Or maybe he's an impolite asshole. Don't know. Don't care. He's required to lend us assistance according to race rules, or he'll be disqualified.

"I'm Diana, you can call me Di if you want. This is my friend Tabitha," Diana broke in eagerly, beaming at him.

He failed to return Diana's smile, instead flickering an assessing gaze over her. Apparently satisfied, he asked, "Where's your canoe?" while glancing up and down the bank.

"We wrecked it. Stupid, huh? So where are we? I mean, where on the river?" Diana babbled. "We're totally lost. Where's Lake Laberge from here? You got maps, right?" She started to bend down toward the canoe, but the man stopped her by gripping her upper arm.

"Don't do that," Yancy said, pulling her away.

"Let her go," Tabitha demanded, her muscles going rigid with the need to strike him. Her temper flared. He hadn't grabbed Diana roughly, but something about the calculating way he stared made her want to punch him in the face.

Yancy released Diana and backed off a pace. "Take it easy, slick," he said. "I didn't mean any harm. Your friend isn't hurt. I'm a private guy, that's all. Don't like people messing with my stuff. Besides, I don't have a map."

No map? That made no sense, Tabitha thought. The Yukon River was complicated with side channels, currents, islands, sandbars and other hazards, especially in the area once called the "Thirty Mile" in the steamboat days—referring to the section between Whitehorse and Dawson where the race took place. No one went out on the river without a map.

Diana appeared unfazed. "How about GPS?" she asked him. He shook his head.

Tabitha's instincts screamed at her that something was off about this man. "Mr. Warner, please excuse my partner," she said, hiding her mistrust behind a bland, smooth-as-cream mask. "We made the mistake of moving off the river a couple of days ago and got lost in the woods a while. We're both kind of frazzled. You understand, don't you?"

"I guess," Yancy replied noncommittally. As soon as he finished speaking to her, he resumed looking at Diana. After a pause, he asked, "You ready to get out of here?"

Tabitha turned to Yancy's canoe, taking her first proper look at the vessel—a tandem canoe, not a solo. Her mistrust deepened. While it was possible for a single paddler to work a tandem canoe, why would a solo racer take on the unnecessary extra weight? Most single paddlers traveled as light as possible.

"Hell, yes, I want to get out of here!" Diana exclaimed. "Preferably to a hotel with hot water and room service."

After scooping up the pack and slinging the rifle on her shoulder, Tabitha went over to the canoe, aware that Yancy's attention remained focused mainly on Diana. She wondered why. Not that Diana wasn't an attractive woman, but his interest seemed a little too intense.

Yancy came up to the other side of the canoe and reached inside to remove a long nylon case with a familiar shape. A rifle case. Tabitha frowned. He glanced at her.

"Bears," he said, propping the rifle case against his leg.

Diana nodded. "We had an encounter ourselves. Nothing serious, but scary as hell." At Yancy's invitation, she stepped into the canoe, settling amidships on a folded sleeping bag.

In Tabitha's experience, Yancy had too few supplies for adventure racing, just the sleeping bag, the rifle, and a single backpack. A military backpack, she noticed, in the mottled green and olive woodland camouflage used by the USMC.

"Marines or army?" she asked in her best casual tone, as if making small talk. Only when she'd spoken did she realize her mistake.

Yancy turned a piercing, narrowed gaze on her for the first time, his expression tightening when he saw the rifle strap over her shoulder. "Army," he answered, his fingers straying to the rifle case leaning against his leg.

Tabitha tensed.

Giving her the same assessing stare he'd used on Diana, he finally shrugged, picked up the rifle case, and shoved it into the canoe's bow. "Got any other questions, better save them till we're underway," he said, bending to start pushing the canoe into the water.

Scrambling to catch up left Tabitha off balance, but before he could make a suggestion or issue an order, she splashed hip deep into the river. The freezing water wrung an involuntary gasp from her, but she pulled herself into the canoe's stern seat, unwilling to sit with Yancy behind her. She needed to keep him in sight.

"Why'd you do that?" Diana asked over her shoulder, grimacing at Tabitha's sodden trousers. "You'll catch a cold."

"I'm fine," Tabitha answered shortly.

The rifle went into her lap. Just a precaution, she told herself. She checked on Yancy. From his position in the bow, he gave no indication he was listening to them, apparently concentrating on maneuvering the canoe into deeper water.

Diana snorted. "By 'fine,' do you mean on the verge of hypothermia? Here, take the sleeping bag. I'm sure Mr. Warner won't mind. I'll just—"

"No," Tabitha interrupted. "Like I said, I'm fine."

"Do we have a problem?" Diana asked, twisting her body around and lowering her voice. "I thought we were okay."

"We are." Tabitha tried to give Diana a reassuring smile. "Don't worry, Di. I'm just a little distracted at the moment."

"Uh-huh, I get it." Diana jerked a thumb at Yancy's back. "Don't want to give the poor guy any ideas about hot, girl-on-girl action." Her leer drove her point home, as did sticking out her tongue and wiggling it. "I'm the soul of discretion," she added.

Tabitha choked and snorted through her nose when her throat clenched on a laugh.

"We'll be coming up on Lake Laberge real soon," Yancy remarked from the bow. He jerked his chin ahead to indicate where the channel widened.

For all their wandering blindly in the woods, Tabitha thought, she and Diana had not really gone that far. Had she known how close they were to Lake Laberge, she might have elected to walk to a spot opposite the checkpoint to try flagging a race marshal or another racer instead of hailing the first canoe that came along.

She recalled a few uncomfortable statistics: over thirty-seven percent of Alaskan women were victims of sexual violence, and incidences of rape in the state were two and a half times higher than the rest of the country. Yancy Warner might be a predator like Robert Hansen, the serial killer who'd murdered at least seventeen women in the Alaskan bush.

On the other hand, there was such a thing as job-induced paranoia. Her instincts could be off the mark. She had no evidence of wrongdoing. In fact, Yancy Warner might be nothing more than a man who found brunettes attractive, hence his fixation on Diana.

A glance at the sky revealed charcoal-colored clouds piling atop one another, a threat of rain blowing in from the mountains. She frowned. A storm over Lake Laberge meant serious trouble. Casting her gaze amidships, she noticed the blade of a paddle protruding under one side of the sleeping bag Diana sat on.

She bent to snag the paddle—navigating the lake under storm conditions required both her and Yancy, one person couldn't do it alone, no matter how skilled—when the canoe rocked violently from side to side, almost pitching her forward.

Sitting up, she saw Yancy standing in the bow, his long legs straddling the seat, and his paddle cocked over his shoulder, ready to swing down on Diana's unprotected head as the storm broke over Lake Laberge with sudden, savage fury.

Cold rain roared out the sky, a solid sheet of water filling the air, running into Tabitha's nose and mouth, choking her with a sensation not unlike being drowned.

Through the muffling curtain of rain, Tabitha saw Diana's hand came up to shield her head, a reflex that wouldn't do a damned bit of good because the edge of Yancy's hardwood paddle would snap Diana's wrist and transfer enough kinetic energy through the bone to crack her skull open. If not, the second blow would kill her, but a strong man like Yancy might not need to hit her twice if his first strike landed in the right place.

A split second to choose. Make the wrong decision, someone dies, Tabitha's rational mind supplied even as she responded to the threat in the way that thousands of hours of training and practice had hardwired into her muscles. Rather than push Diana out of the way, she raised the rifle in her lap and fired over the woman's shoulder in Yancy's direction.

The bullet took Yancy high in the shoulder.

The canoe rocked more violently this time, close to the tipping point when the port gunwale dipped toward the water. Twisting like a cat, Yancy regained his balance and remained on his feet. Tabitha snarled. She'd had no expectation of killing the man with a single shot—an outcome rarer than television portrayed. Instead, she had been trying to distract him. Accidentally coming so close to a kill shot made her angry with herself.

Before he had a chance to ready the paddle for another try, she shoved Diana forward and down as she vaulted up, sacrificing the canoe's stability in favor of speed. She landed with one foot amidships, the other stretched behind her, ankle caught on something under the stern seat. The tendons in her thighs protested the stretch. Pain flared in her overextended knee. Still, she had achieved her goal: putting herself between Diana and Yancy.

Tabitha worked the bolt to eject the shell casing and load a new round. She grounded the rifle's butt on the canoe's deck, pointed the muzzle at Yancy's blurry figure looming in the rain ahead of her, and pulled the trigger, confident of hitting him right up to the moment the rifle didn't fire. With a sinking heart, she realized the magazine was empty.

Unbidden, a memory flashed in a split second across her mind: she and Victoria in a cemetery in Valdosta, dodging headstones in the dark and stumbling over the uneven ground as they played catch-me-if-you-can with Henry Jakes, a murderer and bank robber. She'd heard Victoria grunt and turned to find Jakes grinning triumphantly, holding a dripping knife. Raising her gun, she had squeezed the trigger, her guts churning when all she'd heard was a loud click. In her agitaton, she'd forgotten to take off the safety. Then Victoria, though wounded in the arm, had shot Jakes three times in the chest.

Her mind returned to the present. She couldn't really see Yancy in detail through the blinding rain, but she felt his grin. Rain pelted her head, each drop like a nail driving into her skull. She seemed to move with agonizing slowness as she scrabbled in her pocket, praying to find ammunition before he beat her to death with the paddle. Before she could complete the thought, a furious shriek rang through in her ears, almost making her drop the rifle.

Diana rose from the center of the canoe like a vengeful Fury, her hair sopping wet and hanging in dark strings around her pale, rage-distorted face. She held the spare paddle in her hands. She cocked the paddle over her shoulder and swung it at Yancy like she was trying to hit a home run out of the park. The move unbalanced her, so that she almost toppled over when the current bit into the canoe's keel, sending it skewing sideways.

The blow connected with Yancy's head, a solid crunch that Tabitha heard over the rain. He started to fall. Diana hit him again, the edge of the paddle taking him across the throat. She was winding up for a third strike when the man plummeted overboard and disappeared from view, swallowed by the cold, gray water.

Diana remained frozen in place. The paddle slid out of her hands.

Stunned, Tabitha blinked raindrops out of her eyes. She tried to take a deep breath without also inhaling a lungful of watery mist. When Diana finally leaned carefully over her and put a hand on her back, she felt the tightness in her chest, a constricting band of worry, resolve and anger slowly dissolving. Through the rushing in her head, she heard a whisper of sound. She strained to hear.

"You okay?" Diana asked over the constant, heavy rain sheeting from the clouds. Her mouth brushed Tabitha's ear, a shock of warm contact.

Tabitha nodded, not caring about the rain dribbling down her neck and tracing down her spine like an icy finger. A dam cracked open inside her, spilling want, and need, and so much gratitude and affection she couldn't breathe. Blindsided by the confusion of emotions fighting for her attention, she felt confident of a single fact: somehow, in the space between one minute and the next, she had fallen in love with Diana Crenshaw.

The realization was simple, but unwelcome because of the potential to make her situation with Diana incredibly complicated.

"We're taking on too much water, we need to get to shore," Diana said. She bent closer, her nose almost touching Tabitha's. "Hey, you doing all right? We've got to go, sugar, you hear me?" Her eyes widened. "Did that bastard get you? Swear to God, if he hit you, I'll dive in there, haul his ass out, and whale the living hell out of him again."

Diana's eyelashes were wet, Tabitha noticed in dazed fascination. She roused herself. No point surviving so much danger only to drown or die of hypothermia because she was too busy daydreaming like a besotted teenager to save herself. "Yeah, okay," she said.

Once Diana settled into the bow seat, Tabitha managed to unhook her ankle, sit down in the stern, and begin fighting the current, the rain and the wind to regain control of the drifting canoe. She kept her mind intentionally blank of everything except the moment.

Poor visibility meant she had no idea where they were in relation to the shore. She and Diana might be paddling in circles for all she knew. Peering into the downpour, which continued to drum the lake's surface to a dancing froth, she chose a direction at random.

Three-foot-high waves slapped the hull. Bigger waves splashed over the gunwale, a wash of freezing wetness that raised the water level in the bottom of the canoe to such an alarming degree, Tabitha wondered if she'd have to stop paddling and start bailing.

A tail wind sprang up. For a moment, she thought they might be catching a break, but the wind came at a side angle, sending water slopping directly over her back. The rough chop made her and Diana work for every inch of progress.

The skin of her buttocks and thighs chafed against her soaked underwear and the wet fabric of her trousers. At first, the raw feeling was a minor annoyance, but she knew from experience that if she did nothing, the pain would get progressively worse. Unfortunately, she could do nothing except go on, running on adrenaline fumes. Her arms and shoulders ached while fatigue lit a fire under her ribs that didn't warm her at all.

The tiny muscles around her eyes trembled. The temptation to close them fully snuck up on her, a product of the concussion throbbing in her temples, the never-ending nightmare of wet and cold, exhaustion, and the paddle rising and falling in a mechanical rhythm. Her head nodded. Her eyelids closed. She forced her eyes open, fixed her gaze ahead, and bit her lip until she tasted blood. Doggedly, she began paddling again, relieved to feel the canoe responding to her strokes. At least the rainfall seemed to be softening to a drizzle, she thought, licking the diluted coppery tang off her lips.

At last, the mist began dissipating and the sun broke through the clouds like a hallelujah moment. A few last slanting raindrops sparkled like strings of jewels in the golden light. The surface of the lake settled to a calm, glassy sheen. No longer pounded by waves or crosswinds, the canoe drifted gently along in the current.

The air stilled. In the hush, Tabitha heard the harsh sound of her breathing. Each heartbeat thundered in her chest. She stayed hunched over, her elbows resting on her knees, not knowing or caring if the water dripping off her nose was rain or sweat. Every part of her body hurt, a bone-deep ache from the crown of her head to her toes, as if she'd been carefully beaten by a sadist aiming for maximum pain, minimum damage.

"I'm not sure where we are," she heard Diana panting, "but I think we're way past the checkpoint. What do you want to do?"

Tabitha made an effort to unstick her tongue from the roof of her mouth. She'd spent a lot of time poring over maps of the river, but a printed map differed greatly from the actual physical landscape of a place. Glancing around, she saw no particular landmarks that would indicate their position, just trees, more trees, sandbars and mountains.

She needed to bail out the canoe, determine their current location, put on dry clothes if any could be found, get warm, inventory their supplies, plan what to do next...so many necessary tasks pressed on her, but all she could do was open her mouth and croak, "I don't know," before the lurking darkness at the edges of her vision spilled over, blotting out the sun.

CHAPTER SIXTEEN

"Oh, my God, woman, you keep checking out on me like that, I'll start to think I'm boring you to death," Diana said, looking pinched around the eyes.

Tabitha sighed. She had only lost consciousness for a few seconds. "I'm fine," she said, concealing her uncertainty, "just tired. I didn't pass out. I fell asleep."

Diana eyed her skeptically. "First safety boat I see, I'm flagging it down."

"Of course," Tabitha agreed. "In the meantime, we need to start bailing. We're swamped, in case you haven't noticed. If we take on any more water, we'll be swimming."

Bending forward made her head throb viciously, but she managed to retrieve the pack from amidships. It felt distressingly light. A quick rummage revealed the extent of their supplies: an empty plastic bottle, one freeze-dried meal and the survival kit. She still had the kukri, so she severed the bottle through the middle, offering half to Diana.

The water in the canoe had come to within four or five inches of the gunwale. Tabitha began bailing, scooping water in the halved plastic bottle and flinging it over the side in a motion that taxed her back and shoulders, which already hurt like hell.

After a few minutes, Diana stopped and shook her head. "Hey, sugar, why don't we ground the canoe on a sandbar, tip it over, and dump everything out?" she asked, looking at the improvised scoop with disgust. "At this rate, we'll still be bailing until next week."

Diana's suggestion made sense, but after they'd had so much difficulty getting out of the woods, Tabitha resisted leaving the river now.

Before she had a chance to respond, Diana went on, "Besides, you're soaking wet. You need to dry off, and we sure can't build a fire inside the canoe."

Realizing her teeth were chattering, Tabitha firmed her jaw. Immersed in freezing water, her feet, ankles and calves had lost feeling a while ago. Not exactly numb, she thought. More a disconnected feeling, like the muscles surrounding the bones no longer belonged to her body. Worse, her heart seemed to quiver in her chest, an epicenter of cold that sent subtle shivers rippling under her skin in a way that reminded her of the queasy, creeping flesh sensation she'd suffered while staring into a psychopath's dead eyes.

She sent several more scoops of water flying, but her heart wasn't in it. "Fine," she said at last, "but let's do this quick, okay?"

"Works for me," Diana said. She dropped the bottle to begin paddling toward the nearer shore, her movements stiff and slow.

Tabitha helped as much as she could, chagrined not to have realized that Diana must be cold and hurting too.

When the keel finally crunched on sand, Tabitha levered herself out of the canoe, took hold of the gunwale, and pushed. Nothing happened. Ahead of her, she saw Diana tensing. Still, the canoe didn't move. She tried once more, a massive effort that left spots dancing in her vision. Her breath exploded out of her mouth as she heaved with all her might.

The canoe slid forward half an inch and stopped.

Tabitha closed her mouth over a blistering curse.

"Oh, for fuck's sake!" Diana cried, smacking the side of the canoe with her hand.

"I don't think pimp slapping the canoe is going to help," Tabitha said wearily.

Diana shot her a furious look and sighed, her shoulders sagging. "The way my luck's going, I'd probably break a leg if I kicked the damned thing," she said. "Any ideas?"

"We're stuck on a sandbar, but if we lighten the load, we should be able to get it off without too much of a hassle." Tabitha tried a smile, feeling as if her cold-stiffened face might crack in half. "Maybe we should have kept bailing."

"Excuse me just one second," Diana said sweetly, raising her arms in the air. "Fuck!" she screamed, brandishing her fists. "Fuck, fuck, fucking fuck, fuck, goddamn it, shit, motherfucker, son of a bitch, fuuuuck!" Running out of air, she stood still, breathing hard.

Tabitha kept the amusement off her face and out of her voice. "Feel better?"

"Not particularly, no," Diana replied, lowering her fists. She seemed somewhat calmer after her outburst, the livid red spots on her cheeks slowly fading. "So what now?"

"Anything we need in the canoe?" A sudden, intense desire for warmth struck her, the craving yammering in her blood like an addiction. "I didn't see that Warner had many supplies, just the one backpack. Grab it and we'll head ashore."

Diana stuck her arm into the water amidships, retrieving their would-be killer's camouflage backpack as well as the rifle case. "Let's go. Standing around in the lake isn't doing either of us any good, and I doubt this fucking piece of fucking shit's going anywhere," she said, giving the canoe a light kick as she passed.

Trudging through the forty-degree water to shore sapped the dregs of Tabitha's energy. She managed to scavenge a few pieces of dry wood and scrape a fat handful of the moss called old man's beard from a tree trunk before collapsing against the base of a stunted willow growing above the high-water line.

Diana collected the rest of what they needed, keeping up a running commentary about division of labor under her breath.

"I never did the fire thing," Diana said later, staring at the heap of wood shavings and moss, and the slender sticks, bigger sticks, and branches gathered in neat piles on the sand. She held the magnesium/flint bar from the survival kit. "Correction: I've done the fire thing in a barbeque with lighter fluid and a match. Something tells me this isn't quite the same."

"You'll be fine," Tabitha murmured. "You remember what I told you, right?"

"Right. I can do this, no problem." Bending over the shavings and fluffy moss, Diana tried striking the flint against the magnesium, but her hands shook too much and the flint slid off without effect. Her lips thinning, she struck the flint sharply a second time. An ember jumped through the air, landing glowing in the kindling. Flipping her hair out of the way, she leaned in closer to blow on the glowing red spark. A trickle of smoke rose, quickly thickening to a small cloud as the fire caught.

Diana began feeding sticks to the flames, then branches, and finally a chunk of driftwood. The fire safely established, she grinned at Tabitha. "How's that for a newbie, huh? Must be some pyromaniacs in my family tree."

Tabitha couldn't answer. Both her calves had been seized by agonizing cramps. She fell over on her side, curled into the fetal position and biting her bottom lip bloody while she tried not to scream. The pain felt like stabbing knives. Strong hands took hold of her legs.

"Easy, easy there, sugar," Diana crooned, massaging Tabitha's calves to relieve the cramps. "You feel like an ice cube. You need to move closer to the fire. No, wait…let's get you out of those wet clothes first."

Once Diana wrestled Tabitha free from her shoes, socks, pants, jackets and shirt, she pulled her a few feet over to the fire before opening Yancy's camouflage pack and pulling out items: a mess kit, MREs, two boxes of .338 Lapua ammunition, a Ka-Bar knife, four flannel shirts, four pairs of thick socks, a coil of rope, insect repellent, first aid-kit, and a bedroll. Taking the little metal pot from the mess kit, she stood, obviously intending to fetch water.

"Wait," Tabitha said, wrapping a restraining hand around Diana's pants leg. The waterlogged fabric felt cold. "Get out of that wet stuff, Di. If you catch a fever, we're screwed."

Diana stripped down to her bra and panties without an argument and hastily donned a flannel shirt from the pack. Pulling on a pair of socks, she handed a second pair of socks, another shirt and the bedroll to Tabitha.

"We need something hot to eat, and something hot to drink, and there ain't no room service out here," she said, retrieving the pot. "I'll get water. You get warm."

After dressing in the shirt and wrapping herself in the bedroll with part of it under her to provide insulation from the sand, Tabitha settled cross-legged as close to the fire as she dared. Diana's massage had banished her cramps for now. Warmth, food, and a night's sleep would take care of the rest, she thought.

Extending her leg, she managed to hook the rifle case's strap with her foot and drew it toward her. She suspected Yancy Warner was one of Montoya's hired guns, perhaps the sniper who had shot at them across the lake at the beginning of the race. She recalled her racing canoe with a pang of regret.

I wonder how Vicky's doing with the chemo, she thought while unzipping the case. Her gaze dropped to the rifle inside. She froze, unaware she was holding her breath until she began to feel dizzy. Taking in a gulp of air did nothing to ease the tightness in her chest.

Diana returned, put the pot of water at the very edge of the fire, and added some wood to the flames. Sitting on the ground, she reached for the MREs. "Chili and macaroni, or meatloaf with onion gravy?" she asked, reading the labels.

Tabitha stared at Diana, the woman who had lied to her, who had been lying to her all along. Betrayal hurt like a punch in the gut. Silence stretched, broken by Diana nattering about this and that as she fussed with the fire and the pot of water that was close to boiling.

At last, her questions would no longer wait. When Diana finished poking the fire with a stick, Tabitha asked, "When were you going to tell me the truth, Di?"

The color drained from Diana's face.

Tabitha added, "We've been through so much together, I thought I had a pretty good idea who you are, but Jesus Christ… when I'm wrong, I'm wrong." Pulling the rifle from the case, she pointed it at Diana.

"What the hell…? Have you lost your marbles? Put the gun down, Tabs. If this is a joke, I'm not laughing," Diana said nervously.

Tabitha flipped the weapon around and lay it across her lap. Anger and disappointment had purged her exhaustion for now, lifting the fog from her mind. She knew the feeling wouldn't last, and the crash, when it came, would leave her shattered. That didn't matter. For the first time since the race began, her brain seemed to be ticking over full steam, sorting through the pieces of the puzzle and watching a pattern form.

Take the facts, see how they fit. If something about the case doesn't make sense, you don't have all the facts, or you don't have the right facts.

"This is a British long-range, high-accuracy, bolt-action rifle," she said, "an L115A3, nicknamed the 'Silent Assassin,' and considered the best sniper rifle in the world. With the right scope, under the right conditions, in the right hands, this rifle will hit a target and make a clean kill from a distance of one and a half miles."

Diana gaped. After a moment that lasted a heartbeat too long, her mouth snapped closed. "So?" she finally asked, shrugging with a false confidence that spoke volumes. "What's that to me?" She dumped the MRE entrée pouches into the boiling water.

"This is not a rifle for casual or personal use," Tabitha said, tapping the wooden stock with her finger. "It's a military-grade weapon. Yancy Warner told me he was ex-army and I'll bet he had sniper training. I'll tell you something else: his presence on the river was no coincidence. Montoya must've sent him after

I broke you out of the cabin. I'd say Warner was supposed to patrol a likely stretch of river and pick us up if we surfaced."

"Okay, whatever." Diana made another shrug, but she avoided looking at Tabitha.

"You know, when you first told me the story about the heist, I felt something was off, but I let it slide," Tabitha went on. "This rifle tells me a different story. Warner was a pro, not the kind of person Montoya would hire to take care of a two-million-dollar problem. Frankly, that kind of payoff is hardly worth the expense of putting together a crew, planting an inside man, and risking an armed robbery, let alone following you across the country and paying for hired guns as well as a professional sniper. So how much was the real score?"

Diana said nothing.

Despite the pain clawing at her throat, Tabitha switched subjects, a tactic she'd used in the past to keep a suspect off balance and more likely to make a mistake. The realization she was treating Diana like a suspect brought a wave of fresh hurt. "A well-trained sniper isn't likely to miss many shots, wouldn't you agree?" she asked.

Diana turned her head to the side, a flush mounting in her cheeks. "I don't know—"

"Just after the race began…remember the shots that came so close to hitting us? At the time, I believed the shooter had poor aim, but after seeing the man's equipment, I believe Warner had no intent to kill. He was herding us to shore because Montoya needed you alive and he missed his chance in Whitehorse. But a half hour ago, Warner was ready to bash your skull in with a paddle. Why the sudden change?"

"I don't know!" Diana repeated through gritted teeth.

"I've got an explanation," Tabitha said, erecting a cool, professional façade. "Before I tell you, I'll ask you one last time: how much money did your brother really take from Montoya? A lot more than two million dollars, that's for sure. Tell me the truth, or I swear—"

"He took twenty million dollars," Diana broke in defiantly, folding her arms across her chest. "My dumbass brother stole twenty million dollars from Blair. Happy now?"

Tabitha analyzed Diana's body language, her expression, the timbre of her voice. "I believe you," she decided, although the conclusion did nothing to soothe her broken heart. "That's a bigger haul than the Dunbar robbery in ninety-seven. No wonder Montoya is pissed. For that much money, he'd take apart the world. My next question is, why did Warner try to kill you? Answer: he wouldn't unless you'd already told Montoya the location of the money. Since Montoya has no further use for you, he's tying up loose ends. I guess we're lucky Warner didn't start shooting the minute he caught sight of us, but maybe he figured we weren't worth a bullet. Lapua ammunition isn't cheap, after all."

Diana continued glaring into the fire. "Your trust issues are a pain in the ass."

"My trust issues aren't the point. Tell me, Di, was it really your brother Jack who helped Montoya with the payroll truck heist, or is that a lie, too?"

"Fuck you."

"No, fuck you!" Tabitha shouted, her resolution to stay in control dissolving when her temper flared brilliantly to life. Hurt feelings, resentment and bitter internal turmoil added fuel to the blaze until her rage burned white-hot. A static roar filled her head. "Fuck you! Goddamn it, Diana, you lied to me! I trusted you, I believed you. Everything I had—my body, my heart—I gave to you, and all this time, you were lying through your fucking teeth."

Diana stared, her mouth a round "O" of surprise. "Your heart?" she faltered.

Someone had stolen the air, making breathing difficult. "I thought we were friends, at least," Tabitha said curtly, ignoring the spasm of pain that crossed Diana's face. She pushed aside the black maelstrom of her emotions to concentrate on what was important. "We had sex, it was good, and I mistook that for something deeper. I learned my lesson. I won't make the mistake of mixing business and pleasure again. I'll see that you get safely back to civilization, I'll file a report on Montoya with the authorities. Hell, I'll even help you with a lawyer if you need one. After that, you're on your own." Inhaling, she plowed resolutely on, not giving Diana the chance to comment. "Did you have anything to do with the robbery?"

"No!" Diana blurted, pressing a hand to her chest. "No, everything I told you is the truth except the amount Jack stole. Look, I didn't mean to…I just thought…"

"I'm pretty sure you weren't thinking, otherwise you would have told the truth. Don't bother talking to me right now," Tabitha ordered. She fished an MRE out of the pot. Chili and macaroni, she read on the label. Opening the package, she began eating while trying not to choke on grief.

Showing the whites of her eyes like a spooked colt, Diana retrieved her own MRE from the pot.

Tabitha wolfed down the meal including the fruit cocktail—mostly sweetened diced peaches and pears with approximately one-third of an anemic cherry. Afterward, she added a packet of instant apple cider drink mix to the hot water in the pot and shared the cider with Diana, taking turns with her sipping from the metal mess kit mug. Throughout the meal, she didn't say a word, just ate and drank with dogged persistence.

Once Diana finished her MRE, she rose, tied the arms of another flannel shirt around her waist as a makeshift skirt, and set about gathering long sticks, pushing them into the sand to form a semicircle around the fire. After draping their wet clothing on the sticks to dry out, she cut a length of rope with the Ka-Bar and stretched it across two trees to make a clothesline for the wet sleeping bag. She returned to the fire, sitting close enough to touch. Tabitha decided she wasn't petty enough to turn her back or inch away.

"For what it's worth," Diana said quietly, "I didn't mean to hurt you."

Not trusting herself to speak, Tabitha nodded and focused on the flames.

"This whole mess with Jack," Diana went on, "I just got dumped in the middle without warning, you know? One day, I'm in the lab waiting for results on a sample, next thing I know, he calls me with a wild story about a payroll heist and twenty million bucks he stole from some guy who's…crap, you sure you really never heard of Blair Montoya?"

"Contrary to what Hollywood would have you believe, not every FBI agent knows the details of every single federal case," Tabitha told her. "That's what computers are for."

"Right. Okay. Fine." Diana ran her fingers through her dirty hair, grimacing at the snarls and tangles. She gave up after a moment and kept her hands loosely clasped together in her lap. "At first, I didn't believe Jack. I mean, what with the drinking and the gambling, he's always on about something. Then after he was murdered and I got his letter explaining everything. I finally understood."

"Understood what?"

"I…uh…I didn't tell you everything back when."

"You mean you lied? Again? That's old news," Tabitha muttered. She flinched when Diana laid a hand on her shoulder and leaned in close.

"Blair Montoya isn't the boss," Diana said with unmistakable sincerity. "And the man he's working for is no random criminal, Tabs. He's an honest-to-God terrorist."

Staring into Diana's eyes, Tabitha felt a chill race along her spine.

"Blair Montoya is working for Jesse Wayne Burke, the guy who runs the Trueborn Sons of Liberty Militia," Diana said, pulling her hand away. "You heard of that outfit?"

"Yes, I've heard of them," Tabitha answered, feeding another piece of wood to the fire. The Trueborn Sons of Liberty Militia was a military extremist group being jointly investigated by the ATF and the FBI for weapons smuggling, drug trafficking, conspiracy, assault, murder and a host of other charges including two domestic terrorism plots linked to individuals connected with the organization. No charges pending, as far as she knew.

"Then you know Burke's a real bad man," Diana said, breaking into Tabitha's thoughts. "In his letter, Jack told me Burke needed that money to broker a deal with…let me think, some foreign-sounding name, maybe German, reminds me of those white sausages…"

The light dawned. "You mean bratwurst?" Tabitha asked.

"Yes, like that, but not exactly."

"Bratva?"

"That seems right."

"Shit. Your brother was involved with the Russian mob too?" Diana looked shocked. "The Russian mob?"

"Yes, the 'Bratva' or Brotherhood," Tabitha explained. "Did Jack say what Burke wanted from the Russians?"

"Jack said he'd overheard Burke say he was buying portable atomic bombs from the Bratva. I figured Jack was making up stuff, or maybe he'd heard wrong. I mean, such things don't exist, do they?" Diana asked with a worried frown.

Tabitha spread her hands apart. "That depends on who you believe. The Russian government denies any such devices exist, but according to a high-level defector, the RA-115 portable nuclear devices were developed by the Russian military and controlled by the KGB." She didn't tell Diana that one of her friends in the FBI had participated in an official investigation of the possibility that al-Qaeda had acquired a Soviet suitcase nuke.

"I'm so sorry," Diana said. "I should have told you the truth. I guess I was scared. The cops haven't been very reliable as far as I'm concerned. Besides, Jack's story sounded like one of those spy movies, too crazy to be true. Who'd believe it? I certainly didn't when I read his letter. I just figured Blair wanted his money, end of story. The rest of it was just Jack Crenshaw's typical, patented line of bullshit to make himself sound more important."

"I wish you'd trusted me a little more."

"By the time I knew you well enough to trust you, Tabs, I figured you'd be mad as hell if I changed my story, and I was right."

Despite a lingering sense of shame at how easily she had been fooled, how vulnerable she had made herself, Tabitha found herself softening toward Diana, whose forlorn, frightened expression tugged at her heart. She firmed her resolve. Business only. "Why doesn't Montoya want you alive? What did you tell him in the cabin?" she asked.

Diana shucked off her flannel shirt and held out her bare arms to reveal fresh wounds, already scabbed over. Tabitha examined the odd pairings on each forearm, a set of two round wounds parallel to each other, about three inches apart. The flesh around them looked a bit red and puffy. She prodded one wound gently, thinking about infection. The nearest antibiotics were miles away.

Hissing in pain, Diana pulled her arm out of Tabitha's grasp. "Blair stuck these long needles through my skin," she said, closing her eyes. "Right through to the other side. I thought I was going to puke. He did it just like that, no hesitation, like he was skewering a chicken for the rotisserie. Didn't even ask a question first."

Tabitha's mouth went dry. Diana had been careful to keep her arms covered until the necessity for dry clothes forced her to strip. Still, she should have realized something was wrong. Anger flared, worsened by guilt.

"He told me he'd pierce my nipples next, then my breasts, maybe my liver. After that, he'd use his imagination." Diana sounded faint. Her eyes opened, fixing on Tabitha's. "I'm not a hero. I'm a lab technician and he hurt me. I was scared half out of my mind."

"I know," Tabitha said, giving in to the urge to touch Diana's thigh, to feel the smooth, warm, living skin under her fingertips. She wanted to find Montoya, spend a lifetime making him pay, kill him in the most painful way imaginable, and resurrect him because going to Hell at that point would be too much like a vacation. "Did he do hurt you anywhere else? Are you bleeding?" she asked, making an effort to control herself. Losing her temper would not help.

Diana let out a bark of mirthless laughter. "Blair didn't rape me, if that's what you mean, but he's one cold, mean son-of-a-bitch, and if I never cross his path again, I'll die a happy woman. He kept his men off me too. Said he didn't want me so damaged I couldn't speak or couldn't walk 'cause he was taking me with him. So yes, I told him what he wanted to know. I told him where he could find his damned money."

Reaching out, Tabitha picked up the key dangling on the silver chain around Diana's throat. "You didn't give him this," she said.

"Nope," Diana replied, rubbing her arms as if cold. "Blair thinks it's the key to my car and I didn't see fit to inform him otherwise. As for where Jack hid the money, I told Blair he could find it in Buddy Rinker Jr.'s junkyard in Fort Gill, same as I told you a while back."

"Is that a lie?" Tabitha asked, trying to sound neutral.

"Yes and no," Diana said. She pulled the chain over her head and handed the key to Tabitha. "Blair knows the money's in the junkyard. He just doesn't know exactly where to look because I misled him about that, and he didn't have time to question me more."

"I want the whole story this time," Tabitha said. "No lies, no evasions, no omissions."

Diana nodded. "Buddy Rinker Jr.'s great-grandfather, who started the business, used to make bathtub gin for Kid McCoy during Prohibition. He had a secret way in and out of the junkyard. This key opens the door to a 1921 Birmingham sedan on the north side. Slide through the car and out the other side, and you're in the yard. Once you get inside, you follow the engraved map on the key. That'll take you to a big, old-fashioned, solid steel bank vault that's been sitting in the same spot for a hundred years or so. Great-Grandpa Rinker kept the takings in it when he did business with the Irish mob."

Tabitha squinted at the lines cut into the key's brass surface all along its length. On the other side, she found a series of numbers that looked freshly engraved.

"The vault combination," Diana said in response to Tabitha's raised eyebrow. "Jack got the key from Buddy Jr. back when they were still high school pals. They used to sneak into the junkyard at night with a six-pack and shoot rats with a BB gun."

"And the money from the payroll heist is in the vault."

"That's what Jack told me in his letter. I haven't checked myself."

"What did you tell Montoya?"

"That Jack hid the money in the junkyard's office safe. And I said Buddy didn't know anything about it. Sorry. I didn't know what else to say and I sure didn't want him to lay hold of that money after he killed my brother."

Contemplating the key, Tabitha considered what she'd been told. Her nerves seemed to vibrate like piano strings. This was bad. Very bad. She'd heard an ex-CIA analyst at a recent seminar set the value of a black market Soviet RA-115 at around ten million dollars—he'd joked that the economy affected everyone. A domestic terrorist with twenty million dollars at his disposal might be able to buy two tactical nuclear devices from the Russians.

She was certain Jesse Wayne Burke planned to take out a major target once the purchase was made. As far as she remembered from the seminar, each RA-115 would yield about a kiloton each. By contrast, the atomic bomb dropped on Hiroshima had a yield of sixteen kilotons. The RA-115's value lay not in its explosive capability, but in the radioactive contamination that could spread twenty-plus miles from ground zero, more so if wired to additional dirty bombs. Washington, D.C. was a target-rich environment, but wherever Burke decided to use his devices, severe disruption, destruction, chaos, injuries and death would be the inevitable result, essentially creating a nationwide war zone.

"So Warner was left here to tie up loose ends," she murmured. "I'll bet Montoya is headed to the US right now." A pain in her hand made her realize she was holding the key in her fist so tightly, the sharp edges had cut into her palm.

"I'm sorry," Diana repeated. "What are we going to do?"

Tabitha let the key drop. "We're not going to let Montoya get away with it," she said, taking a box of ammunition from Warner's backpack and loading the dead man's rifle.

She owed Blair Montoya a bullet in the head.

CHAPTER SEVENTEEN

Despite her declaration, Tabitha knew going after Montoya was not possible. Stumbling through the wood on a chase when she had no back up, no clear idea of the terrain, and no way of locating her suspect was a formula for disaster. Thinking about what Victoria might say about such foolhardiness made the corner of her mouth twitch.

The smartest move would be returning to the lake at dawn, paddling until she and Diana encountered a safety boat or a checkpoint, and using a satellite phone to alert her boss to the threat. Given enough warning, the FBI could put agents in place in Fort Gill before Montoya arrived, or better yet, locate and confiscate the money. That way they stood a good chance of nipping Burke's plot in the bud.

If there is a plot, she thought, setting the loaded rifle aside. Jack Crenshaw, the main witness and co-conspirator, was dead. She had only Diana's word—the word of a proven liar, she reminded herself. Diana's testimony about what her brother overheard was hearsay unless the letter was produced or the testimony corroborated with other evidence.

Long practice at stakeouts and painstaking investigations allowed her to remain calm despite the itch to take immediate action. A touch on her wrist caught her attention.

"Do you think you can help me with these?" Diana asked, shrugging off the shirt and holding out her arms. "You know, cover up the holes or something. Do we have bandages?"

The sight of the livid wounds jolted Tabitha out of her brown study. She had to stamp on the sparks of renewed anger to answer, "Sure," while reaching for Warner's backpack. The first-aid kit inside a waterproof pouch was brand new and fully stocked. She donned a pair of purple nitrile gloves and tore open a foil package of antimicrobial wipes to clean Diana's wounds. The sharp chemical smell stung her nostrils, a vivid reminder of visits to the emergency room to speak to victims or witnesses. Finished with the wipes, she dabbed triple antiseptic ointment over the scabs.

Diana said through gritted teeth, "That stuff burns like hellfire."

"Sorry," Tabitha replied. She taped sterile gauze dressings over the injuries. Snapping off the gloves, she glanced up. "There's a couple of acetaminophen here. You want 'em?"

"Don't get me wrong, sugar, being stabbed by foot long needles doesn't feel good, but I reckon we'd better save the pain medicine until one of us really needs it," Diana replied. "Thanks, by the way."

"You're welcome."

As Tabitha put the kit away and tossed the used paper wrappers into the fire, Diana pulled her shirt on without bothering to button it.

"Do you think you'll ever forgive me?" she asked.

Tabitha almost asked, "For what?" but understood Diana's meaning in time to say instead, "I'll think about it."

Diana made a face. "You said we were fr—"

"Don't," Tabitha warned, humiliation surging afresh. "Please don't. I made a mistake. I invested a little more in you than I should, given that we hardly know each other, and apart from paddling a canoe, getting lost in the woods, and running away from a bad guy, the only interaction we've had is a single sexual encounter."

"My, my, Miss Priss, can't you just say we fucked like bunnies?"

"I'd rather not."

"You regret what we did." Diana's tone made it a statement, not a question.

"In a way, yes, I do. A one-night stand doesn't mean anything deeper than we had a good time," Tabitha said, getting more uncomfortable the longer the conversation continued. She braced herself, determined to clear the air. "Di, I find you appealing on a lot of levels, but intense situations, physical danger, relying on each other for survival…these things can form an emotional bond that's deceptive in—" She broke off when Diana kissed her.

Diana's lips were warm and smooth. A tingling swept over Tabitha's skin. Her nipples tightened. God help her, she couldn't resist leaning in, increasing the pressure a little, and tilting her head so their mouths sealed together. She knew she shouldn't let this happen. She had far too many reasons why sleeping with Diana was the epitome of a bad idea, but neither her brain, her heart, nor her libido seemed to gave gotten the memo.

After a moment, she felt Diana's teeth biting gently on her bottom lip. Tabitha trembled, unsure if the rising goose bumps on her flesh came from the wind or the velvet tongue that slid into her mouth when she parted her lips. Despite the chill, she felt sweat gathering in her hairline, under her arms, in the valley between her breasts.

"Let me," Diana murmured against her mouth, fingers busy on her shirt buttons. "Let me in, Tabs. I need to touch you."

Tabitha barely stopped herself from panting in her eagerness. Regardless of the arguments she had marshaled against it, she wanted Diana. She wanted to do wanton, morally reprehensible things to her, lick her clean, invent new obscenities, and start over until neither of them could walk straight. She wanted to go to sleep and wake up with Diana in her bed, in her arms, in her life. The heat of desire scorched her.

Diana scooted closer, mouthing at the base of her neck, nipping her collarbone.

Mustering ever particle of willpower she possessed, Tabitha wrenched herself away. "We can't," she blurted.

"Yes, we can," Diana replied, her eyes wide, achingly blue, and fever bright. "We're grown women. We can do what we want and right now, I want to do you."

"Don't make jokes, Di. It's not funny."

"Look, just tell me you don't want me. Tell me you don't want this." Shrugging apart the sides of her open flannel shirt, Diana took her breasts in her hands, her fingers curving over the shells of her bra cups. Her dark rose nipples were visible as shadowy bumps pushing against the fabric. "Tell me, and I'll let it be."

Tabitha's resolve crumbled.

"You don't want this? You sure about that?" Diana crooned. She wantonly spread her tanned thighs to flash the crotch of her panties. Rising up on her knees, she dipped a hand under the elastic at her waist.

Her breath catching, the blood rushing to her head, Tabitha watched the long, slow glide of Diana's fingers under the white cotton, imagining her playing with herself, smearing wetness around as she rubbed her clitoris in circles.

She tasted a ghost of Diana's essence on her tongue, the remembrance of musk and salt turning her insides to liquid heat. Her head demanded one thing, but the rest of her body, including her heart, knew what it desired. She felt like she'd been scooped up by a wave and left hanging on the crest, balanced between treacherous waters and a turbulent shore.

"Just tell me, sugar. Say you don't want me and I'll never, ever ask you again," Diana said, the movements of her hand inside her panties quickening.

The wave crashed. Tabitha broke. Lunging at Diana, she knocked the laughing woman on her back and sprawled on top of her, biting at her mouth and the hollow of her throat. Diana's legs wrapped around her waist, the muscles shifting and bunching under the skin.

When she tasted rusty iron, Tabitha drew away, holding herself above Diana on braced arms. "Why?" she asked, tracking the tiny smear of blood on Diana's bitten lip. "Why now? Why me? I won't leave you here, if that's what you're worried about."

Diana's eyes flew open. "You think I'd whore myself out to buy your protection?" she asked, baring her teeth. "Should I be insulted or flattered? You're not the only one who's a little too invested in someone they barely know and don't have much reason to trust. And may I remind you, you didn't tell me you were an FBI agent until you couldn't hide the truth anymore, so I'd say we're about even in that department."

Caught by the exasperation, affection and lust that made Diana's gaze incandescent, Tabitha couldn't speak. She took a quick, sharp breath, inhaling the scents of river and forest: spruce trees, decaying leaves, and the earthy fragrance of the woman beneath her.

Turning her head on impulse, she nosed at Diana's hand where it lay on her shoulder. The index and middle fingers were coated with a subtle sheen. Diana had shimmied this hand inside her panties. She sniffed again, the heady smell bringing a gush of wetness from her sex. Unable to resist, she touched Diana's finger with the tip of her tongue, gasping as the taste of female arousal exploded on her palate.

Snatching at the remnants of control, Tabitha sat back on her heels, feeling hot and flushed, but in control. "Sure, I didn't tell you I'm an FBI agent at first," she said, lightly rubbing Diana's thigh. No freckles here, just skin tanned the color of caramel, paler at the crease where thigh met torso. She longed to kiss that tender spot. "It doesn't change the fact that this… this attraction between us can't go anywhere good, for you or for me."

Diana remained sprawled on the sand, her dark hair spread around her head like the tendrils of some exotic creature washed up by the sea. "Speak for yourself, chicken heart. I don't see why not," she said.

"Accessory after the fact? Aiding and abetting?" Tabitha retorted. "All felonies carrying penalties under the law."

"Aw, the district attorney won't charge me."

"Try federal prosecutor. Robbing an armored car is a federal offense. There's a halfway decent case since you knowingly concealed Jack's crime. If you withheld information about the money because you planned to keep it for yourself, that may add to the charges."

"Oh, for fuck's sake, Tabs!" Diana sat up, scattering sand everywhere. Her mouth twisted into a frown when she continued, "For somebody who's so horny she's practically dripping, you're making a damned fine argument against getting laid!"

Her face burning, Tabitha stood, took the bedroll, and quickly walked away.

CHAPTER EIGHTEEN

Summer nights never became truly dark in Alaska, Tabitha thought, staring at a ribbon of dying sunlight rippling bronze and silver on Lake Laberge. Picking up a stone, she flung it into the water, wishing the temperature were a little more tropical. Her ardor had cooled to an uncomfortably cold stickiness that made her long for a bath.

Worse, her mild headache had redoubled with a vengeance, viciously throbbing in the space behind her eyes as if her brain was determined to kick its way out of her skull. She'd have traded her soul for a Vicodin.

"Are you done sulking?" Diana asked, plopping down on the ground next to her. Almost as soon as she sat, she jumped back up again, muttering about sharp rocks.

Tabitha scooted over, offering a corner of the bedroll. "I'm not sulking." Part of her was glad for the distraction. Another part wished she didn't have to face Diana so soon.

Diana sat on the bedroll, this time a bit more gingerly, and settled so her shoulder bumped against Tabitha's. "What was her name?" she asked. "I'm referring to the criminally inclined bitch who broke your heart and made you skittish."

Tabitha returned her gaze to the river. "I've never fallen for a felon, a witness, a victim or a suspect," she replied, deciding to be honest. "Been attracted to, yes. I'm human. It happens. Have I been stupid enough to jeopardize my career that way? No. Never."

"Not even for love?" Diana asked frankly.

"I don't know if what we have is love, or just infatuation brought on by stress and adrenaline," Tabitha confessed. She drew up her legs and rested her chin on her knees. Her headache receded a little. She sighed. "I'm even inclined to think I might be going crazy."

Diana smiled. "Here's what I know: I like you, Tabs, even when you rile me up so much, I want to punch your stupid face in," she said. "The sex is better than good and I want more, please. Apart from that, I want to spend a whole lot of time getting to know you better outside the bedroom because I think you're interesting."

"You want to date?" Tabitha felt her eyebrows climbing toward her hairline.

"Of course! Dinner, a movie, dancing…you have a problem with that?"

Tabitha started to answer, but closed her mouth, considering what she wanted to say and how she wanted to say it. "I like you," she said at last. "I really do. I'm just not sure if it's wise to get involved. Apart from your legal issues…" She paused when Diana snorted loudly and continued, "Like I said, there's your legal situation. Dating a woman found guilty of multiple felonies will pretty much end my career. Hell, even if you're charged and later acquitted, my bosses will take a dim view. It may not be fair, but that's the reality."

"I hate to admit it, but you've got a point," Diana muttered. "A point that sucks to the power of infinity, mind you."

"Second, long-distance relationships rarely work," Tabitha went on, trying to formulate and articulate her objections in order. "You live and work in Canada, while I'm based in Florida.

I can't move. I won't leave the state. My family's all down there, and so is Vicky. I won't abandon my partner, not for anyone, love or no love."

"Nobody's asking you to pull up stakes. If it came to that, I don't have a problem leaving Canada. I'm a skilled technician. I can find work just about anywhere. Besides, I'm not sure I have a job anymore," Diana added ruefully. "Not like I applied for vacation time."

"What if we try and decide to call it off?" Tabitha asked, the question popping out before she could smother it. Christ, I sound like a whiny teenager, she thought, cringing.

Diana seemed to agree. "Sweet baby Jesus in velvet pants! Did you miss the 'grown women' part? Now you're really scraping the bottom of the excuse barrel." She frowned. "So basically, you're afraid if we take our mutual attraction out for a slightly more serious spin, you'll lose your job and/or turn into my jailhouse wife, or possibly both. You'll be dragged kicking and screaming to Canada or elsewhere that isn't the land of retirees in socks and Bermuda shorts. And if, at some point in time, we happen to mutually end our connection, your delicate heart will be broken, shattering your entire life to pieces. Is that about right?"

Tabitha's cheeks heated unpleasantly. "When you put it that way…"

"What silly objection will you come up with next?" Diana asked with a sigh. "Look, I'm not asking for your hand in marriage, the keys to your condo, or for your immortal soul. If you don't want us to go any further than a roll in the hay, that's fine. Just say so. But if you'd like to explore the possibilities with me, I'm open to the idea. That's all." She patted Tabitha's leg and she rose to her feet. "You let that simmer in your pointy little head a while."

"Yeah," Tabitha said, feeling even more of a fool.

Diana stood with her hands on her hips. "Come to bed," she said, "such as it is. Only to sleep," she emphasized. "I'm tired, you're hurt, I'm cold, and I'm done with analyzing stuff to death. No decisions have to be made tonight, or anytime soon, for that matter."

Sleep sounded good, Tabitha thought. No, better than good. She was stiff from sitting in the chill and the damp, her joints and muscles protesting as much as her head. Groaning under her breath, she tried to work out the soreness while trudging to the fire, where she leaned against a tree while Diana retrieved their dried clothes.

Her skin crawled at the thought of putting on her filthy trousers and underwear, but a soaking in the rain had helped slightly, and at least the clothing was warm. She refused her fleece jackets, preferring to keep the more comfortable flannel shirt for sleeping. Her shoes were still wet, so she left them by the fire to dry out overnight. As a precaution, she ensured their packs were left close to the shoes, in case she and Diana had to leave in a hurry.

After sinking to her knees, Diana added some thicker sticks to the fire and used her hands to scoop out a long hollow in the sand, removing any rocks or gravel. She took the remaining two flannel shirts out of Warner's pack and used them to line the hole. She took in her work with a satisfied expression. "The bedroll's still damp, but I thought we could use your jackets as blankets," she said, lying on her side in the hollow. "I've slept on worse beds, and if we share body heat, we'll be warm enough." She looked at Tabitha, the flames mottling her face with shadows and gilded light. "You want to be the big spoon or the little spoon?"

Tabitha chuckled and slid in behind Diana, who immediately snuggled closer, making a contented noise low in her throat. A moment later, her flailing hand snagged the jackets, drawing them over their bodies like blankets.

Heat bloomed after a short while. Little by little, Tabitha relaxed, tucking herself closer to Diana's back. She closed her eyes and felt a light brush against the back of her hand. A bug? No, Diana's fingertips, she realized, tracing circles on her skin.

Keeping her eyes closed, she turned her palm over, her hand sliding of its own accord to cup Diana's breast through the layers of clothing. At least, that's what she told herself as she lay pressed against the curve of Diana's spine, surrounded by languid warmth. Like the two of them were hidden from the world, apart from everything except the safety of this space. She buried her face in Diana's hair, blotting out the firelight, and just breathed.

Diana tried to turn around, but Tabitha tightened an arm around her waist, stilling her. She could not bear conversation or confrontation. Either might shatter the fragile bubble that sheltered them. When Diana relaxed, she pressed a kiss to the baby soft skin behind her ear, adding the barest hint of teeth to make her shiver.

Tabitha insinuated a hand under Diana's shirts, gliding a flat palm over the smooth waist and up the torso to full breasts confined behind a sports bra. The row of tiny clasps between the cups was too fiddly to open, so she simply slipped her fingers under the cup, working her hand inside until she felt a rubbery nipple.

A sharp pinch wrung a gasp from Diana. The sound made Tabitha's throat thicken with something like desperation, but not the same white-hot blaze as before. Her blood turned molten, running sluggishly through her veins. Rather than searing her in its greed, her desire had tempered to a low hum of appetite and anticipation.

Diana whispered, "Yes, yes, do it."

Tabitha shushed her.

She felt lazy, emboldened and empowered by the dark and its illusion of anonymity, fancying herself a demon lover. The observation seemed apt, somehow. She, the predator. Diana, the feast laid out for the taking. Her imagination hadn't usually been allowed such freedom, but at the moment, rational thought had been banished in favor of want and need.

The slow, slick, throbbing pulse between her legs could wait.

Leaving Diana's breast, Tabitha managed to unsnap and unzip Diana's pants, tugging at the waistband until the garment slid a little past her hips on one side. A prickling flush broke out all over her skin when she wormed a hand into Diana's panties.

The position was awkward at best. Her elbow stuck out at a painful angle, her wrist was strained, and Diana couldn't spread her legs much, but she continued pushing until she felt crisp pubic hairs tickling her fingertips.

Ruffling the hairs, Tabitha used her first two fingers to delicately part the folds of Diana's sex until she found the yielding bump of clitoris. Her mouth filled with saliva. The discovery that Diana was wet sent pleasure coiling low through her belly. She propped herself up on her other elbow, the better to lean over and kiss the shell of Diana's ear.

Diana panted, choked animal sounds coming out of her mouth to blend with the snapping of a branch in the fire that spilled sparks over the sand.

Tabitha stroked Diana's clitoris harder and faster. The muscles in her forearm burned while Diana squirmed against her. She felt a deliciously warm, melting sensation spreading through her body. Light-headed, she squeezed her legs together to increase the pressure.

Letting out a low, thin whine from behind gritted teeth, Diana came, grinding down on Tabitha's hand until she was trembling and sated.

Tabitha grinned against Diana's neck, feeling smug, powerful, and as satisfied as if she had experienced the orgasm herself.

CHAPTER NINETEEN

"That wasn't very nice of you," Diana said the next morning after she and Tabitha bailed out the canoe, pushed it off the sandbar, and readied the vessel for travel.

Tabitha stole a glance at the woman seated next to her by the fire. Diana looked the way she felt: frazzled, somewhat worn, but filled with the banked glow of satisfaction. "I think that was very nice of me," she said, giving Diana an arch look.

Diana poked her in the ribs. "Whatever happened to 'this is not a good idea?' Or is what happened last night a farewell-to-thee?" At Tabitha's glare, she held out her hands and laughed. "Look, sugar, with the way you're blowing hot and cold, I don't know which direction you're gonna jump next. I'm just asking for some clarification."

Sighing, Tabitha glanced at the lake. From this position, she could spot any craft that came along. She picked up a long stick and pushed the pot of simmering water closer to the fire, willing the MRE pouches to heat up faster. She wanted to go. Every moment's delay meant more time for Montoya to acquire a suitcase nuke and deliver it to Jesse Wayne Burke and the Trueborn Sons, but she needed food to power the effort.

"I do want you," she said, coughing to clear her throat when the words caught. Christ, how she longed for a cup of coffee. "I do. I was thinking—"

"Should I alert the media?" Diana interrupted.

"—and we can't really make many plans for the future until we have more information," Tabitha continued, ignoring the banter. "You have to admit there are some issues to be addressed, such as whether or not you'll be spending time in jail."

"Suppose I'm in legal trouble," Diana said. "What then? Will you drop me?"

Holding Diana in her arms last night, Tabitha had spent precious sleeping time considering her options. "No, of course not, what do you take me for?" she asked, hurt by the suggestion. "I'll do everything to help you get the best deal. Probation, preferably. But…"

"But what?"

"Any deal will more than likely include you giving testimony against Montoya."

"Will he be charged with my brother's murder?"

"I don't know what's what in your brother's murder case," Tabitha said, pulling a warm MRE pouch out of the pot and juggling it between her hands. She peered at the label. Vegetable Stew with Beef. Doggedly, she tore open the pouch, gave the contents a stir, and began to spoon up the stew with a plastic spoon. "If the police have evidence against Montoya, he'll be charged," she said between bites. "If not…well, considering he'll be going down for conspiracy to commit terrorism, I'm pretty sure he won't see daylight this century."

While Tabitha talked, Diana removed her own MRE from the pot, opened it, and took a spoonful. "Turkey chili," she muttered, making a face. She began to eat. "So I'll testify about the money, right? Produce Jack's letter, that kind of thing?"

"Very likely. Don't worry right now, okay? It's just speculation at this point. First, we have to alert the FBI to Montoya and his boss, Burke. We have to arrest them before they acquire a nuclear bomb to use on American soil."

Diana shivered. "Jesus, that's scary," she said, her eyes growing wider.

"Tell me about it." Finishing the stew, Tabitha rose and offered Diana a hand. "You ready to go?" she asked, kicking sand over the fire to smother the flames.

"Let me visit the little girl's bush first," Diana said, walking up the gravel bar and behind a tree. "So does this mean you're my girlfriend?" Her voice floated out of the woods.

"Yes," Tabitha answered, unable to prevent a grin despite her lingering doubts. Could they make a relationship work? How deep did her feelings for Diana run?

Diana returned, straightening her clothes. Like Tabitha, she wore two flannel shirts and a fleece jacket over their long-sleeved shirts and trousers. Warner's backpack had also provided them each with a pair of clean socks. While pulling her hair into a ponytail and fastening it with an elastic band, she said, "I don't lie to my girlfriend." She came to stand right in front of Tabitha, chest to chest. "I don't cheat. I don't steal. I don't abandon. And I try my damnedest not to disappoint."

"Thank you," Tabitha replied, brushing stray grains of sand off Diana's cheek. "I promise the same. We'll get through this, Di. Together."

Leaning in the fraction of an inch necessary to bring them into contact, Diana kissed her, a firm press of mouth against mouth more comforting than dazzling. Tabitha returned the kiss with interest. At last, Diana broke free.

"Daylight's burning," she said, grabbing both packs on her way to the canoe, "and I'd like to leave before the mosquitoes wake up."

Tabitha followed, taking the rifle case. Happily, her concussion headache had lessened overnight to a faint shadow of irritation in the back of her mind, easily ignored in favor of more important concerns.

The late Yancy Warner's canoe was not as good as her lost Double Jeopardy, Tabitha decided when she and Diana set out on the lake. She chose a course that would keep them within a hundred meters of shore and set an easy paddling rhythm. They had agreed last night that getting in contact with US authorities took priority over all else.

Lake Laberge was one of the most dangerous spots in the race, so there ought to be a half dozen or so safety boats patrolling for stragglers. The volunteers carried satellite phones in case of emergency. The second either she or Diana spotted a motorboat, they would signal for help. In the meantime, a tailwind had picked up, an advantage to be exploited.

Her muscles stretching and singing as she worked, Tabitha cleared her mind and let the paddle in her hands fall and rise.

Some time later, hearing an engine noise, Tabitha glanced up at the sky to see a Cessna 180 bush plane flying in low from the south. Seagulls dipped, dodged and wheeled out of the way. The plane's wings waggled once when it sped overhead, the wind of its passage flattening her hair. She ducked instinctively, though she'd never been in danger, and waved her paddle wildly, yelling despite knowing the pilot couldn't hear her.

When the plane continued north, she subsided into her seat. "Shit! Did he even see us?" she asked.

"Had to, he waved at us," Diana replied, twisting around in the bow seat to face her. Her expression cleared. "God, I must be having a senior moment. We missed the checkpoint ages ago, remember? I'll bet the plane is part of a search party looking for us."

"I forgot about that too." Tabitha watched the sky a moment longer, but the airplane didn't reappear. "Stay put or go on?"

"Stay put," Diana decided. "The pilot should've radioed his base. I'll bet they're sending boats our way right now."

Tabitha agreed with a sense of relief. Their wilderness ordeal was almost over. In an hour or so, she'd have made her report and would be in the hotel soaking in a hot bath, ordering a steak from room service, drinking a beer…and what? Calling Victoria came first on her list. Second, making a start at sorting out Diana's problems, unless she was needed to assist in the apprehension of Blair Montoya and Jesse Wayne Burke.

With the FBI's focus on preventing Montoya from buying any RA-115s from the Russian mob, or if not then arresting Burke before his organization could use them, she believed the organization most likely to want Diana in custody was the district attorney in Georgia. Or possibly the US Attorney. She intended to devote some time to legal strategies, including which attorney to hire to represent Diana.

About a hundred yards away, Tabitha caught sight of a Voyageur canoe gliding past, and paused her thoughts to admire the traditional wooden craft. The tall rounded bow and stern gave the twenty-eight foot long canoe a pleasing grace, but also a tendency to catch the wind. Voyageurs weren't the fastest on the river, but they were sturdy and beautiful. Her breath caught when she watched the crew's paddles rising and falling in unison.

The sight was so mesmerizing, she almost missed a smaller white canoe slipping into the Voyageur's wake. Three people inside, she noted at a glance: stern and bow paddlers, and another person sitting amidships. The oddity struck her at once. In a race, no one carried passengers, and the conclusion flashed through her mind that these men might be tourists, since journalists or photographers would have hired a motorboat.

In the next second, she realized no tourist would have reason to draft off another craft on the river, possibly interfering with the race. Putting all her attention on the canoe, she recognized the man seated in the center. Her stomach plummeted.

Blair Montoya.

CHAPTER TWENTY

Tabitha dropped the paddle and picked up the rifle case. She paused with her fingers on the zipper tab. Hitting a moving target, even at relatively close range, was too tricky to attempt, especially with the white canoe so close to the Voyageur. She wasn't a trained sniper. Besides, if she killed Montoya now, she would face a murder charge.

She didn't think Diana had seen him. For a long moment, she wavered. Remain here, wait for rescue, alert law enforcement as soon as she had access to a phone? The thought of letting Montoya go free to do his dreadful business left a taste like ashes in her mouth. But pursuit was neither practical nor recommended. She had no jurisdiction in this country. She couldn't arrest Montoya or extradite him to the United States.

Watching the canoe disappear into the distance ate at her, a curl of flame in her belly, the sourness of bile in the back of her throat. With deliberate movements, she set the rifle case aside, removing temptation from her immediate grasp.

A half hour later, when the safety boat arrived, she found it difficult to celebrate. Returning Diana's brilliant smile hurt her face. Huddled in a warm blanket, she said little until the safety boat reached the checkpoint, where she immediately asked for a satellite phone.

"I'm sorry," said a race marshal, a middle-aged man with a bristling mustache that reminded her of a walrus. "Unless you have a medical problem, we're not allowed to let anyone borrow the phone. We can arrange transport back to Whitehorse in the morning—"

"I must get in touch with the RCMP," Tabitha insisted. Irritation fizzed along her nerves, threatening to escalate her minor headache. In the corner of her eye, she watched a volunteer fussing over the bandages on Diana's forearms. She turned her attention back to the race marshal and continued, "I'm an agent of the Federal Bureau of Investigation and this is an emergency situation."

He frowned. "I don't suppose you have identification."

"In my hotel room in Whitehorse," she said, making a poor attempt to conceal her impatience. "I need to report a murder, sir. Where is your phone?"

"A murder?" His eyes rounded. "Oh, that can't be right. You must be mistaken. I read in the newspaper there was only one murder in the Yukon Territory last year."

"New year, new statistics," Tabitha told him dryly. She caught him glancing across the tent. She followed his gaze to a tall, well built man standing beside the tent opening near a table holding a coffee urn, paper cups, sugar, creamer and trays of sandwiches and doughnuts. The way the man had positioned himself to command the entrance and cover his back, as well as his tight crew cut and his constant surveillance shrieked cop to her.

Leaving the race marshal behind, Tabitha walked up to the other man, privately amused to see him turn so that one hip—likely his gun hip, though she didn't see a holster—was kept angled away from her. That instinctive move, meant to prevent someone from grabbing his weapon, seemed to confirm that her guess was right.

"Excuse me," she said, taking another step to bring them closer together and pretending not to notice him stiffening, "you're RCMP, right?"

He nodded cautiously, studying her with a lawman's eye.

"I'm Special Agent Tabitha Knowles, FBI."

"Constable Anderson."

She maintained a professional demeanor in the face of his skepticism. "I need your help," she said, going on to give him a bare-bones account of her ordeal in the forest, the run-in with a dangerous criminal, the murder, the body in the woods. She kept the Trueborn Sons of Liberty and suitcase nukes out of her story, deciding to keep matters as simple as possible to avoid any international bureaucratic tangles.

"A suspected robber and murderer is escaping on the river with the help of accomplices," she told Anderson. "I spotted him in a canoe at the location we were found by the rescue plane." She went on to explain the payroll truck robbery in Georgia, her meeting Montoya during the race, the chase through the woods, and the murder of one of Montoya's guides—greatly simplified, of course, with many details left out.

"I'll have to verify your identity before I can do anything," Anderson said when she finished, exactly as she'd expected.

"The suspect will have crossed the border by the time you have a search party organized. On the other hand," Tabitha said with a twist of her head inviting him to a confidential distance, "in the spirit of cross-border cooperation, I can give you my badge number, you can check my ID with your headquarters, then you can lend me a phone so I can call my boss and we'll catch this guy pronto."

Anderson hesitated. He leaned slightly away from her. Realizing her nose had become inured to her own stink, which must be appalling by now, Tabitha tried not to blush.

"What's your badge number?" he asked at last, pulling a notebook and pen out of his jacket pocket. "And where were you staying in Whitehorse?"

Carefully swallowing a triumphant grin, she answered his questions.

Once Anderson left to make his phone calls in private, Tabitha looked for Diana and couldn't find her in the tent. She left to search the area and found her at a makeshift first-aid station, just several folding chairs, a card table, a cooler and a medical kit. Diana sat on one of the chairs with her shirts off, bandages gone, and a blanket clutched to her bare chest, while a First Nations woman wearing nitrile gloves rubbed a wet sterile pad on her injuries. The sharp, chemical reek of disinfectant reached Tabitha at the tent flap.

"Take a seat," the woman said after glancing at her. She tossed the used pad into a medical waste receptacle and tore open another package. "Dr. Hewitt. Be right with you." She began winding a fresh bandage around Diana's left arm.

"I'm fine," Tabitha said.

"You are not," Diana protested, far too vehemently for Tabitha's liking. "Doctor, she hit her head hard enough to lose consciousness."

Finished with Diana's bandages, Hewitt snapped off her nitrile gloves and discarded them. She pumped a couple of squirts of antiseptic gel from a dispenser and rubbed it into her hands, donned another pair of gloves, and swiveled in her seat to face Tabitha.

"Come here into the light," she said, her brow creased with concern. "You feeling any nausea now? Dizziness?"

"No."

"Double vision? Blurred vision?"

"No."

"How long were you out?"

"Not long, I guess."

Diana shook her head. "Maybe ten minutes or so. I'm not sure, but it wasn't more than a half hour. And don't give me the stink-eye, Tabitha Knowles. You know you whacked your noggin hard enough to see a whole galaxy's worth of stars."

Tabitha fidgeted while Hewitt shone a light into her eyes, checking her pupil response. "Look, I hit my head a couple of days ago," she said in what she hoped was a reasonable tone. No point antagonizing the person in charge of your health. "I'm really okay."

Hewitt grunted and continued her examination. "You've got a concussion," she told Tabitha. "How's your shor- term memory? Had any seizures? Any disorientation?"

"Not at all," Tabitha answered.

"No problems with coordination or balance?"

"None."

Hewitt nodded. "Okay, you'll probably live," she said, her brown eyes filled with good humor, "but be sure to follow up with your own doctor. If you have any problems, seek medical help immediately. Now, any other injuries I need to look at?"

"Just scrapes and bruises, nothing serious." Tabitha considered wheedling some acetaminophen from the doctor— her head still hurt somewhat, especially behind her eyes—but she needed food and rest more urgently, preferably in that order.

Preparing to leave the station, she saw that Diana had already left.

While walking away from the first-aid station, she wondered where Diana had gone, annoyed with herself not to have noticed. A passing volunteer pressed a sandwich in her hand, which she devoured without noticing the filling or the taste. At last, she stopped the race marshal with the bristling walrus mustache.

"Remember the woman I came in with?" she asked, praying for a hint of recognition in his face. When he nodded, she continued, "Have you seen her? We were separated."

"She took off," he said. Oblivious to her surprised gasp, he went on, "She left the checkpoint with a couple of gentlemen about fifteen minutes ago. Beautiful white tandem canoe. Handmade, I think. Very sleek. Pity they weren't in the race. Tourists, I guess. Well, one of them I knew on sight, a local hunter-cum-guide named Barry Tsosie. The other fellow must be his employer. Hey, are you okay?"

Feeling the blood drain from her face, Tabitha fought to remain upright.

For the second time, Diana had been taken by Blair Montoya.

CHAPTER TWENTY-ONE

"All right, Agent Knowles, tell me again what happened," Constable Anderson said in a calm, reasonable tone. His voice was accented with broad, rounded, and raised vowels, every word pronounced with a precision most American speech lacked.

She made an effort to regain her composure. Shrieking and yanking at her hair in frustration would only make him label her an hysterical woman, and therefore too easily dismissed. Besides, it was good police work to make a witness recount their story a few times to reveal inconsistencies. Reigning in her impatience, she told him again about Montoya, though she said nothing about Diana's abduction. The news that a wanted criminal had taken a hostage would light up the local police department like a whorehouse on payday. Despite the need for discretion, she chafed at the delay, needing to do something productive.

Anderson jotted a few lines in his notebook. He looked thoughtful. *Probably checking the details against what I told him before,* she said to herself.

"I've relayed your request to headquarters in Whitehorse," he said after a few moments. "I'm waiting for a call back confirming your credentials."

She nodded, wishing every paper-pushing bureaucrat in Canada to be cursed with shingles, ingrown toenails, abscessed molars and a thundering dose of the clap, but any unprofessional behavior or angry outbursts on her part would rouse Anderson's natural suspicion that she was not who she claimed to be.

Besides, she understood the RCMP's caution considering the current headache faced by both Canada and the United States: a rise in human trafficking and the smuggling of drugs, cigarettes and firearms both ways across the border. Her presence might be a decoy meant to concentrate their attention in one direction, thus drawing personnel and resources away from illegal activity in another location. Until her identity was confirmed, she would be treated politely, the same as any tourist.

"Is there any way to expedite that confirmation process, constable?" she asked. "You know there's a need for speed in this matter."

"Which is why I've been authorized to grant you access to a telephone," he said, offering her a cell phone. When she reached out to take it, he held it firmly in his grasp, his gaze cool but not hostile. "By now, my commander will have sent a constable to your hotel in Whitehorse to make inquiries. If you are impersonating a United States federal officer, now is a good time to retract your statements."

"I am a federal officer, constable."

"Please be aware any calls you make will almost certainly be monitored."

"Fine, monitor to your heart's content," she said, snatching the phone from him. "You have any problem with me making a long distance call?"

He shook his head. "I must also warn you that the consequences of filing a false report—"

"Understood." She dialed her office number from memory, adding her boss's extension. When Special Agent in Charge Ted

Strickland answered, she snapped, "This is Knowles. We've got a real hot situation in Canada and it's headed your way."

His quick indrawn breath sounded loud, but he covered it with a cough that rang in her ear. "Hot situation" was interdepartmental code for a possible nuclear threat. "Who are the parties involved?" he asked.

She blessed his intelligence. Ted Strickland understood she couldn't be frank over an obviously unsecured line and would ask no awkward questions. She gave him Blair Montoya's name. "Connected to a payroll truck robbery near Fort Gill, Georgia," she added. "He's going over the border into the US but I don't know where he intends to attempt entry."

"Well, the man has over five and a half thousand miles of border to choose from. Is he coming by sea, air or land?"

"Probably air for the trip to Georgia, but I think he'll stick to land for the border crossing from Canada. Airport security is too tight."

Strickland fell silent. At last, he said, "We'll do our best to narrow down the possibilities for an entry point. Is Montoya armed? How many in his group?"

"He has rifles, maybe small arms. I can't confirm any other weapons, although I suspect he'll be acquiring more serious firepower once he's home. As for accomplices, two locals for sure. I don't know if he plans to bring them into the US"

"Very well, agent. Anything else we need to know?"

She considered what might be safe to say. She dared not tell him about Diana or the nuclear threat, or risk the Canadian Security Intelligence Service becoming involved. The more agencies competing for the arrest, the greater chances of the operation going wrong. Not a law enforcement officer in the United States had forgotten the tragedy Ruby Ridge.

"Just be aware of the Liberty boys, sir. They're suspected of collusion in the situation," she said. "J.W.B. is almost certainly in this up to his neck."

"Of course," Strickland replied.

She hoped she'd given him enough clues to identify Jesse Wayne Burke and the Trueborn Sons of Liberty without giving anything away to whoever was monitoring the call. "You'll probably want to look into a Russian connection too."

"Russian?" He sounded startled. "Ah, yes. We'll check it out. Let's keep the news under wraps for now. No need to forewarn our felon. And you should stay put in case our operation requires someone on the ground in Canada. Where are you?"

She gave him the name and telephone number of her hotel in Whitehorse, but she had no intention of remaining in Canada despite Strickland's orders to the contrary. Stay here and hear about Diana second- or third-hand? Stay here twiddling my thumbs? Not a chance. Feeling she had told him everything possible, she ended the call.

Anderson took the phone when she offered it to him. "Have you finished? Is there anyone else you'd care to call?" he asked politely.

"For the moment, I'm done. What I need now is a lift back to Whitehorse."

He shook his head. "I'm not authorized—"

Tabitha made sure neither her expression nor her tone betrayed the frustration bubbling like acid in the pit of her stomach. "Where can I hire a boat or a plane?"

"Everyone in the immediate vicinity has commitments to the race."

"Look, I just need a little help. I'm not asking the RCMP to subsidize my trip, okay? I've got a credit card and cash in my hotel. I'll gladly pay."

"I will be happy to provide assistance once my commander has verified your credentials. As you are no doubt aware, interagency cooperation is very important—" He broke off when his phone rang. Walking away from her, he answered the call.

"Goddamn it," Tabitha muttered. She had not felt so helpless since…well, she could think of a few cases that had left her wrecked, sobbing on the bathroom floor with a towel pressed to her face to muffle the sound. She'd recovered each time, stronger and better for the experience, but if Diana came to harm, she didn't know how she could bear the loss.

She wished she had her cell phone. Victoria always knew how to talk to her, how to channel her energy in productive ways, how to recall her if she wandered too far off track. If it came to that, if the worst happened, Victoria would comfort her.

She abruptly rejected the what-ifs and gloomy predictions. She wouldn't let herself dwell on something that hadn't happened yet. She had to focus on keeping Diana alive and rescuing her from Montoya. Any other outcome was unacceptable.

Diana's absence felt like a deep, lightless hole in her belly carved all the way to her backbone. She had no appetite, but she managed to force down another dry sandwich and a cup of sludge-like coffee while waiting for Anderson to finish his call. The bitter, scorched flavor of the coffee lingered unpleasantly on her tongue.

Her heart leaped when Anderson closed his cell phone and turned to face her, his expression much friendlier. "Welcome to Canada, Agent Knowles. How may we assist you?"

Flooded by relief that things were finally going her way, she could have hugged him.

CHAPTER TWENTY-TWO

"Are you one hundred percent sure?" Special Agent in Charge Ted Strickland asked.

Seated in a chair opposite his desk in the Orlando field office, Tabitha maintained a cool façade with an effort while burying her impatience and worry.

"Yes, sir," she replied with all the confidence she could muster. She hadn't been able to give him many details over the phone, and of course he wanted her to brief him. "Blair Montoya is working for Jesse Wayne Burke, who plans to purchase at least one nuclear device, possibly two, from Bratva using the payroll robbery money. That's the gist of it."

Strickland grimaced. "We failed to intercept Montoya at the border, more's the pity. By the way, agent, you went off the radar when I told you to remain in Whitehorse. I was almost at the point of requesting the CSIS to investigate your disappearance."

Tabitha knew better than to shrug. She returned Strickland's stare calmly. Remaining in Canada had not been an option. It had taken her almost a day and a half of nightmarish, nonstop travel to return to Florida, organized by the efficient Constable Anderson: a motorboat to Whitehorse, a plane from Whitehorse to Calgary, then to Salt Lake City with a three-hour layover before boarding a nonstop flight to Orlando.

Fear for Diana's safety remained lodged like a cold stone against her heart. As a concession to her haste, she'd gone home from the airport for a quick shower and change of clothes before heading straight to the office. She hadn't even called Victoria yet.

"I'm sorry, sir," she said. "I felt my presence here would allow me to be more productive than staying in Whitehorse. And the Canadians seemed eager to see the back of me. I got the impression they preferred to kick the matter over the border where it belonged."

His grunt told her the matter was closed, but not forgotten. "Alice Gable in the Georgia field office is in charge of the case, but I've been read in due to your involvement. Here's where we stand," he said. "The Counterterrorism Division has an undercover agent in place with the Trueborn Sons as well as a reliable confidential informant. Neither source is able to confirm Burke's intent to purchase nuclear devices. However," he added, holding up a hand to forestall her protest, "I'm told there's been some chatter from the Russians, specifically a Russian gang based out of Atlanta headed by Anatoly Revnik. We've had our eye on his gang. They're involved in human trafficking and the manufacture and transportation of methamphetamine. Recently, investigating agents monitoring a wiretap intercepted messages about a major deal going down soon. A twenty-million-dollar deal."

Tabitha understood the figure's significance, but she also knew it was a tenuous connection. "Do we have any intel from the Russian government?" she asked.

Strickland snorted. "Regarding suitcase nukes? You know the Russians have always officially denied the existence of portable tactical nuclear weapons. On the other hand, Revnik's brother-in-law, Vasily Varenkov, is a nuclear scientist who used to hold a high position in the communist government until his forcible retirement last year." He gave her a significant look. "At the moment, our sources indicate Moscow—in particular the Federal Security Service—is scrambling to locate Varenkov, who disappeared shortly after a break-in six days ago at a military facility in Sevastopol leased by the Black Sea Fleet."

"What was stolen?"

"No details, but from the CIA reports I've read—about which you did not hear from me—whatever Varenkov took from a secure, top secret location has the FSS reacting like a kicked anthill. This particular facility is believed to store radioactive materials, though that's unconfirmed. Our ambassador was contacted early this morning by the Director of the FSS acting in an unofficial capacity, asking for assistance in locating their runaway scientist, but he refused to reveal the reason." He slid a tablet PC across his desk.

She took it, examining the picture on the screen: a heavy built, heavy boned Caucasian male with dark hair and Slavic features, no visible marks or tattoos.

"Vasily Varenkov," Strickland said. "He arrived in the United States yesterday at Hartsfield-Jackson International. That picture was taken at the airport. He breezed through Customs, exited the airport, got into an SUV, and vanished."

Tabitha returned the tablet PC to him. "Varenkov couldn't have flown a nuke out of Sevastopol," she commented. "Not on a commercial flight, anyway. A device like that would've lit up airport security and caused a panic even in the Ukraine."

"He chartered a private plane, paid for by Revnik who transferred the necessary funds from an offshore bank account. The license plate on the SUV that picked him up in Atlanta is registered to one of Revnik's known lieutenants. And it's interesting to note that Revnik made a twenty-second phone call to Jesse Wayne Burke this morning."

"Not much of a conversation."

"Revnik said only, 'I am not without sins.' No further communication since."

The phrase sounded familiar. "Is that a code?" Tabitha asked.

"A quote from the late Alexander Lebed," he said, "former Secretary of the Security Council and governor of Krasnoyarsk

Krai. He was one of the few Russian officials to admit the existence of suitcase nukes, though his claim was disputed by his government.

"As of this morning, Burke and his second-in-command, Johnny Salyers, are on the road, headed southeast toward Fort Gill, Georgia. They've got two other people with them—one man, one woman. We're trying to identify them." Strickland tapped the tablet PC, and showed her more pictures, obviously taken by a surveillance camera. Not the best resolution, but she recognized both people sitting in the truck's backseat.

"Blair Montoya," she said around the knot in her throat, "and Diana Crenshaw."

Strickland's frown deepened. Turning to his office phone, he pressed the intercom button. "Jeremy," he said to his administrative assistant, "I need everything we can get on Diana Crenshaw. Preferably five minutes ago."

Tabitha waited until he finished speaking before she said, "Crenshaw's a civilian."

"The woman whose brother conspired with Montoya to rob the payroll truck?"

"Yes, sir."

"She may be an accessory."

"I believe she's a kidnapping victim in possession of unique information desired by Montoya and Burke, information which will aid them in obtaining the money," Tabitha said, somehow managing to speak the words without gagging. "Montoya tortured her when we were in Canada. I assure you, sir, she did not leave willingly with him."

"Did you witness the torture?"

"No, sir, but I saw the wounds. They were genuine."

"Very well, I'll make sure the agents on the ground are aware of Crenshaw's status."

Tabitha tried not to appear too eager...or too pathetic, she thought. "I'd like to request permission to join the team in Georgia," she said. In response to Strickland's raised eyebrow, she added, "I spent a lot of time with Diana in Canada, sir. She trusts me. And I have this." Pulling the key on its chain from beneath her shirt, she let it dangle. "The key belonged to

Diana's brother and unlocks a hidden way into the junkyard, as well as the safe where the money's hidden. Could be very useful to the team."

Strickland considered her for a long moment, long enough to make her suppress the urge to squirm in her seat. "You and Crenshaw are…close," he said, hesitating as if choosing the word with care and discretion.

She understood the question he was too professional to ask. "We're friends," she said, more of a half-truth than an outright lie. If Strickland knew she and Diana were lovers, he'd never allow her to stay on the case. "Sir, I want Burke and Montoya in custody, on trial, and in federal detention. I will do nothing to jeopardize that goal."

He continued to examine her closely. Finally, he nodded and said, "If at any time you feel you're skirting the edge of conflict of interest, you are to inform SAC Gable immediately and follow her instructions to the letter. Don't force me to put a reprimand in your file, Knowles. You're a good agent, but you and I both know there are people in this office more concerned with politics than performance. I think you understand me."

"Yes, sir." She appreciated the warning. Botching up the case for any reason, especially a personal one, would torpedo her career. As much as she resented the political creatures above her in the office hierarchy who would gladly use any legitimate excuse to see a lesbian gone, she would not back down. Her job was important to her, but so was Diana. Staying in Orlando and doing nothing went against the grain. "Thank you."

"I'll inform Gable that you're on the way. If you leave now, you should reach Fort Gill in about six hours or so."

Tabitha wasted no time getting out of Strickland's office, feeling slightly queasy with gratitude, hope, and most of all, apprehension.

CHAPTER TWENTY-THREE

The Special Agent in Charge of the Atlanta field office, Alice Gable, didn't seem to like Tabitha very much. The black woman's expression suggested she had bitten into a lemon and found it even more sour and bitter than expected.

"I hear from your SAC that you're hip deep in the Burke case," Alice said without preamble as soon as Tabitha stepped into the temporary command center, an auto showroom in downtown Fort Gill that looked as if it had been standing empty a few months. The space contained tables, folding chairs, phones, a coffeemaker, and a variety of computer equipment requiring a fat bundle of electrical cords snaking across the carpeted floor.

"You could say that," Tabitha replied, maintaining a careful neutrality in her tone and expression. "Recently, I was in the Canadian Yukon participating in a canoe race when I met Diana Crenshaw, the sister of—"

"I've been briefed," Alice interrupted, flapping a hand. Her critical gaze fell on Tabitha's travel-rumpled DKNY suit.

"We've got rooms at a decent local hotel. Head on over there, Agent Knowles. Eat a meal, take a shower and get some sleep. There's a pretty good pizza place close by that delivers, if you like that kind of food."

Tabitha shook her head. She hated seeming contrary when she'd only just met Alice, but she was not going to slink off to a hotel. "Ma'am, I didn't come here as window dressing," she said, attempting to convey respect as well as determination. "I'd rather help the team, lending you my knowledge and experience, rather than take a nap and watch bad TV."

Alice's brows rose. She stared at Tabitha, who held her breath while she waited for a decision. At last, Alice nodded and said, "Very well, Agent Knowles. Make yourself a cup of coffee, then sit down and tell me what you know."

"What about Burke? Isn't he here?" Tabitha asked, not really eager to sample the dark liquid in the coffeepot, which had an unpleasantly scorched aroma.

"Not yet."

"Are you sure? He ought to be here by now."

"Believe me, Agent Knowles, if Jesse Wayne Burke breaks wind, my people will tell me what it smells like about ten seconds later. A minute after that, I'll have a report in my hand from the lab techs telling me what the man had for lunch." Alice sat in a plastic chair facing Tabitha, her slender legs crossed, looking cool and professional in a Versace jacket and skirt with polished leather pumps on her feet. "This morning, Burke's truck suffered a breakdown in Pine Corner," she went on, "some itty-bitty town about twenty-five miles north of Fort Gill. No car rental places. The town mechanic's fixing the problem, but Burke's stuck there, at least until tomorrow. I'm hoping he takes a room at the fleabag motel next to the liquor store. If so, we'll send in a tactical team, take him while he's asleep."

Thank God it's not over yet, Tabitha thought, sitting down in a chair before her knees gave way. All the way to Fort Gill, she had fretted about arriving too late, her mind's eye conjuring images of Diana dead or wounded that tore at her heart.

"You know Diana Crenshaw is a hostage, correct?" she asked.

"There's some debate about her status," Alice told her, "but at the moment, we're treating Ms. Crenshaw like a civilian hostage. Should later facts indicate otherwise…" Her voice trailed off, but Tabitha got the message.

"Do you have any questions for me?" Tabitha asked, straightening her spine and clasping her hands together on the table in front of her.

Alice took a sip of coffee from a travel mug, leaving a smear of bright red lipstick on the rim. "I'll leave the question of your involvement with Ms. Crenshaw in Canada to your own SAC," she said, showing a flash of disapproval so quickly concealed behind a bland mask that Tabitha wondered if she'd seen it at all.

She said nothing, waiting for Alice to continue.

The woman let her wait for what felt like a good long while before saying, "Strickland told me about your partner, Victoria Wallace. I'm very sorry for—"

The statement hit Tabitha like a fist to the gut, almost making her double over as pain and grief blazed in her chest, burning her heart and turning part of it to ashes. "Oh, my God," she gasped, "poor Vic, my poor, poor Vic…Christ!"

Obviously concerned, Alice leaned forward, almost knocking over her travel mug. "Agent Knowles, listen to me," she said, reaching across the table to grasp Tabitha's wrist. "Agent Wallace is alive. I apologize if I gave you the wrong impression."

"Victoria's alive?" Tabitha managed to ask through the constriction in her throat.

"Yes, she's alive, she's undergoing chemotherapy. Haven't you spoken to her?"

Tabitha accepted a paper napkin from Alice and wiped her eyes. The agony receded, leaving her relieved and slightly annoyed that Alice had misled her, even accidentally. She needed to concentrate on Diana, she reminded herself. "There's been no time," she said, balling up the napkin in her hand before tossing it overhand into a wastebasket.

"Perhaps you'd like to call Agent Wallace when you get a chance," Alice said, releasing her. "I'm sure she'd appreciate hearing from you."

"I'll do that tonight, thank you." Tabitha tried to compose herself. She found it difficult with Alice's unwavering gaze fixed on her.

Alice gave her a few minutes' grace, sipping coffee while Tabitha forced down the embarrassed heat in her cheeks, feeling like a fool for losing control.

"Before my promotion," Alice murmured at last, "I lost my partner to prostate cancer. I'd been nagging him forever about his diet—I swear, the man hardly ate anything that wasn't deep-fried—and when he told me he had cancer, I punched him. Jesus Christ, I was furious! But we stayed close until…until the end. I know how helpless a loved one with cancer makes you feel. You ever want to talk about it, Agent Knowles, I'll listen."

"Thanks," Tabitha whispered. She cleared her throat, determined to address a topic she believed might make Alice distrust her more. Nevertheless, the air needed to be cleared. "I'm not sure what you think you know about Diana Crenshaw and myself—"

"I don't know anything," Alice said, putting emphasis on the word, "except you and she were lost in the woods together. Furthermore, I don't care. It's not my problem. As long as you don't do anything stupid, anything that jeopardizes my operation, my people, or yourself, what happened in Canada stays in Canada as far as I'm concerned. Am I clear?"

"Clear as crystal."

"Good."

"Would you mind filling me in on your operation?"

"I have a tactical team at the junkyard. The plan is to take Burke when he shows up, unless we can do it earlier at the motel."

"What if he doesn't take a motel room? Have you thought about intercepting him somewhere in Fort Gill before he reaches the junkyard?"

"Are you questioning my plan, Agent Knowles?" Alice asked, her upper lip curling. It seemed their rapport was at an end. "There are too many ways for Burke to get into Fort Gill, we can't cover every route. If the motel falls through, our best bet is to take him in the junkyard, which we've already evacuated. Once Burke and his people go inside, we'll box him in. I find that preferable to a running gun battle in the streets."

Tabitha had to accept the plan. She pulled out Diana's key. "This will provide access to the junkyard. There's a vintage car on the north side which acts as a secret entrance. The key has a map engraved on it that leads to a safe where Jack Crenshaw hid the robbery money." She put the key on its chain in Alice's palm. A phone rang. Not hers, she realized.

Whipping a cell phone out of her pocket, Alice answered the call. She kept the key in her hand while she spoke, absently rubbing it between her thumb and forefinger. "Where?" she asked. After listening for a moment, she said, "Keep me informed," and returned the phone to her pocket. "No motel for Burke, I'm afraid," she explained to Tabitha. "That was one of my surveillance guys. Burke must've given the mechanic in Pine Corner some powerful incentive to fix his truck pronto."

"Burke's on his way to Fort Gill?"

"He just rolled into town. Our team is in place. I'm headed over there to join them."

Tabitha stood at once. "I'm going with you," she said firmly. On this point, she remained inflexible. If Alice didn't like it, she could go to hell.

Fortunately, Alice merely nodded. "I've got an extra bulletproof vest in my car and we'll issue you a firearm, if you want." Her expression turned grave. "You are not to interfere in any way, Agent Knowles. It may take me off your boss's Christmas card list, but if you mess with my operation, I'll charge you with obstruction. Do as you're told, when you're told, and nothing else, or I will break you," she added, her glare as unyielding as black stone.

"Yes, ma'am."

"Let's go."

Praying Diana would remain safe, hoping she would find her lover unharmed, Tabitha followed Alice outside where the strong sunlight made her blink.

CHAPTER TWENTY-FOUR

The junkyard stood on a big patch of ground near one of Fort Gill's worst neighborhoods. The site was completely surrounded by a twelve-foot high fence topped by coils of razor wire. From behind the closed gates, Tabitha heard the frantic staccato of dogs barking. The sound had an edge of madness. Dobermans, she thought. Maybe rottweilers.

Standing beside her, Alice Gable leaned over to say, "That's a recording to ease Burke's suspicions. The real dogs—vicious sons-of-bitches—have been confined. Now go do what we discussed, and don't mess up." She gave Tabitha a warning glance and walked away.

Tabitha had forgotten how hot a Georgia summer could be, different than Florida's humid, dirty wet mop of an atmosphere. Oppressive heat shimmered off the asphalt, ripples rising to blur her vision, clench in her throat, and wring the sweat out of her. The sun, as white as a blast furnace, paled the sky to a trace of blue. Not a breath of wind stirred.

She shrugged to settle her heavy bulletproof vest, and double-checked the magazine in her SIG Sauer P225, a slim-line model easier for someone with smaller hands to handle than the standard issue Glock.

Around her, other FBI agents looked at their equipment, sipped coffee from a nearby shop, and talked to state and sheriff's department officers. To minimize potential targets and causalities, Alice had decided to hold local law enforcement in reserve unless needed. As far as Tabitha knew, apart from the secret entrance accessed by the key Alice had returned to her, the gates were the only way in or out of the junkyard. If Burke and his associates tried to make a run for it, they'd meet a lot of officers itching to get in on the action.

She glanced at the mobile command center set up by a SWAT team from Atlanta. The vehicle resembled a white bus with blacked-out windows, and sported a small satellite dish on top. She'd seen Alice step inside, no doubt to enjoy the air conditioning and consult with the tactical unit's leader, Captain Simon King—a real peach of a good old boy whose ego entered the room before his body reached the door. Watching the SWAT team members loitering around the command center and pointedly ignoring FBI agents and police, she grimaced and hoped interdepartmental rivalries didn't endanger the operation.

Or Diana, she thought. Worry and exhaustion had taken their toll. She felt wrung out, her nerves strung tight as wires and buzzing with nervous energy. When she'd tried to sleep on the plane during the flight from Canada, torturous nightmares had played out behind her eyelids. The victim was always Diana screaming, crying, or mute and staring, a broken thing.

Shaking her head to rid herself of memories best forgotten, Tabitha went to join Marty Coombs and Taylor Broadstreet, two FBI agents from the Atlanta office. She had been assigned to help them infiltrate the junkyard using the secret entrance. Alice wanted their small group to cover that entrance in case Burke tortured the knowledge out of Diana. The thought made her want to shoot something or more specifically, someone.

"You ready?" she asked Broadstreet.

"Yeah, we're good to go," the tall, well-built, dark-skinned man drawled. A sheen of sweat gleamed on his forehead. He passed a handkerchief over his brow and glanced at his partner, Coombs: shorter, wiry, blond and blue eyed, with a peeling, sunburned nose.

Coombs shrugged and slipped on a pair of sunglasses. Unlike Broadstreet, who defiantly wore a suit and tie despite the heat, he was dressed in cargo pants and a lime green polo shirt. Tabitha thought his decision wise considering they were about to prowl around a junkyard. She'd bet a hundred dollars that Broadstreet would either lose the jacket and tie at some point or keel over from heat exhaustion.

She took the lead, walking north around the perimeter of the junkyard. Coombs and Broadstreet followed, the partners chatting about the heat, a baseball game, a pawn broker named Lew…she let the conversation roll in one ear and out the other, keeping an eye peeled for the Birmingham. She'd looked up the model on the Internet before leaving Orlando.

Here and there, holes in the fence had been patched with an odd assortment of objects: a steel refrigerator door welded across two poles, a pile of car tires filled with concrete, a single ornate cemetery gate, a heap of crushed metal cubes bristling with rebar. As she continued to walk, she became more and more concerned. Where was the Birmingham?

"Hey, Knowles, you sure you don't need to stop and ask directions?" Coombs wisecracked. "You know women can't navigate worth shit," he added to Broadstreet.

Fuck you very much, Bubba, Tabitha thought. "There's supposed to be a vintage car on the north side of the junkyard," she said without betraying her anger. No need to let him know he'd gotten to her. "A nineteen twenty-one Birmingham. That's the way in."

Broadstreet brightened. "My uncle restores old cars," he said to Tabitha. "Want me to call him? I'll bet he knows what a Birmingham looks like."

Before Tabitha could reply, Coombs broke in. "That the uncle who married the exotic dancer who used to work at the Stag Knight? Man, you know, the one with the big—"

"Be careful, Marty," Broadstreet rumbled. "My aunt Shanice found Jesus after she married Uncle Jerome and quit the club, and I don't want to hear no disrespect out of you."

"Oh, c'mon, Taylor, Shanice is hot."

Again, Tabitha tuned them out and continued checking the fence while she walked. After turning the first corner, her concern increased. Diana had told her the car was on the north side, hadn't she? Recalling the confession, she felt certain she wasn't wrong, but a few minutes later, doubt began creeping in. Could Diana have been mistaken?

"We've been circling this junkyard for ten minutes," Coombs complained, coming up to grab Tabitha's elbow. "You got no idea what you're doing, do you?"

Tabitha refrained from shaking off his grip. "Agent Coombs," she said with frigid politeness, "my source is impeccable, my intel is good."

"So where's this mythical car?"

"I'm looking for it. May I suggest you do the same?"

Broadstreet moved to stand next to her, his big, bulky body casting a stripe of shadow on the sidewalk. Tabitha felt grateful for the shade. "Marty, lay off," he said, staring pointedly until Coombs removed his hand. "We've got a job to do. We sure as hell won't get it done standing here bitching. Pardon me," he added to Tabitha.

Taking out her cell phone, she discovered there was no WiFi in the area. They must be too far away from the mobile command center. Without the ability to grab an image off the Internet, she would have to do this the low-tech way.

"You guys know what a Model T Ford looks like, right?" she asked. When Coombs and Broadstreet nodded, she went on, "We're searching for a vehicle that looks something like that. A four-door sedan with running boards. I think it's been here a long time, so look for an old but intact vehicle that's practically rusted into place."

"Why do you think it's been here so long?" Broadstreet asked.

"I was told the owner's great-grandfather worked for the Irish mob during Prohibition," she replied, "and he used that car to transport illegal alcohol."

"Grandfather," Coombs said as if correcting her.

The single word made Tabitha's brain freeze and her blood turn sluggish in her veins. After a moment of struggling with a horrible presentiment, she managed to unclench her jaws enough to say, "You mean great-grandfather."

Coombs narrowed his eyes at her. "Knowles, I grew up in Petersonville, which is next door to Fort Gill," he snapped, his fists bunched on his hips. "My daddy collected junk for Old Man Rinker. Daddy used to do two things on a Friday night: drop off his collection and collect his pay, and go get blind, stinking drunk at O'Malley's while I sat in the back room eating peanuts. I'm telling you, it was Old Man Rinker—Buddy Rinker Sr.'s grandfather—who did business with Kid McCoy back in the day." His belligerent expression softened. "The old man used to tell great stories. Bullshit, most of 'em, but what kid doesn't like hearing about Al Capone and Meyer Lansky? Get your facts straight."

"Oh, my God," Tabitha breathed. For an indescribably long moment she felt like she had been thrown from a great height, falling weightless and helpless with nothing below her but air. She experienced the world with crystalline clarify, the heaps of metal in the junkyard, a dandelion defiantly poking its yellow head out between two pavement slabs at her feet, the exhaust stink of passing traffic. At last, reason rushed in to claim her, body and mind.

"Agent Knowles, you okay?" Broadstreet asked.

"Jesus, Knowles, your face...you're as white as a sheet," Coombs said. "You pregnant? No, I'll bet it's the heat. Maybe you need to sit down, have a cold drink or something. Don't you faint, you hear me? 'Cause I am not toting your ass around—"

Pivoting on her heel, Tabitha turned and began running back toward the mobile command center. She had enough presence of mind to call over her shoulder, "It's the wrong junkyard, goddamn it! The wrong junkyard!"

Diana's words to her in the Canadian woods slammed into her mind over and over, spurring her to greater speed. You go to Buddy Rinker's junkyard. Junior, not Senior.

Tabitha ran like someone else's life depended on it.

CHAPTER TWENTY-FIVE

Reaching the mobile command center out of breath, Tabitha pounded her fist on the door. Her mouth was dry. Her head hurt, the pressure of panic and haste tightening in her temples until she imagined the crack and creak of splintering bone.

"Damn it, open up!" Allowing herself to lose a smidgeon of control over the beast raging at her core, she drew back her foot, preparing to kick the split panel doors apart when they suddenly flew open, revealing an angry-looking Alice Gable standing on the steps.

"Knowles, I assume you've got a good explanation for your behavior?" Alice asked, a fire smoldering in her dark eyes that promised consequences beyond official reprimands.

Tabitha lowered her foot. She started to speak, but the scorching air caught in the back of her throat, tickling as if she'd swallowed a mouthful of feathers. An explosive coughing fit made her bend over, hacking and sobbing for air. Through her watery vision, she saw Alice watching her, the corners of her red lipsticked mouth turned down.

At last, the coughing eased enough for her to gasp, "What junkyard is this?"

Alice snorted. "Buddy Rinker's junkyard, Agent Knowles. What the hell kind of game are you playing? We're in the middle of an op with national security implications—"

"Junior or Senior?" Tabitha asked urgently.

"I beg your pardon?"

Tabitha made an impatient gesture. "There are two junkyards in Fort Gill. Buddy Rinker, Sr. and Buddy Rinker, Jr. Where did you set up the operation? Where are we?"

"I don't…did you say two junkyards?" Alice's irritation abruptly turned to surprise, and sharpened into horror, anxiety and a slow burn of anger not directed at Tabitha.

"Hey, why'd you take off like that?" Marty Coombs asked, coming up behind Tabitha.

She ignored him and paid no attention to Broadstreet when he came walking up to join his partner. "We're in the wrong junkyard," she told Alice. "The money is in Buddy Rinker Jr.'s place, and I'll bet by now, so is Burke."

Alice whirled around, shouting a rapid-fire string of orders as she disappeared inside the command center. Not waiting for an invitation, Tabitha followed, driven by impatience and the knowledge that Diana remained in even greater danger now that the plan to apprehend Burke had failed. Christ, what a fuckup, she fumed savagely. If anything happens to Diana, someone's going to pay.

The doors slapped shut almost on her heels. Moving past the empty driver's seat into the vehicle's blessedly dim interior, she shivered when cool air from the overhead vents slithered over her face and down her neck. Her skin erupted in gooseflesh. Her sweat dried in an instant. Despite the relief from the heat outside, inwardly she boiled.

The command center's interior consisted of a row of computer and communications equipment on one side, the flat-screen monitors manned by three men in police uniforms. On the other side of the aisle, a dry erase board and a couple of cabinets hung above several long, rectangular lockers she assumed held firearms and other equipment.

She found Alice standing behind one of the seated computer technicians, hovering over the man's shoulder while he spoke into a headset microphone.

"And tell Harris and Perry not to do anything else until the cavalry arrives," Alice concluded. When Tabitha approached, she glanced up. "Agent Knowles, it seems a typographical error by a clerk in my office has caused a problem."

"Problem? I'd say that clerk of yours has put us neck deep in shit and the tide's rising fast," Tabitha replied with real venom. Fear gripped her like cold, dead fingers squeezed around her soul. "Jesus Christ, what a cluster fuck! Tell me, what kind of goddamned incompetent, piece of crap outfit are you running here, Gable?"

The computer technician gave her a startled look.

Alice drew her to the back of the command center. "I get that you're upset, and rightly so," she said in an iron-clad voice, "but we are professionals, Knowles. We don't throw tantrums. We are respectful to the chain of command. Human error happens, plans change, you know that. And if you ever—I mean ever—speak to me that way again, you're gone."

"I understand," said Tabitha at last, the only thing she trusted herself to say without turning the air blue with obscenities since she was too angry and worried to apologize.

"Having said that, when this operation is over, I assure you the clerk and I will be having a serious exchange of words," Alice said, her nostrils flaring.

Registering the banked fury in Alice's expression, Tabitha felt a little less like snarling. "Okay," she said, "tell me what to do."

"Good." Alice inhaled deeply and let her breath out in a sigh. "They'd better have a whole bottle of aspirin in here 'cause I'm going to need it," she muttered, pinching the bridge of her nose. To Tabitha, she went on, "Your assignment remains the same. You, Coombs and Broadstreet infiltrate the correct junkyard using the secret entrance you told me about. I'll radio your new positions before we move in."

"Where's Junior's junkyard?" Tabitha asked, unwilling to take any chances this time.

"I'm sure Agent Coombs knows the location, but…" Her voice trailing off, Alice went over to speak to the computer technician. After a moment, she returned with a piece of paper. "Here are the GPS coordinates to Buddy Rinker Jr.'s junkyard. It's across town. We'll be right behind you, Knowles. Don't do anything to get yourself or my people killed."

Snatching the paper from Alice, Tabitha hurried out of the command center. She found Coombs and Broadstreet waiting outside. "Come on," she snapped at them, "we're at the wrong place, the operation is moving, we need to go, right now."

"Yeah, okay, no problem, our car's over there," Broadstreet said, beginning to walk toward a dusty black Crown Victoria.

Coombs talked on his cell phone while he jogged past them to reach the car first. He snapped the phone closed. "SAC's got a major bug up her ass," he said to Broadstreet while digging a ring of keys out of his pocket. "Jeez, can you believe some dumbass secretary messed up the location? We're supposed to be at the son's yard, not the father's."

Broadstreet shook his head and moved around to the passenger side.

Left to the backseat, Tabitha climbed into the car, silently urging Coombs to hurry, but the man wasted no time driving out of the parking lot. When the Crown Victoria pulled into traffic, she tried to relax, to no avail. You failed, and Diana's dead, pessimism insisted. You'll save her in time, optimism countered. The conflict raged inside her head, warred in her heart, and left her feeling sick to her stomach. Thinking about the ways Burke and Montoya might kill Diana hurt her like a knife slowly splitting her heart in two.

Coombs remained silent while he drove, swerving around slower vehicles, skimming around corners, and ignoring stop signs. Despite his gratifying speed, Tabitha chafed at every minute's delay. She found it hard to concentrate. Her hands needed something to do. Taking out her SIG Sauer, she ejected the single-stack magazine. Eight rounds, she counted, exactly the same as the other three times she'd checked. Replacing the magazine, she returned the SIG to her shoulder holster, aware of the weight of extra magazines in her jacket pocket.

A muscle in her face twitched. Blowing out a sigh, she squelched the impulse to squirm in her seat, jiggle her leg up and down, bite her fingernails, or just give in to the bright scarlet madness lurking in the back of her mind.

"We're here," Broadstreet announced, his cheerful statement shattering her thoughts.

Opening the door, Tabitha exited while the Crown Victoria was still coasting to a stop. She staggered when her shoes hit the sidewalk and met Newton's First Law of Motion.

The junkyard seemed twice the size of the former lot, bounded by a twelve foot high, chain-link fence festooned with barbed wire and razor wire. A surveillance camera set high on a pole stared down at her. Other cameras reared above the fence roughly twenty feet apart.

"Shit," said Coombs, coming up from behind. "Looks like Junior's got the place surrounded by surveillance. Our guys won't be able to make a move without Burke seeing it."

"Do we know for sure he's inside?" Tabitha asked.

Coombs jerked a thumb at Broadstreet who stood on the sidewalk with a cell phone pressed to his ear. "Bet that's the boss," he said. "We'll soon find out what's what, but me? I trust my gut, Knowles, and my gut tells me Burke's in there already."

Tabitha stared at the closed gates and forced herself to wait despite her near overwhelming need to be inside.

"Harris and Perry haven't found a way into the junkyard yet," Broadstreet said to Coombs after finishing the call. To Tabitha, he added, "They were assigned to tail Burke."

Tabitha nodded. She reminded herself to stay firm, stay in control—stay fucking frosty, for God's sake—and do what had to be done. Without question, her first priority was rescuing Diana, though capturing Burke, Montoya, and anyone else involved in the plot ran a close second. "So we're good to go?" she asked.

"Boss says we find that secret entrance, we secure the safe if we can," he replied.

"What about the hostage?" A realization crossed her mind. Tabitha didn't allow him to answer before going on, "I didn't see anyone from Critical Incident Response. Shouldn't they be here? Who knows how many people are in the yard with Burke—"

"SAC told me Harris reported no customers in the junkyard, only two employees. And CIRG is coordinating two raids. Burke's out of the picture right now, and so's his second in command, so another team's raiding the Trueborn Sons of Liberty's main compound. The second raid is on the home of a Russian mobster they think is holding the RA-115s Burke was going to buy," Broadstreet said. "Homeland Security's in on that one too."

Coombs gave Tabitha a reproachful look. "Hey, we got a job here," he said, "so let's quit farting around and get to it, Knowles. You gonna show us this mythical car or what?"

Tabitha headed north around the junkyard's perimeter. She found that by sticking close to the fence, she remained out of the cameras' field of view. Telling Coombs and Broadstreet to follow her lead, she trotted on until she spotted a rusty, dilapidated 1921 Birmingham with sheet metal soldered over the windows. The car was shoved sideways into a hole in the fence. Miscellaneous junk was cemented on the roof to block access.

A real old-fashioned box on wheels, the Birmingham: all squared off angles apart from the graceful curve of fenders over the flat front tires. The vehicle reminded her of Prohibition, of Eliot Ness and the Untouchables, and the St. Valentine's Day Massacre.

Thinking about the massacre made her shudder.

"This is it," she said, yanking the chain over her head. Warm from her body heat, the key seemed to sear her palm. She eyed the Birmingham's door doubtfully. Was the lock too rusty to open? No, the lock looked almost new. Inserting the key, she turned it. To her mingled surprise and elation, the door swung open on oiled hinges.

Broadstreet whistled. "Somebody's been taking care of business," he said.

"Cool," Coombs said, his face lit up with awe. "Really cool. Jeez, this is like a movie or something." Before Tabitha had a chance to protest, he slid onto the torn front seat and slipped over to the passenger side. That door opened easily, too.

Tabitha followed, crawling over the seat. Broadstreet waited until she stood in the junkyard before making his own way through the secret entrance.

Drawing her SIG, Tabitha glanced around. All the cameras were focused outside the fence, not inside, so she and her group could move as they pleased. The place looked like a labyrinth with solid walls of wrecked cars piled atop each other, up to twelve deep in some places, plus other heaps of junk with aisles of clear space between.

Turning to Coombs, she asked, "Are you familiar with the yard? Where's the office?"

"Is the safe in the office?" Coombs countered. "Because unless our SAC was talking Greek, I'm sure we're supposed to cover the safe with twenty million dollars inside, which I know from the briefing is on the southwest side of the yard, and that ain't anywhere near the office. Look, if you've got any cowboy thoughts, Knowles—"

"Broadstreet needs to contact SAC Gable, tell her the team's got a way inside now, and help her coordinate the arrest," she said, summoning every ounce of persuasion at her command. "You need to stay here to guide our people to the right safe and secure it." She pressed the key into his hand. "There's a map engraved on the other side. Can you follow it?"

Coombs stared at the key, and finally looked at her, his expression hardening. "Does a polar bear crap on ice? But I'm thinking you aren't gonna come with or stay put. Whatever you're planning, don't even think you're gonna swoop in on Burke like John fuckin' Rambo and screw the pooch on our operation, 'cause I will cuff you and leave your ass in the car."

Tabitha glanced at Broadstreet, but the man had turned away to make his call. Returning her attention to Coombs, she said, "I'm just going to do a little reconnaissance, okay? Get eyes on the hostage and the hostiles so SWAT has some idea what's going on. What if our team walks into a trap? Somebody has to scout ahead." In the face of his skepticism, she radiated innocence, taking no offense at his warning. He didn't know her, had never worked with her, and had no reason to trust her.

Finally, Coombs reluctantly relented. "Okay, okay, but I am serious, Knowles, serious as a goddamned heart attack—you be careful, you be quiet, you don't get caught, you don't spook the bad guys, you don't do anything that'll make my job harder or give Gable a reason to rip me a new asshole."

"I promise," Tabitha said, meaning to keep her word. She had no intention of endangering Diana as a result of foolhardy behavior. "I'll update Gable on the situation as it develops. Where's the office?"

Coombs told her, a shadow of suspicion still lurking in his eyes.

Tabitha took off, following his directions at a near run through the aisles carved out between the stacked cars. Heat poured down from the cloudless sky, rolling over her head and shoulders like a sweltering wave. The walls cast little shade, and the sultry air smelled of sun-baked metal and rust, difficult to draw into her lungs without her feeling the urge to cough.

She held the SIG in both hands, the muzzle pointed at the ground, ready to snap up at the first sign of a threat. Reaching a point near the battered trailer on blocks that housed the office, she slowed and picked her way closer step by step. Nothing moved. From the trailer came the sound of music, brassy *musica de banda* with a heavy Latin beat.

Hearing a voice, Tabitha stopped. Her heart jumped in her chest. The trailer stood in a clear patch of dirt that provided no cover. She strained to listen. Was someone headed her way? It had to be Burke or one of his men, she decided. They were smart. Securing the employees and any customers in the junkyard would be their number one priority.

She squeezed into a narrow space between two cars at the bottom of a pile of junkers. The wrecked cars pressed against her front and back, almost as constricting as a metal corset.

She tried to take shallow breaths and forget about the weight of metal that hung inches above her head, but the math swept insistently across her mind.

The average automobile weighed 3,600 pounds. The eleven cars in the pile over her equaled 39,600 pounds. If anything happened to upset the balance, she'd be squashed. Closing her eyes, she willed away the unwanted memory of autopsy photos from the murder of a counterfeiter last year. The man had been secured to the top of a shipping container by a gang and another container dropped on top of him. The remains hadn't looked human.

Just breathe, she told herself. Stay still. Be ready.

Her eyes opened at the crunch of footsteps on the ground. A man passed by, thankfully not glancing in her direction. She recognized him at once. Blair Montoya.

She let him go. While she'd take great personal satisfaction in putting him down now, she could not afford to alert Burke and his second-in-command, Johnny Salyers, who were both likely inside the trailer and armed to the teeth. In addition, Montoya carried an M16A2 assault rifle with the air of a man used to handling automatic weapons. She'd hadn't seen him use a firearm in Canada, but she couldn't assume he was inexperienced.

When Montoya disappeared from sight, she slipped out from her hiding place and took a single step forward, only to halt when a large, black, dog-shaped shadow raced over the ground to her right. The sun was behind her, so that meant...

She turned, raising her gun just as the Doberman leaped, and stepped backward, her free arm rising to shield her throat. The Doberman jerked to a halt mid-air, little puffs of dust rising when he fell and hit the ground. Her gaze went to the thick leather collar around the dog's neck. The collar was fastened to one end of a taut chain that disappeared around the corner. Her pulse slowly returned to normal.

She lowered the SIG, wondering why the Doberman, who eyed her with a red pinprick of murder gleaming in its dark eyes, remained silent. This close to the office, either a barking dog or a gunshot would set all hell loose.

She took another step away, and another, half expecting the Doberman to burst out in a frenzy of violence, but the dog stayed quiet and alert, nostrils quivering, lips lifting to show curving canines capable of slicing flesh from bone.

Perhaps Rinker trained his guard dogs not to bark when they were chained, she thought. That made sense considering the junkyard would be busy with customers during the day and a hysterical watchdog might frighten people away.

Deciding it was safe to go on, Tabitha left the Doberman behind and continued walking cautiously toward the trailer.

CHAPTER TWENTY-SIX

The closer she came, the louder the volume of music pouring through an open window. A *narcocorrido*, she thought, an accordion ballad with a polka-like beat that snared the feet while a man lovingly sang about murder and drug smuggling.

She moved to a spot at the end of the trailer near a window air-conditioning unit jury-rigged to fit into a hole cut high in the aluminum siding. The air conditioner wasn't running, but a drying puddle on the ground below indicated the unit had been switched on recently.

Pressing her ear to the trailer's siding, she made out muffled, unintelligible voices drowned by the music. She hadn't expected to hear much without a listening device, but it would have been nice to know what Burke, Salyers and possibly Montoya were doing inside.

How could she get eyes on the situation, she wondered. She walked around to the back of the trailer and paced to the other end where she found a window. She frowned. The blocks under the trailer raised the structure enough to make it impossible for her to simply look through the window. She needed a ladder, a stepstool, or something solid for her to stand on.

Holstering her SIG, Tabitha scouted around the immediate area for a suitable object, finally deciding to cobble together a platform out of a stack of tires and a plywood board. Assembly took her several minutes. Finally, she climbed on with care. The platform wobbled with each shift of balance, threatening to tip over. Despite the difficulty of moving around while wearing a bulletproof vest, she managed to steady herself.

She peered through a gap in the dingy curtain. At first, she could see very little of the dim interior, then her vision adjusted, giving her an excellent view of the trailer's occupants. She recognized the major players and was grateful Alice had given her access to the case files.

Tall and well built, his blond hair cut to within an inch of his scalp, Jesse Wayne Burke leaned a hip against a cluttered desk about ten feet from the door. He held a fat cigar between his thumb and forefinger, the ember glowing like a hot red eye. Johnny Salyers—saturnine and wiry with the bad complexion of a poverty-stricken childhood—sat behind the desk pecking at a computer keyboard. Two unidentified men stood with their faces pressed to the fake wood paneling as if closely examining the naked centerfolds and Pirelli calendar stuck to the wall. Their hands were secured with zip ties behind their backs.

Hostages. Must be Rinker's employees.

Finally, Tabitha let her gaze drink in the sight of the dark-haired woman bound to a wooden chair in the middle of the room.

Her heart clenched with a complicated mix of longing, pain, fear and anger at the vivid bruises on Diana's face. Bile scalded her throat. What else had Burke and Salyers done? She forced her mind to calm, to focus on her goals. Rescuing Diana. Arresting Burke, Montoya and Salyers. Ending the plot to buy suitcase nukes for domestic terror purposes.

While she watched, Burke straightened and walked over to Diana. His lips moved. To her frustration, she still couldn't make out anything. Burke spoke again. This time, Salyers rose from behind the desk, moving to kneel in front of the chair. He picked up one of Diana's bare feet and held it firmly, his hands wrapped around her ankle.

Burke spoke to Diana, who shook her head, her lips pressed together. Shrugging, Burke leaned over, the glowing end of his cigar hovering just above the ball of Diana's foot. He was patient, gauging the slow burn like an expert. Tabitha choked on a flood of curses, silently damning Burke while watching a thin thread of smoke curl into the air. A circle of Diana's skin turned red, blistered, and eventually crisped to black.

Over the song blasting through the stereo, she heard Diana's scream.

Hatred poured through her, a rising black tide carried on the music.

"*Por vengaza*," cried the singer. "*Lo mataron a traición…*"

Her hand shook. She gripped the SIG so hard, her knuckles hurt. She could squeeze off a shot. At such close range, even with the added challenge of shooting through the window glass, she could kill Burke. Put a bullet through his head or his heart. She desperately wanted to paint the wall with his blood. Take the shot, her rage said in a smoky whisper so seductive, she raised the gun. A moment later she rejected temptation.

Just live, she willed, wishing Diana had the ability to read her thoughts. Survive. That's all you have to do. I will make Burke pay for every time he touched you.

At last, Burke removed the cigar. Diana convulsed a final time. A dribble of vomit trickled down her chin. Blank-faced, Salyers let her foot drop and stood, stretching his back before returning to the computer. Burke spoke to him. Salyers shrugged, his attention already fixed on the computer monitor. Shaking his head, Burke took a puff on the cigar.

Tabitha pulled out her cell phone and speed dialed Alice's number. As soon as the SAC answered, she said, "It's Knowles. I've got eyes on the office in the junkyard where three hostages are being held by Burke and Salyers."

"The tactical team is getting ready to go in, Knowles," Alice said, the spotty reception adding a sharp crackle to her voice. "I want you out of there."

"No," Tabitha said flatly. She would not leave without Diana. In some previously unknown, superstitious part of her soul, she feared that if she left Diana here alone, she'd never see her alive again. Her heart turned to stone at the thought.

"Please relay my intel to the tactical team," she went on. "I'll remain on site until they arrive." Not giving Alice the chance to argue, she told her about the weapons she'd seen in the trailer: a pair of M16A assault rifles, one with an optional grenade launcher attached, and a semiautomatic in a holster on Burke's belt and Salyers' revolver.

"Listen to me, Knowles," Alice said when she finished, "you come to the command center right now, or you can kiss your career goodbye, do you hear me?"

Tabitha hung up without answering, unable to muster any regrets for sending her FBI career up in flames. She returned her attention to the window and the view inside the trailer. Diana's eyes were closed, her breath coming in rapid pants. Her body shook with occasional tremors. Her head hung low, her face veiled by her hair. Was she sobbing?

The idea hurt Tabitha more than she'd thought possible.

Burke joined Salyers behind the computer. What were they looking at? The video camera feed? While she considering the possibilities, her gaze traveled unbidden to the M16A rifles leaning against the desk. She felt like she'd forgotten something.

A warm, metallic touch on the back of her neck made her flinch.

"Drop your gun," Blair Montoya ordered. "Looks like I've caught a spy." He gestured her to climb off the platform.

Tabitha shuffled backward, letting her SIG clatter to the top of the platform next to her knee. She deliberately shifted her weight to one side. The stack of tires wobbled. From behind, she heard an annoyed and clearly impatient Montoya tell her to be careful. She paused and said over her shoulder, putting a fearful whine into her voice, "This isn't exactly stable. I'm gonna fall, I know it. A little help over here?" She stuck out her ass, practically wiggling it in his face. Take the bait, asshole.

Cursing under his breath about stupid blond bitches, Montoya took a step closer. His rifle swung down on its nylon strap. He reached up a hand to her.

A certain kind of man always underestimated women, Tabitha thought. She'd pegged Montoya as the type. Even better, he had no idea she was an FBI agent.

Grasping his offered hand, she threw all her weight on one knee and extended her other leg to kick him hard in the face. At the same time, the tire stack swayed and toppled over, spilling them both on the ground.

Tabitha landed badly, almost falling when her foot hit the dirt at an awkward angle. Thank God she'd had the presence of mind to snatch up the SIG before she fell. Straightening, she turned to find Montoya and aimed the gun at him while he lay sprawled on his back, his nose bleeding. The M16A rose to aim at her, his finger on the trigger.

She shook her head. "Is today a good day to die, Blair?"

Montoya froze, his eyes searching hers.

Dropping the cool, professional mask that normally concealed her emotions from suspects, she let him see the black, howling heart of her rage.

He shrugged the strap off his shoulder, let rifle fall, and pushed the weapon toward her, carefully keeping his finger away from the trigger. He stood up, glaring at her.

Tabitha knocked the rifle further away with the side of her foot, wondering what to do. She couldn't cuff him and leave him here. He'd raise the alarm the moment she was out of sight. She finally elected to remain there to keep him covered until the tactical team arrived on the scene to take charge of her prisoner. The decision cost her a pang. She hated leaving Diana in the trailer with Burke and Salyers, but didn't feel she had a choice.

Glancing at Montoya, she saw his gaze appeared fixed on her chest. What the hell was he looking at? In a split second, she realized her bulletproof vest was emblazoned with big white letters: FBI. She looked up and met his triumphant grin. He knew she was a federal officer, thus required to arrest him, not shoot him in cold blood.

Shit.

Montoya shouted, "FBI! Burke, the FBI's here!"

She had no doubt Burke heard him above the music. Spinning around, she darted away from the trailer, choosing a course that would let her evade the Doberman, still straining at the end of its chain. She prayed Burke wouldn't think of releasing the dog, or any other toothy canines Rinker might keep around for guard duty. Although the animals were just as likely to turn on Burke than hunt her, he might take the risk just to sow confusion.

Crap! Crap! Crap! ran through her head. She rounded a corner, trying to remember the way to the secret entrance. Had she blown the operation? Certainly she'd alerted Burke to an FBI presence in the junkyard, destroying the tactical team's element of surprise.

Hearing a chatter of gunfire in the distance, she took cover behind the bulk of a '57 Chevy. The vintage car was pitted with rust and falling apart, but back in the day, American automakers built with Detroit steel. Should slow down a bullet, she thought, fumbling her cell phone out of her pocket and dialing Alice. She held the phone pinched between ear and shoulder to keep her hands free for her gun.

"What the hell is going on, Agent Knowles?" Alice demanded without preamble.

"I was spotted," Tabitha confessed. "Burke's been warned. Where's SWAT?"

Alice cursed. Her voice grew muffled when she relayed orders to someone else, and louder when she returned to Tabitha. "SWAT's getting into position, which is beside the point. Where are you?" she asked.

"Out of the line of fire, I hope."

"Don't you dare joke about that, Knowles. Is my team walking into a trap?"

Tabitha swallowed. Guilt clawed at her insides. If any law enforcement officer died because of her... She rallied to answer Alice, saying truthfully, "I don't know. Burke's aware I'm here, he knows I'm FBI. Maybe he thinks I'm alone."

"For the last time," Alice said coldly, the sound of her leashed fury sending chills down Tabitha's spine, "get out of there unless you want to be arrested."

"The hostages—"

"You mean Diana Crenshaw," Alice interrupted. "Strickland warned me you might have a conflict of interest given your sexual orientation, but he had no proof and you've got such an excellent record, I decided he must be mistaken, that you'd act like a career FBI agent instead of a teen with a crush. Well, fool me once, Knowles. You won't fool me twice."

Wincing at Alice's ugly tone—not entirely undeserved, she admitted to herself—Tabitha shifted to ease the cramp in her neck and said into the phone, "Three hostages, actually. Burke has also taken two junkyard employees captive."

"I stand corrected."

"I won't interfere, but I'm remaining on site. When the hostages are safe, I'll come out, apologize to you, turn in my gun and badge, and send a resignation to Strickland."

"Agent Knowles, you are hereby—"

Tabitha ended the call. She had done her best to warn the tactical team. As for Alice's threat to have her arrested, she didn't think SWAT or any other officers involved in the operation would let themselves be distracted by a rogue agent when Burke remained a far more serious threat. If she kept her head down and stayed out of the way, she should be fine. Besides, the risk of being escorted out of the junkyard in handcuffs paled beside the possibility of Diana in a coffin because she hadn't been there to save her.

After a few minutes, her phone vibrated, startling her. Tabitha checked the caller ID. Cold rushed over her. Victoria Wallace. She answered the call. "Hello, Vic."

"Hi, Tabs," Victoria replied. "I hear you're in some trouble."

"Goddamn it," Tabitha said softly. Her throat hurt with the effort not to yell. "Did Gable put you up to this? Shouldn't you be, I don't know, resting or something?"

Victoria made a scratchy sounding laugh. "I'll rest when I'm dead."

Tabitha sucked in a shocked breath. "You shouldn't say things like that."

"Why not? It's the truth. I'm dying, Tabs. I'm dying, you're dying, we're all dying, just some of us are doing it sooner than others."

"Vic, don't."

"Even if the treatment's successful, the cancer will probably return. Maybe I've got six months. Maybe a year or two. Maybe longer. Who knows?" Victoria took a breath and let it out in a sigh. "Yes, I talked to Alice Gable. She thinks you went crazy in the Canadian woods. I told her crazy is your default mode."

"She shouldn't have involved you."

"When, Tabs? When should Gable have told me my partner is trying to get herself killed? And don't tell me you're just doing your job."

"I'm just doing my job," Tabitha said with a straight face, though she knew Victoria couldn't see her.

"Liar," Victoria said. "At least tell me this Crenshaw woman's dynamite in bed."

Tabitha chuckled. "Fat Man and Little Boy combined."

"That good, huh? Well, now I understand why you're trying to get yourself killed…not. C'mon, Tabs. There's no reason for you to flush your career like a stale turd. There are agents on the ground who have expertise in hostage situations. You're putting everyone, including Diana, at risk by staying there against orders."

"It's not like that—" Tabitha started to answer. She broke off when she caught a whiff of cigar smoke. Burke. She closed the phone, cutting off the call, and slipped away. She paused in her flight when Burke began to speak.

"I don't know exactly who you are," he said, "or how many of you are in this junkyard, but I know you're all flunkies of the tyrannical New World Order. FBI or ATF?"

She didn't reply. Taking a few more steps to the side, she found a hiding place behind a bulldozer's heavy yellow body.

"Doesn't really matter," Burke called out. "The point is, I know you're here and I know what you want, but you aren't going to get it. As an emancipated, sovereign citizen of this great country, I am answerable only to common law, not your corrupt federal statutes. Big Brother can run along home with his tail between his legs."

A waste of rhetoric, Tabitha thought, and froze. Why was Burke expounding to an invisible audience? The answer came in a flash: a delaying tactic while his men searched the area. When she heard a guttural voice with a Russian accent, she realized that Burke may not have found the vault yet, but Anatoli Revnik was here to do business anyway.

Instead of facing a couple of antigovernment militia members armed to the teeth, she now had the Russian mob standing between her and Diana.

How many of his men had Revnik brought to the meeting? She had no doubt the Russians were at least as well armed as Burke and his boys. Did the SWAT team know? Before she had a chance to find her cell phone, gunfire erupted. In the same moment she realized no one was shooting directly at her, she heard return fire. SWAT must have engaged a target, either the Russians, Burke's men, or all of the above.

She decided now was an excellent time to double back to the office.

CHAPTER TWENTY-SEVEN

Choosing her route by the metallic thunks of bullets chewing into scrap metal, Tabitha attempted to avoid wandering into the middle of the firefight. When she rounded a corner on the way to the office, her heart leaped into her throat at the sight of a man holding an FN F2000 Bullpup assault rifle, the weapon very distinct with its oddly modular stock and short muzzle. She tried to duck out of sight, but he spotted her.

A series of three-shot bursts from the FN F2000 stitched the side of a car high in the stack behind her. A split-second thought ran through her head: the guy might have a cutting-edge weapon, but he was obviously unused to it. A little more practice on the gun range and he'd have blown a fist-sized hole through her head.

She dropped, took aim with her SIG, and shot at him. Her first bullet took him in the chest. The second bullet caught him on the shoulder, forcing him to drop the assault rifle when his arm went limp. A spate of choked Russian ended in bloody froth spilling from his lips. He collapsed on his knees and fell over. She moved on.

While she stalked through the aisles, it seemed to her that her senses expanded in all directions, scanning the environment for potential threats. Her autonomic nervous system kicked up several notches to high alert. Her skin prickled with clammy, cold sweat. Her chest tightened. She felt so hyped on adrenaline, she imagined she could bench press an SUV.

At last, she reached the trailer. Caution dictated she hide behind a couple of broken soft drink vending machines and wait, straining her eyes and ears for the presence of danger. The area seemed deserted, not even a sign of the Doberman she'd encountered earlier, but someone had turned the radio to a different channel and lowered the volume.

She took a step out of her hiding place, tripped on something, and sprawled flat on the ground, almost biting through her bottom lip. As she fell, she heard a shot from nearby. A quick glance at the trailer showed one of the windows open and a glint of light on a gun barrel. Montoya or Salyers? She discounted Burke. He was out there with the Russians. Had one of Revnik's mob boys been left to guard the trailer?

Tabitha crawled backward over the dusty ground, flinching each time the unknown gunman popped off another shot. He missed, sometimes by inches. When she reached the safety of the vending machines, she stood.

"Asshole," she said, wiping the blood off her mouth with the back of her hand.

As if he heard her, the gunman's next bullet slammed into the vending machine closest to her. Inside, she heard the explosive hiss of a burst cola can.

Tabitha spat out saliva tinged with blood. Her lip throbbed, pulses of pain like a second heartbeat. She needed to get into that trailer, but a frontal assault was out of the question and she dared not return the gunman's fire. Diana might be hit, or the gunman might decide he'd rather kill his hostage and try to escape rather than stay put and fight his way out.

Worry tugged at her to attempt infiltration, but common sense reminded her the trailer was small, leaving her nowhere to hide if she went inside. Her options were limited to do nothing and wait for backup, open negotiations with the gunman to buy time, or… An idea struck. She decided she'd take the third option.

The gunfire exchange between SWAT and the Russians had died down to sporadic cracks and the occasional split-second flurry of bullets from some idiot emptying the magazine on a full-auto weapon. Tabitha figured the tactical team would be here soon. She adjusted her grip on the SIG, waited an extra moment to be sure the gunman wasn't about to emerge from the trailer, and backtracked down the aisle.

She circled through the junkyard, taking a roundabout route to the back of the trailer. As she had hoped, she found a door, but it was high off the ground, almost five feet. No steps like the aluminum set standing at the front of the trailer. She could probably pull herself into the trailer by main strength if she could open the door, but she'd have to have the jumping ability and hang time of Michael Jordan just to reach the knob, much less finesse the lock.

Tabitha didn't think she had time to gather materials and build a makeshift platform like the one she had constructed earlier. The longer she delayed, the lower Diana's odds of survival dropped. SWAT wouldn't try a frontal assault, but if negotiations failed and the subsequent raid went bad, the gunman would have ample opportunity to kill Diana.

Her mind chugged along furiously. She considered and discarded a number of plans, none of which possessed enough safety factors to suit her. At last, she holstered her SIG and fell to her knees to peer into the twilight gloom of the crawlspace beneath the trailer. Visions of snakes, spiders, roaches, rats and other horrors invaded her head. Her flesh rose in goose bumps. She steeled herself. She was a grown woman, not a child.

Rolling over onto her back, she used her heels and elbows to scoot into the crawlspace, hampered somewhat by the awkward weight of her bulletproof vest. Slightly moist, cool air feathered across her face. She closed her eyes against a wave of revulsion when she thought she felt a wriggling touch on the back of her neck. Even years of living in Florida hadn't inured her to creepy-crawlies. She scooted further under the trailer, her skin trying to hump off her bones.

Just enough light filtered in for her to see the shadowy outline of a trapdoor, exactly what she'd hoped to find. She studied the latch and reached for her SIG. Her hand brushed against something slimy and definitely alive.

A scream tried to erupt from her throat. She locked her teeth over it and choked, setting off painful spasms in her chest until she caught her breath. Thank God for the music filtering through the floor above her, a country thump and twang that ought to drown out almost anything except the full-throated, fear-fueled shout of an entomophobe.

Shuddering, she withdrew her hand from the squishy, squirming whatever-it-was, found the grip of her SIG, and pulled the gun out of the holster before trying the trapdoor latch. Unlocked. Her luck seemed to be turning. With aching slowness, she pushed on the trapdoor, swinging it up on its hinges. Every creak made her muscles tense. If the gunman was standing anywhere near, he'd see the trapdoor open. He could be waiting just out of sight and have a clear target at point-blank range.

When she wasn't immediately greeted by a bullet, Tabitha slowly and cautiously climbed inside the trailer. The moment she drew her legs up, she caught sight of a silhouette in the living room at the end of a short corridor. Whipping around so quickly her back muscles protested, she aimed the SIG, but recognized Diana, still bound to the chair. She didn't see the two junkyard employees she had noticed earlier.

Somewhere in the room, someone tuned the radio to a different station.

Diana's wide blue eyes held fear, hope, and a concern that touched her.

Tabitha put a finger to her lips, indicating silence. Diana didn't nod or otherwise acknowledge the command. Instead, she glanced away from her when an unseen man said, "Yeah, how you doin' with the feds out there, man? Got a clear shot at the money yet?"

He didn't sound like Burke or Montoya. Johnny Salyers, most likely. The man's accent sounded West Virginian to her ears, a strong "R" and nasal resonance flavored by generations of families laboring in the coal mines. She listened to the one-sided conversation almost idly, using his distraction to move closer to the living room. One more step and I'll have him. This whole nightmare will be over.

She froze when Salyers laughed and continued, "Damn, Jesse, don't you wish you could see the looks on their faces when the bomb goes off?"

The ice holding her in place crackled, split and shivered into splinters when she took a last step forward, the SIG in her hand pointed at the man with the cell phone.

Salyers held the phone to his ear. His gaze remained locked on hers, but he didn't seem alarmed. "Got a fed in here already, Jesse. Seen her poking around outside some." He grinned. "Took a few shots at her for practice. More fun than shooting crows, I tell you."

"Federal officer. Put the phone down, John Salyers, you are under arrest," Tabitha said, putting an edge in her voice. "Keep your hands where I can see them."

He didn't drop the instrument as ordered. Instead, he ended the call and faced her, keeping his thumb on a speed-dial button. "How about a counterproposition?" he asked with an unnerving degree of good humor for a man facing imminent arrest, a slam dunk conviction, and a life sentence in the federal Supermax prison in Colorado.

She stared at him, hardening her expression to let him know she meant business. "I said, drop your cell phone right now, Salyers."

"Can't do that, boss lady," he replied, smirking. "See, this phone is connected to a bomb. A nuclear bomb right here in Fort Gill."

Tabitha felt the blood drain from her face.

"Old Jesse there, he told the Russians he wanted to sample their wares, make sure the bombs were legit 'cause God knows, them nukes have been sittin' on a shelf somewhere in Commie pinko land for years and years. He ain't paying millions for a dud. All I got to do is press this little button right here," he flourished the phone, "and boom! No more Fort Gill."

"Where's the bomb?"

He shook his head. "You think I'm gonna spill my guts just 'cause you asked?"

Nervous tension thrummed in her neck and shoulders. Was he telling the truth? His assertions seemed improbable, but not beyond possibility. "Listen to me, Salyers. Be smart. If you surrender right now, come in and cooperate, the US Attorney will take the death penalty off the table, guaranteed. Maybe even give you immunity in exchange for your testimony. How'd you like a new life anywhere you please, courtesy of the US Marshals? But if you do this, if you set off a nuclear bomb, nobody can help you, understand? You'll be one of the most wanted men in America. When you're caught, you will get the needle, but only after they let you rot in Guantanamo for a good long while."

"First they got to catch me," Salyers taunted. "I reckon your folks'll be busy digging mass graves for the dead. Won't have time to worry too much about little old me." He sneered. "You put down your gun or I will press this button, my hand to God."

"Are you so eager to commit suicide?" She blinked sweat out of her eyes. "Radiation poisoning is a nasty way to die."

"Better call off your federal pals too," he said, ignoring what she'd said. "I see any more cops, I'm liable to get nervous, then Fort Gill's a ghost town, I flat-out guarantee."

Tabitha took a moment to study Salyers. He gave her a jailhouse stare, his hooded eyes giving nothing away. She tried to judge his sincerity. If she got it wrong, the minimum safe distance was two hundred fifty miles from Ground Zero. There'd be no time to warn anyone, no time to evacuate the city, not even time enough to kiss her ass goodbye. She decided to err on the side of caution. No point rescuing Diana only to perish with her in a nuclear fireball because she read a man wrong.

"Okay, okay, we got no problem here," Tabitha said, loosening her grip on her gun. She offered it to him butt first, though every instinct resisted being left helpless. He took the SIG and dropped it on the desk behind him.

"Now get on your phone and call off the other feds," he instructed.

She reached into her pocket and with infinite care, drew out her cell phone and pressed the speed-dial button. One ring. Two rings. After three rings, Alice Gable answered.

"Agent Knowles, you are disobeying a direct order," Gable said.

Tabitha interrupted. "I'm with John Salyers in the junkyard office. He's in possession of a remote detonator and claims a nuclear device has been planted in Fort Gill."

She heard nothing, not even breathing, for several long moments. Finally, Alice asked in a remarkably calm tone, "Do you have visual confirmation of the bomb?"

"No, I haven't seen it. According to Salyers, the nuke's been hidden somewhere in Fort Gill, location unknown. He is prepared to detonate if his demands are not met."

"What does he want?"

"At the moment, he wants the tactical team to evacuate the junkyard."

Salyers snatched the phone out of her hand. "Tell your people to leave the yard. You hear me? I see a hair of a federal head and I will press the button, and we'll all go bye-bye." He listened for a moment. "Uh-huh. Well, you see, Special Agent in Charge Gable," he pronounced the title with careful disdain, "seein' as how I'm the man with my finger on the trigger, maybe you ought to let me dictate the terms."

Tabitha tuned him out.

While he continued his conversation with Alice, she turned her head slightly and caught Diana looking at her. Diana's eyes flicked downward for an instant and an eyebrow quirked in a silent message. She followed Diana's line of sight. On the floor, just poking out from under the desk, she spied the yellow plastic case of a Taser.

Her spirits rose.

Did the Taser belong to the junkyard employees? Salyers? Or Burke? He had been here before the fighting erupted outside. She dismissed her speculations to concentrate on a more important question: how could she put her hands on the Taser without alerting Salyers? And once she had it, would the defensive weapon be effective in this situation?

She considered the facts. The Taser would discharge an initial 1,200 volts into Salyers, severely impairing his muscular control and preventing him from pressing the speed-dial button unless he managed to push it in the split second before his body locked up.

If that happened, if she failed to stop him…she shuddered, recalling photographs of Hiroshima and Nagasaki. Of course, delivering one-fifth the yield, a suitcase nuke wouldn't have quite the same destructive effect on the city, but the citizens of Fort Gill and beyond would still suffer. For those people caught in the actual blast, a blinding white flash and instantaneous death. Further out, potentially lethal radiation exposure and severe burns. The wind would spread radioactive dust to other populated areas outside the city limits.

Her jaw popped painfully. She realized she had clenched her teeth together. Taking action against Salyers might result in a nightmarish disaster, but doing nothing might prove equally fatal. Could Salyers and Burke really be trusted to keep their word? Were they just buying time to get clear before setting off the bomb?

When Salyers finished the call, he tossed the cell phone back to her, startling her out of her thoughts. "Now we've got that shit settled," he said with evident satisfaction, "you go over there against the wall." When she hesitated, he added, "Your boss has pulled her people out like I asked, so I'm not making the good citizens of Fort Gill glow in the dark like she asked. Are you seriously going to fuck up all that goddamn goodwill we're building here?"

Tabitha shook her head and obeyed, moving to stand with her back to the wall as directed. In hostage situations, the most fundamental rule was simple: don't get anyone killed.

She met Diana's steady gaze. *I should have just shot Salyers when I had the chance.* She risked another glance at the Taser. Burke was probably on his way to the office with the Russians in tow. Once they arrived, it would be her against three or more suspects, and she was unarmed. If she was going to make a move, it had to be soon.

Waiting for Salyers to settle down and take his attention off her, she went over the little she knew. Burke had asked the Russians for a suitcase nuke to test. Did that mean he intended to set the bomb off inside Fort Gill? Thinking about it, the plan made no sense. Fort Gill wasn't a strategic target. Destroying the small town would be a tragedy, but not on the same level as bombing a larger city or a state capital.

Wipe out a state capital and you wipe out a hefty chunk of the state's infrastructure. She paused. Burke had supposedly planted a nuclear device in Fort Gill, which seemed wasteful at best when much more tempting targets were available.

Furthermore, once a nuclear bomb went off, every federal agency and branch of the American military would bring every resource to bear in the mad scramble to hunt down Burke, his followers, and his known associates and contacts. Under that kind of pressure, it would be almost impossible for him to conceal a second bomb anywhere in the country without being seen, recognized, and arrested or killed.

The more she considered the problem, the more she came to believe that Salyers was lying to get the FBI's tactical team off Burke's back. The bomb threat had to be a bluff to give his boss more time to find the money and broker a deal with the Russians.

Tabitha glanced at Salyers. He noticed her looking and said, "Whatever's runnin' around inside that head of yours, better get rid of it." He waggled his phone.

"I'm just wondering, what is Jesse Wayne Burke holding over you, John?" she asked, maintaining a bland expression. She kept her tone almost friendly. "How did he get you by the short hairs? I mean, you seem like a smart guy. Why would you throw your life away on a man who couldn't organize an orgy in a whorehouse?"

He bared his teeth at her.

Undeterred, she went on, "By the way, where is Mr. Burke? Shouldn't he be here to share in the historic occasion?" When

Salyers' nostrils went white with strain, she added, "Oh, wait, I forgot…there's twenty million dollars at stake. That kind of money buys a lot of protection from the authorities for a man who skips to another country."

"Shut up."

"Ever seen twenty million dollars, John? A man could live like a king. Steak for breakfast every morning. All the women he wants. If I were Burke, I'd pick a patsy, some redneck peckerwood who's too stupid to realize he's been had. I'd set him up to take the fall while I got the hell out with all those sweet, beautiful millions. I'll bet Burke's already gone, John. He's on the highway, headed to the airport right this minute with a trunk full of untraceable cash and a one-way ticket to Belize in his pocket."

"I said, shut up!" A vein throbbed in Salyers' forehead. A muscle worked in his jaw.

Tabitha bit back a grin. In his eyes, she glimpsed a glimmer of doubt. If she kept chipping away, she might get a result. "Maybe not Belize. Some countries in Africa don't have an extradition treaty with the US. Mexico isn't bad if he avoids the federales, but the kind of money he's carrying will grease a lot of local palms. Can you see it, John? Can you smell the suntan lotion, hear the music, taste the margaritas, feel that pretty señorita nestled warm and soft in your lap? Burke can. Hell, he's one flight away from living the good life while you stand here like the world's dumbest criminal.

"Burke talks the talk, I know. He says he's a patriot. He says he'll sacrifice himself to bring down the government and set the people free. But really, John, think about it. If Burke really meant all those things he said, wouldn't he be here now, ready to die with you?"

Salyers took a step forward. She tensed, expecting him to swing at her. Instead, he halted, the tension in his body drawing his shoulders tight and his mouth into a straight line.

She sensed he was close to the edge. Clearly, Salyers hadn't invested himself totally in Burke or his organization. The man's trust was not absolute. She did a quick adjustment of her assessment of him. Not a fanatic foot soldier after all, but an opportunist seizing the advantages Burke offered. Someone like that was a gift.

"He's long gone. I'll bet he took off the second the tactical team pulled out. Tell me, did Burke promise you a share of the money?" she asked, doing her best to sound sympathetic without overdoing it. "A chance to dip your beak before the Russians put their sticky fingers in that twenty-million-dollar pie?"

The way Salyers looked at her was more eloquent than a shout.

"Really, John, I'm surprised," she said, raising her eyebrows. "Don't you know there's no honor among thieves?" She let him stew over that idea a moment. "Face it. Burke's gone."

Tabitha recognized the moment his self-control broke. His gaze left hers and cut to the cell phone clutched in his hand. Got you, she thought, mentally pumping a triumphant fist.

"Give me your phone," he said at last.

"Come and get it," she retorted.

Salyers didn't move—smart man to stay out of arm's reach— nor did he threaten her with his gun, which she'd thought would be his first option. He simply repeated his demand. She repeated her refusal. The stalemate lasted approximately thirty seconds. Finally, he licked his lips. Sweat shone on his forehead. Without speaking another word, he retreated behind the desk, picked up the SIG, and aimed it at her while he dialed his cell phone.

She allowed him time to be distracted by the call before she dove for the Taser. Landing on her stomach hurt like a bitch and knocked the wind out of her. No time to think about anything, just action and reaction. Her hands closed over the Taser's plastic grip. When Salyers shouted, she snapped up the Taser, planted her elbows on the floor, pointed the business end at him under the desk, and fired.

A pair of electrodes burst from the Taser in a confetti flurry of antifelon ID tags and flew the short distance, striking Salyers in the inner thigh to the left of his crotch. He screamed, a horrible, high-pitched wail that filled the trailer and echoed back from the thin walls. His body went rigid. The SIG and the cell phone dropped.

Tabitha scrambled under the desk on her hands and knees, the Taser abandoned in her eagerness to secure the phone. The moment her fingers closed over it, she pushed herself backward and away, rolling to her feet while Salyers fell with a thump that shook the trailer and knocked the radio off the windowsill. The music faded and died.

She stuffed the cell phone in her pocket and snatched up the SIG from the top of the desk where it had fallen. For a brief moment, she stood over Diana, thinking furiously. Knife, knife, where the hell can I find a knife? Her gaze lit on a carpet knife half buried under a mound of manila folders on top of a filing cabinet. She used it to carefully cut the duct tape binding Diana's wrists and ankles to the chair.

"You okay?" she asked while she worked. She squatted beside the chair and kept an eye on Salyers, who appeared semi-conscious. She hoped his balls were smoking. If the bastard so much as twitched, she'd put a bullet in him.

"Never better, sugar," Diana answered, giving her a trembling smile. Her bare foot, the same one Burke had burned with a cigar, spasmed once.

Tabitha gripped the carpet knife more tightly.

Once free, Diana took a few extra seconds to locate her shoes and slip them on before following Tabitha outside. She paused on the top step.

"Sweet baby Jesus in velvet pants," she said, lifting a hand to shade her eyes against the strong sunlight. "I feel like absolute and utter shit." She glanced at Tabitha sidelong. "If I catch that son-of-a-bitch Burke, I owe him for a lot more than killing my brother."

Ordinarily, Tabitha would have discouraged death threats, but she nodded and shrugged. "I'll hold him down, you kick him to death." She wasn't entirely joking.

"In these shoes? I'll break my toes. Better wait till I get some steel-capped boots." A slow, vicious smile spread across Diana's face. Her blue eyes took on a distant look that Tabitha had seen in torture victims. "Blair Montoya...now him I'd like to gut slow, real slow, with a sharpened spoon and with exquisite attention to detail."

"Don't get your hands dirty," Tabitha murmured. She pulled Diana into a hug, relieved beyond measure when she didn't stiffen or pull away. "Are you really okay?"

Diana kissed her, dry and chaste, but welcome. "Nothing time, a hot bath and a stiff bourbon won't fix."

Reluctantly, Tabitha ended the embrace. "Come on, we need to get out of here," she urged, herding Diana away from the trailer.

She kept her SIG in her hand. As far as she knew, the Russians were still in the junkyard with Burke and Montoya, and as soon as Johnny Salyers recovered, he'd be coming after her with revenge on his mind. While walking through the maze of junked cars, she remained on high alert, every sense she owned working at peak performance. Had a mouse broken wind within ten yards, she'd have heard it and probably shot the gassy little bastard.

Diana suddenly stopped. "We have to go this way," she said, pointing to a side path flanked on either side by lines of obsolete motorcycles powdered with rust.

"Why?"

"The safe."

"Forget about the safe, Di. Forget about the money. Come on."

Diana resisted her tug. "I went through hell in that trailer," she said, her breath catching on a sob. Her spine stiffened. "I went through hell in Canada, too, and all because my stupid, greedy, demented screw-up of a brother couldn't quit gambling and fucking around with his life, and ended up stealing millions of dollars from a dangerous man.

"I know I can't spend the money," she continued, her fingertips soft and warm on Tabitha's arm. "It's not mine. But I want to be the one who opens that safe door. I want to put my hands on those stacks of bills and just pretend, for one second, that I'm going to drive to the airport in a limousine, get on a private jet to Europe, and spend the rest of my days wallowing in pure, unadulterated, and very expensive vice."

Tabitha shook her head. "There's a Russian gang running around here armed with automatic weapons and God knows what else. The only place we're going is out of here. Sorry, Di, it's not possible. Let's go."

"Ah, well, if wishes were fishes…"

"Beggars would be pescetarians."

Finding the exit proved harder than Tabitha expected. She dared not try for the front gate, assuming the Russians had men posted there. Her best chance lay in locating the Birmingham that guarded the secret entrance, but she'd gotten hopelessly turned around.

"Oh, for God's sake," Diana yelped after a while, either not noticing or not caring that her voice carried and echoed off the piles of junk. "I swear we've passed that same rusted out VW bus three times already. Do you even know where you're going?"

"Not like I can stop and ask for directions," Tabitha muttered, wiping her sweaty forehead on her shirtsleeve. The unrelenting heat made her feel unpleasantly deep-fried.

"Goddamn it, Jesse!" she heard Salyers shout, too close for comfort. "I catch that bitch, I'm going to cut her into strips from the toes up!"

"Be easy, brother," said Burke. "You'll have your vengeance and your glory, too. Just stay the course."

"Shit," Diana whispered. White-faced, she clung to Tabitha's hand, her grip grinding the bones together.

Tabitha endured the pain. "This way," she said in Diana's ear, tugging her over to the next aisle. She froze. Blair Montoya stood with his back to them, smoking a cigarette. Oh, how she wanted to empty her SIG's clip into that miserable son of a bitch and kick him while he bled out in the dirt! She lowered the SIG, deciding it was wiser to move around Montoya and avoid a confrontation than alert the bad guys with a gunshot.

Wrenching herself away from Tabitha as if she'd read her mind, Diana started toward Montoya in complete silence, her hands raised, the fingers curled into claws.

Tabitha recovered from her surprise almost at once and stumbled forward a few clumsy paces before regaining her balance. Fortunately, Diana's burned foot left her unable to manage more than a fast hobble, not quick enough to avoid a desperate grab. Latching onto the back of Diana's shirt, she dragged her to a halt.

To her relief, she realized Montoya hadn't heard them. He seemed engrossed by whatever he listened to a portable media player, and his earbuds blocked outside sounds. She pulled Diana gently but firmly in the opposite direction and around the corner, not stopping until they were a safe distance from Montoya and anyone else.

Diana glared. Eventually, she subsided. "I guess that wasn't my brightest moment," she said, her shoulders slumping.

"Not really, no," Tabitha said. "Let's try not to get killed, okay?"

"Yeah." Diana shook herself all over, like a dog shedding water. When she finished, she gave Tabitha a small, somewhat embarrassed smile. "Good thing I didn't have a gun."

Tabitha indicated they should go on. While they wandered the junkyard maze, she watched Diana walking beside her, taking in the lank hair, the dark circles under her eyes, the bitten lips, the clothes that had seen too many days' wear. None of it bothered her. Affection swelled inside her chest, warm and tender.

"You're safe. You know that, right?" she asked, searching Diana's expression.

"I knew you wouldn't leave me, sugar," Diana replied, a strange quality in her glance that Tabitha hadn't seen before and wasn't sure how to interpret. "I knew you'd save me come hell or high water." Her voice dropped to a murmur. "I never doubted you. Never."

Diana's reply certainly gave Tabitha hope. "When this is over, are you going back to Canada?" she asked.

"I don't…I don't think so," Diana said hesitantly. "I mean, I doubt I still have my old job considering I took off without notifying anybody. And besides, I'm considering moving somewhere warmer—" She stopped and glanced at their surroundings. "Hey, I think I recognize that car crusher. Jack brought me here about a year ago and things change around the yard with the speed of a glacier. Anyway, we're close to the safe."

Tabitha turned her mind back to the business of escape, recalling the engraved map on the key. "Okay, if the safe's in that direction and we go this way, we should find the Birmingham in a few minutes."

"But we have the combination," Diana said, "and it won't take a minute, I swear."

"We've had this conversation, Di. As soon as the FBI takes control of the yard, they'll send a team after the stolen money. Believe me, when that happens, you do not want your fingerprints anywhere near the safe or the money."

"Yes, but—"

A man's voice interrupted. "Did you know that by my count, there are fourteen safes in this damned junkyard?" Jesse Wayne Burke asked, walking out from behind a backhoe. He was flanked by Johnny Salyers and Blair Montoya, who gave Diana a wink. Behind him came a group of well-armed men, one of them carrying an oversized backpack.

Diana made a strangled gasp.

Tabitha retained her grip on the SIG, even when Salyers gestured with his gun. She had no doubt he would cheerfully cut her down where she stood. Everyone gets out alive, she reminded herself. Still, she wouldn't surrender her weapon for the second time that day unless she had an overwhelming reason to do so.

Salyers grinned and raised his Beretta.

Burke waved a hand. "I'm sure we're all reasonable people here, John. The agent knows she can't shoot her way out. The odds are against her. I expect she doesn't want to get herself or her friend killed so she'll drop that gun right about now." He smiled at her. The expression seemed genuinely friendly, but something sharp lurked behind it, a shark's grin looming out of murky waters.

She bent to place the SIG on the ground.

Burke seemed shorter and more solid in person, thick through the chest and shoulders with small hips and bowed legs—a typical redneck build, Tabitha thought. His beefy arms were covered in age-dulled patriotic tattoos. He seemed fairly unremarkable until she looked into his eyes. A hot, unwavering spark glowed in the depths of his gaze. Her stomach sank when he turned that fanatic's glance on her.

"Thank you, agent, for your cooperation," Burke said, sounding as polite as if they'd met during a church social. He turned to the other men and went on, his voice falling into the smooth pattern of a pastor delivering a sermon, "It's like I told you, boys. The illegitimate, tyrannical government of this country uses violence against its citizens every day, violence perpetrated by hapless drones subverted by these same conspirators who have usurped the American citizens' rights. It is our clear duty to liberate the government, but those dupes who act in ignorance may be given mercy if they choose not to oppose us."

The Russians shrugged. Montoya nodded. Even Salyers, who had been giving Tabitha a hateful glare, subsided and lowered his gun to hang loosely at his side.

"Now that you federal folks are cooperating, I believe our operation may commence," Burke continued, returning his attention to Tabitha. He fairly glowed with righteousness.

She took Burke's measure in an instant. He had meant every word he said. In his mind, his cause was just. He was a freedom fighter battling a dictator. He would detonate a nuclear bomb and wipe out a city without a qualm if it served his ultimate goal. He didn't believe himself a bad man, but a man on a mission as sacred and holy as any handed down by God. No sacrifice was too great, no atrocity unthinkable.

Burke did not fear capture either, she guessed. He did not fear death. The only thing he feared was failure, but she considered the men with him and thought they didn't feel the same.

"Stash these ladies somewhere, John," Burke said, turning to leave. "We'll question both of them in due time."

She let him get six steps away before she charged the Russian with the backpack.

Suicide wasn't her intention. Nevertheless, as she ran toward the bristling gauntlet of automatic weapons, Tabitha wondered whether today might be her time to die.

Surprise kept her opponents paralyzed for a crucial moment, long enough to plow through the group and reach the man holding the backpack. He was burly, squat, and probably weighed a good three hundred pounds. She drove her elbow into his face, feeling the satisfying crunch of his nose breaking under the blow. When he staggered back, she darted around him to use his body as a shield and grabbed the backpack, yanking it away from him.

The weight dragged down her arm. Had to be fifty pounds or more in there, she thought, keeping hold of the strap with an effort. Her imagination conjured up a brief image of a bomb: a tangle of wires, shaped explosives charges, and the heavy, grapefruit-sized sphere of weapons-grade plutonium or uranium at the core of the device.

Her mouth went dry at the thought of radiation, but her rational mind insisted the nuclear device had to be shielded somehow, otherwise it couldn't be safely carried by an operator. Her monkey brain, on the other hand, gibbered in terror.

A glance over the man's shoulder showed a lot of guns pointed in her direction. Burke, Montoya and Salyers were already moving away, probably headed to the safe to take the money and run while leaving the Russians to clean up the mess.

Tabitha took a deep breath and punched the man who shielded her, driving her fist into his kidney. He doubled over, gasping. She darted to the hydraulic car compactor, urgency lending her strength and speed, and tossed the backpack inside. A couple of bullets zinged off the metal sides, thankfully not coming close to the bomb or her.

Grabbing the yellow control box that hung from a thick cord, she put her thumb on the green button. The Russian men confronting her halted, their weapons raised but no longer firing. She motioned Diana to come closer.

"Any of you guys speak English?" she asked the group.

The man who had carried the backpack glared at her and wheezed, "Kill the bitch."

"I wouldn't if I were you," Tabitha warned. "I don't need to explode the bomb to screw everybody up for what's left of their lives. See, if I breach the containment with this car crusher, the whole area will be saturated with radiation…and so will you."

Several of the Russians took a step backward when the man made a rapid-fire translation of her words. The language sounded like stones gargled deep in his throat.

"Anatoli says you will not do it," said one of the others. He squinted at her, his skepticism clear.

"Won't I? I'm going to die anyway, and I'll at least take you bastards with me." Simultaneous rushes of hot and cold ran under her skin. "Put down your weapons and leave this area right now, or I'll push the button."

"Maybe I shoot you first," sneered Anatoli.

Tabitha sneered back at him. "Then my final act will be to send you to hell." She stared at him defiantly when he raised a pistol and aimed at her. The simmering tension grew moment by moment until she felt it coming to a boil, her nerves on fire.

The Russians seemed to hold their collective breath.

A shadow slipped across the ground, a bird flying overhead. The movement made Anatoli jerk, breaking the mood. Spitting out what sounded like an annoyed curse, he put the pistol away, and Tabitha's heart began beating again.

The Russians argued back and forth. Anatoli grew increasingly agitated. Tabitha didn't know the language, but from the gestures, facial expressions, and the rising volume of their voices, she thought they were discussing whether or not the crazy American woman would really commit suicide by nuke.

Further conversation wouldn't help her case, so Tabitha maintained a cool expression, letting them read whatever they wanted in her relaxed body language. She maintained her hold on the control box, letting the men see her thumb on the button that activated the compactor. Let them picture the backpack crushed and ripped apart, lethal levels of radiation spilling out to contaminate everything and everyone within a hundred yards or more. Acute radiation syndrome. Rapid death. Let them think about that, too.

The debate continued furiously. By now, two of the men had stepped away and turned their backs—a clear indication that they wanted no further part of the situation.

Finally, one of his fellows grabbed Anatoli's shoulder and shouted a stream of Russian. Anatoli shook his head, looking uncertain. Time to go for the kill, Tabitha thought.

"Know what? Fuck it. Boom!" she shouted, mashing the button. To a man, the Russians yelled and pelted away, scattering like pheasants startled from the bush. She stopped the compactor.

Beside her, Diana broke into giggles. "Boom?"

"Okay, so I bluffed, but I got the bomb, didn't I?" Tabitha grinned and rubbed her sore bicep. "Think I pulled something heaving that sucker into the crusher." She reached into the compactor, groaning a little when her muscles protested, and snagged the backpack.

"Remind me not to play poker with you."

"Duly noted. Let's get out of here before they work up the nerve to come back."

Diana stuck by her side while they hastened away from the area. Going past a towering heap of discarded refrigerators and washing machines, Tabitha had to squint against the sunny reflection from the white surfaces. "Too bad about the money," she said.

"What?"

"I have a feeling that by the time we find our way out of this maze, Burke and his boys will be long gone and twenty million dollars richer."

Diana shrugged. "Do you care? The bank's insured."

"By the federal government, which I work for," Tabitha pointed out. "And most banks have to pay hefty deductibles on a robbery claim."

"Know what this is?" Diana held out her hand, her thumb and forefinger rubbing together in tiny circles. "It's the world's smallest violin playing 'My Heart Bleeds For You.'"

"Very funny."

"I thought so. With the bonuses those guys hand out to themselves like hundred-dollar bills grow on trees, I reckon they can afford a deductible. Pay it out of petty cash, probably."

Tabitha nodded. Despite the circumstances, bantering with Diana felt good. "My second point was, if Burke walks away with twenty million, he won't be going to Disney World. Want to bet he'll use the money to fund some other illegal scheme?"

"No bet."

"Smart girl. Hey, how are you holding up?"

"My foot hurts like a bitch," Diana said, grimacing. "I stink so much, I think I saw a love-drunk skunk following me. I'd shove my grandmother under a train for a halfway decent shower. My hair is past salvation. Do not ask me about the state of my underwear, which will be burned later. I'm hungry, I'm thirsty, I need to pee, and—"

Tabitha cut her off with a hug. She'd found Diana and rescued her. The nuclear bomb was in her possession, and Burke's terrorist threat was ended. He still had to be apprehended, but she thought she'd done enough for one day. Of course, she had yet to face the fallout for her escapade. Only in an alternate universe would her FBI bosses shake her hand and give her a promotion. The prospect of joblessness curdled her stomach, but she was unwilling to puncture her happiness balloon just yet.

Releasing Diana, she went on a few paces before realizing she was alone. "Come on, Di," she said over her shoulder. "Let's beat feet out of here."

"Listen, I need to tell you something."

"Can it wait?"

"You can't guarantee I won't be arrested as soon as we're out of here, right?"

"Damn it. Why do we have to have this conversation right now?" Tabitha complained, but she didn't wait for an answer. She dragged Diana over to a niche created by a gap between two stacks of cars. "Since you insist, I'll give you a few minutes, then we are leaving. Deal or no deal?"

"It's important," Diana insisted. She hesitated.

"Well?" Tabitha chafed at the delay.

"We had a talk, remember? On the sandbank. Back in Canada."

"After Yancy Warner tried to kill us. Yes, I remember it vividly."

Diana flushed at her dry tone. "We said we were attracted to each other, right? And maybe we wanted to try dating. Getting better acquainted, so to speak."

Tabitha barely registered the words. She felt antsy, as if the world and time had left her behind while they spun ahead. Any minute now, as soon as the negotiator deemed the hostage takers unreachable and the standoff phase ended, SWAT and a few dozen other federal and state law enforcement officers would start sneaking through the junkyard hunting the bad guys. They'd arrest everyone they found on principle.

She said, "We can talk about whatever topic you choose, just later, okay?"

"We can't!" Diana's hands balled into fists. Her glare recalled Tabitha from her musings. "Goddamn you, Tabitha Knowles, I need to tell you that I lo—"

The full-throated roar of a nearby explosion erased whatever else she meant to say.

To Tabitha's amazement, scorched and burning fifty-dollar bills fluttered down from the sky, littering the ground around them.

CHAPTER TWENTY-EIGHT

"Burke and his guys captured Broadstreet and Coombs, and blew the safe door with C-4," Tabitha told Diana much later in a motel room, sharing a bed while the muted television's flickering light painted their skins in shades of blue and silver. "They'll be vacuuming up bits of that heist money from here to Atlanta."

"And the nuclear bomb?" Diana asked.

"There was only one, thank God. It's in the FBI's hands. And the Russians were arrested. So were Burke, Montoya and Salyers. A clean sweep. You're safe."

Diana relaxed against her, warm, shower fresh, and smelling of motel soap.

Tabitha sighed, remembering how an FBI agent in the junkyard had stumbled on her and Diana in the minutes after the blast. The sweating, red-faced man, clearly rattled by the explosion, had nearly shot them before she had a chance to surrender.

Placed under arrest, she and Diana spent the night in the local lockup. The next morning at the Atlanta field office, Alice Gable left her stewing alone for three hours in an interview room with only a cup of vile coffee to keep her company.

She'd eventually learned that Alice had been in contact with Strickland in Orlando, and the two of them had hammered out a deal that covered them with glory while also covering Tabitha's butt. For services above and beyond, she could keep her badge and her pension. For disobeying direct orders, she'd receive a black mark in her file that effectively ended any chance of further promotion. She was surprisingly okay with that outcome.

For the moment, Diana was not under arrest or facing prosecution, but she'd have to make an official statement about her brother's part in the robbery soon.

So far, so good, Tabitha thought drowsily, letting her eyelids drift shut. She would call Victoria tomorrow and give her the news.

Despite the desire to doze, a niggling sense of discontent pricked at her. Had she missed something? Recalling the chaotic events of the past several days, she wouldn't be surprised. All at once, a memory surfaced, rousing her.

"Di, you awake?" she asked, giving Diana a little shake.

"Oh, damn your eyes, Tabs, I was dreaming." Diana sat up and yawned.

"About what?"

"Does it matter? Cabana girls in skimpy bikinis serving me banana daiquiris. Or was it winning the lottery so I can wear a monocle like Uncle Moneybags in the Monopoly game?"

Tabitha smiled. "Do you remember the junkyard? I mean," she hastened to add at Diana's thunderous frown, "right before the explosion. You were bound and determined to tell me something important."

"Oh, that." Diana fiddled with the cotton sheet covering her breasts.

"Yes, that. Come on, quit stalling."

"I was going to tell you that I'm leaving Canada for good."

"Are you?" Tabitha didn't actually squeal in delight, but her heart began to thud.

"Yeah. I had a chance to call my boss this morning, and he basically told me I'm fired. No surprise there. But I've got other job offers, so that isn't a problem. And besides, I have to testify in Blair's trial in about six months anyway."

Tabitha waited a beat for her to continue, but Diana resolutely stared at the television as if the inane talk show host was the most fascinating person she'd seen this decade.

"So, um, where are you moving to?" Tabitha asked after an awkward, silent stretch of time had passed.

"The Sunshine State. I hear the winters aren't so cold in Florida." Diana glanced at her. "Quit grinning like that. Who says I have to live near Mickey-ville?" She smiled when she spoke, giving Tabitha a floating feeling.

"Hey, that's Mr. Mouse-ville to you." Abruptly sobering due to the loving emotion she glimpsed in Diana's expression, she continued, "I'd like you to live in Orlando very much." Her mouth dry, she waited for an answer to a question she hadn't asked.

"How much?" Diana finally whispered.

The air seemed dangerously thin. "Infinity, squared."

Diana's smile turned incandescent.

Light-headed in relief, Tabitha laid an open-mouthed kiss on Diana's freckled shoulder and began tugging the sheet down an inch at a time, past her breasts, past her waist, past her hips and thighs. Beautiful, so beautiful...

Growling impatiently, Diana kicked the sheet off the bed, leaving their naked bodies exposed. She rolled over, settling between Tabitha's thighs.

Skin on skin felt so damned good, Tabitha thought, flattening a hand against Diana's back to urge her closer. Sparks of contact ignited everywhere they touched. She shivered. Feeling playful, she strained her neck and licked a stripe up Diana's throat, over her chin, and on her lips, letting out a muffled yelp when Diana gently bit her tongue.

"Want you," Diana murmured. Her eyes burned blue fire, warming Tabitha to her soul.

Tabitha's playfulness vanished under a curl of pleasure so addictive, she instantly craved more. She tilted her head, inviting a kiss. Diana obliged. The kiss was sweet, tender and caring, making Tabitha's desire blossom.

Diana continued to kiss her, slower, longer, taking her time as if trying to map the inside of her mouth and the shape of her lips. Tabitha melted under the attention. Her body turned pliant, yielding to the caresses. She felt no urge to take control. The room receded until she dwelled solely in her own skin, nothing but nerves and sensations.

But Diana didn't seem satisfied with her surrender. The kisses became fierce and hungry, Diana silently insisting that she rise to the challenge. When Tabitha felt the thin skin of her lower lip split under worrying teeth, her appetite roared to life.

She fisted a handful of Diana's hair and pulled firmly until she stopped biting. Diana gazed down at her, panting. Tabitha opened her fingers. The slightly damp strands stuck to her palm and clung to her wrist as if reluctant to be released.

Diana looked wrecked already, wide-eyed and desperate, but overwhelmed, too, like a starving woman at a feast who couldn't decide where to start.

"It's okay, we'll get there. We'll get there, I swear," Tabitha said, tracing the line of Diana's spine with her fingertips, from the nape of her neck to the dimple just above her buttocks. "I'm right here. I've got you, baby."

Diana shifted position to hands and knees, straddling Tabitha's leg and pressing an impossibly hot, impossibly wet sex against the top of her thigh. "I've got you too," she rasped, beginning to move.

Between the television light behind her and the hair falling over her shoulders, Diana's face was cast in shadow. Arousal and heat spilled through Tabitha. She imagined that hidden, greedy gaze devouring her mouth and straying to her tight pink nipples. Her breath caught.

She offered encouragement by tensing the muscle in her thigh until it trembled. Diana's hips gyrated in circles. The pressure of her sex felt like juicy, pulpy fruit sliding on Tabitha's skin. She reached up and cupped Diana's breasts, stroking the soft flesh, keenly aware of the body quivering and swaying above her.

She started when Diana's hand skimmed her pubic bone, callused fingers moving down to the top of her slit and slipping inside. Her clitoris felt swollen, fat with unfulfilled need. Diana rubbed—too hard, not hard enough, wrong angle—but she cried out when her pleasure spiked anyway. A final spasm and her orgasm hit, battering her in waves.

Tabitha's breath came fast and uneven while Diana ground down on her thigh, racing to her own climax. Afterward, Diana slumped sideways and fell on the bed, shaking.

"Tabs," she whispered. In the limited light, her face seemed colorless. She took Tabitha's hand and held it in a cold grip. "I need to tell you something. In the beginning, when all this started, I wanted to run away. Be safe. And you took me in, sugar. You saved me. More than that, we made a real connection. I'd be a fool not to admit it. You're the best thing that's ever happened to me. I don't know how you feel, but I know I'm in lo—"

"Shh," Tabitha interrupted, laying a hand across Diana's mouth to prevent her from speaking. "I hear you, Di. You don't have to say it. I hear you loud and clear. And you know what?" She tenderly brushed a lock of hair out of Diana's face. "I feel exactly the same."